A
Hundred
Flowers

A
Hundred
Flowers

Gail Tsukiyama

St. Martin's Press ≋ *New York*

This is a work of fiction. All of the characters, organizations, and events portrayed in this novel are either products of the author's imagination or are used fictitiously.

www.stmartins.com

Library of Congress Cataloging-in-Publication Data

Tsukiyama, Gail.
    A hundred flowers : a novel / Gail Tsukiyama. — 1st ed.
        p. cm.
    ISBN 978-0-312-27481-8 (hardcover)
    ISBN 978-1-4299-6169-1 (e-book)
    1. Families—China—Fiction.   2. China—History—
20th century—Fiction.   I. Title.
    PS3570.S84H86 2012
    813'.54—dc23

                                        2012021274

First Edition: August 2012

10 9 8 7 6 5 4 3 2 1

For Tom

Acknowledgments

I would like to thank my editor, Hope Dellon, along with Sally Richardson, George Witte, Joan Higgins, Merrill Bergenfeld, and everyone at St. Martin's Press who made this book possible.

I'm very grateful to Jane Hamilton, Nancy Horan, Elizabeth George, and Anne LeClaire for their support and sustenance and to Thrity Umrigar and Carol Cassella for their invaluable assistance. Thank you also to Walter Shui Heng Yong for answering my numerous questions and, along with Jack Dold, showing me China.

For their ongoing care and encouragement, many thanks to my family and to my agent, Linda Allen, and to Abby Pollak, Blair Moser, Cynthia Dorfman, and Catherine de Cuir, who continue to guide me through those difficult first steps.

Let a hundred flowers bloom; let a hundred schools of thought contend.

—Mao Tse-Tung, 1956

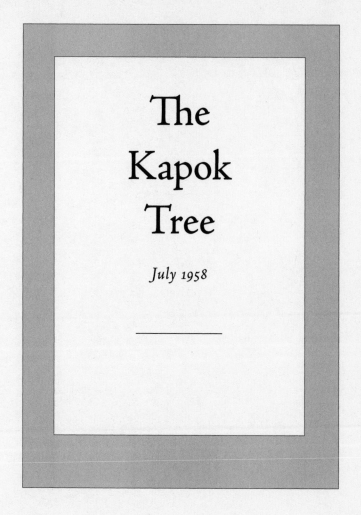

The Kapok Tree

July 1958

Tao

THE COURTYARD WAS STILL QUIET SO EARLY IN THE morning, the neighborhood just waking as Neighbor Lau's rooster began to crow. The air was already warm, a taste of the heat and humidity that would be unbearable by midday. Seven-year-old Tao knew he had little time to climb the kapok tree before he'd be discovered. He glanced down at the gnarled roots of the tree and felt strangely comforted, a reminder of the crooked ginger roots his *ma ma* sliced and boiled into strong teas for her headaches, or when his *ba ba* complained of indigestion.

Tao wasn't afraid as he shimmied up the kapok tree's slender trunk toward the broad branches, avoiding thorns on the spiny offshoots of the same tree his father had climbed as a boy, his heart thumping in excitement at the idea of seeing White Cloud Mountain from up so high. From the time he was two, his father would lift him up to look out his bedroom window, or from the second-floor balcony, as they searched for the mountain in the far distance. His *ba ba* always told him that if he looked hard enough, he could see all of Guangzhou and as far away as White Cloud Mountain on a clear day. With its thirty peaks, the mountain was a magical place for him, and his eyes watered with an effort to glimpse just a shadow of an elusive peak.

Tao could still feel the rough stubble of his father's cheek against his, like the scratchy military blankets they used at school during naptime when he was younger. But last July, just before his sixth birthday, everything changed. Angry voices filled the courtyard early one morning, his father's voice rising above them all, followed by the sound of scuffling. He looked out the window to see his *ba ba*'s hands bound behind his back as he was dragged away by two unsmiling policemen in drab green uniforms. He saw his grandfather trying to push closer to his father, only to be roughly shoved back by one of the policemen. "Where are you taking him?" his mother's lone voice cried out from the gate. But all he heard was a roar of the Jeep, and then they were gone.

After his father was taken away, when his mother and grandfather thought he was still asleep, Tao heard their low whispers, but when he made his way downstairs, the whispering had stopped. He saw his mother crying and his grandfather sitting in the shadows as still as stone. He wanted them to answer all his questions. "Where did *ba ba* go? Why did those men take him away? When will he come home again?"

Before he could say a word, his mother pulled him toward her and hugged him. "*Ba ba* had to go away for a little while," she told him. He smelled the mix of sweat and the scent of boiled herbs in her hair and on her clothes and he blurted out, "Why didn't *ba ba* tell me he had to go away?" But she held tightly on to him and a strange sound came from her throat.

Only then did he understand his father was really gone and his questions would remain unanswered. He squeezed his eyes shut so he couldn't see her crying.

From that day on, his father was no longer there to tell him about White Cloud Mountain. At first Tao was scared and confused, wanting only to feel his *ba ba*'s warmth beside him and to hear his laughter coming from the courtyard. Tao searched for his father in all the places they had gone together: down by the tree-lined canal, through the alleyways that separated the red-brick apartment buildings, in and out of the crowded, narrow streets lined with restaurants, and in the small shop where his father always bought him sweets filled with red bean and rolled in sesame seeds on their way to Dongshan Park. It was as if they were playing a game of hide-and-seek; he thought his *ba ba* would have to come out of hiding sooner or later. But he never did.

Mr. Lam, the shopkeeper, brought Tao safely back home, but not before he reached up to the shelves and took down a glass jar and slipped him a piece of candy, the same sugar candy that his mother's patients often sucked on after drinking an especially bitter tea.

"Don't worry, your *ba ba* will be back soon," he said reassuringly.

Tao nodded, but all he tasted as he sucked on the hard candy was grief.

For a whole year, his *ba ba* returned to him only in dreams. Tao felt his presence in the shadows, the calm of his voice, the safe, solid grasp as he lifted him up and into the air, and the sweet scent of his cologne. The idea of climbing the tree had come to him in a dream just that morning: he was perched at the top of the kapok tree and could finally see all the way to White Cloud Mountain and there on one of the peaks stood his father waiting for him.

Tao suddenly heard the slow whine of a door opening and peered anxiously at the balcony. He held his breath and waited, but no one emerged as the air seeped slowly back out from between his lips. Sometimes his mother stepped out in the mornings to check the weather, or to see if she had any patients waiting. On this particular morning, he was relieved to see that the neighborhood was slow to wake.

His mother, Kai Ying, was something of a well-known herbalist and healer in their Dongshan neighborhood, where the quiet streets were lined with once-stately red and gray brick villas that surrounded their courtyard. She was known for her restorative teas and soups that cured many of the neighbors' ailments. People came and went through the courtyard all day long, wanting her advice to treat some pressing malady. On any given morning there would likely be a patient or two already waiting anxiously at the gate to see her. But only after his mother fed him and his grandfather breakfast did she walk out to unlock the gate and let the first patient in. And it wasn't until she ministered to the last person waiting that she locked the gate again at night.

According to Tao's grandfather, it was his great-grandfather, a wealthy businessman, who built one of the first villas in the Dongshan area, once a remote and isolated part of Guangzhou where mostly military families lived. By the 1920s, there were hundreds of villas in the area. Most were two or three stories, designed in the European style with high ceilings and columned balconies. Tao's family still lived in the same brick villa that was built by his great-grandfather, whose portrait hung on their living room wall. And though his great-grandfather had died long before Tao was born, he felt as if he knew the white-haired, stern-looking man wearing a dark blue silk *changshan*, standing tall in his long mandarin gown as he gazed down at him. He always thought of his great-grandfather as an intrinsic part of the house, just like the faded redbrick walls, the sweeping stairway and square-paned windows, the second-story balcony, and the wide-open courtyard that was specifically built around the kapok tree. Dongshan was the only district in Guangzhou that had houses with large, open courtyards.

After the Communists came into power in 1949, the two-story redbrick villa had been divided among three families. Tao's now lived on the top floor that opened up to the second-floor balcony. Auntie Song lived in a smaller apartment facing the backyard, and Mr. and Mrs. Chang, an older couple who were currently away visiting their daughter in Nanjing, lived in the rooms downstairs. They all shared the kitchen, though the Changs kept to themselves and usually took their meals in their room. Auntie Song occasionally ate with them, but preferred to cook the vegetables she grew in her backyard garden on a small hot plate in her apartment. Tao's grandfather often told him that when he was a boy, the entire house belonged exclusively to his family. Tao couldn't imagine what it must be like to have so many rooms to run through.

Lately, he noticed his grandfather was repeating the same old boyhood stories, many of which took place in the courtyard, where the tall, spiny-armed kapok tree stood guard. He knew his grandfather was an only son, though he had five much older half sisters. Tao imagined the kapok tree had provided his grandfather with company, just as it did for him. "The tree has been here for a very long time," his *ye ye* repeated, just yesterday. "Think of all it has seen over the years, all that it has heard," he added. His grandfather gazed up at the tree as if he could see the past in each of its limbs.

"A tree can't see or hear," Tao said.

His grandfather looked down at him and smiled. "How do you know? It's a living thing. Just because it doesn't have eyes and ears the way we do, how can we know it doesn't feel things in other ways?"

Tao thought about it for a moment. "Just like we can't see how water and sunlight make it grow?" he asked. His grandfather, Wei, and his father, Sheng, were both teachers. Ever since Tao was a very little boy, he felt their joy every time he asked questions and was eager to learn something new.

"Yes," his grandfather said, and clapped his hands once. "Exactly like that! So many things happen around us without our seeing or knowing."

"How old is the tree?"

His *ye ye* stroked the gray hairs on his chin. "Let's see," he said, "I would say it was planted during the Ch'ing Dynasty, the last great Chinese dynasty, so well over a hundred years ago."

Tao nodded and counted in his head. His grandfather was seventy-one and he was going to be seven. The tree was older than both of their ages combined.

His *ye ye* and his parents constantly reminded him of how thankful he should be to be surrounded by nature, and how lucky they were to share it with their neighbors. Just four months earlier in the heart of March, his grandfather had marveled at the kapok's red blossoms that were in full bloom, bold and unafraid. Known as Guangzhou's city flower, it was a splendid sight. Now its branches looked like a completely different tree, the nut-size pods replaced by lance-shaped green leaves that wavered and blurred in the heat of summer.

Tao climbed upward now, quick and agile, careful not to look down at the stone pavement below. He grabbed hold of another branch and pulled himself up and onto it, then paused for a moment to look over the concrete wall of their courtyard, which was topped with the same weather-beaten red tiles as many of the other old villas in their neighborhood. His grandfather had told him that each villa's design was based on the courtyard and garden it contained. Theirs was a remnant of the old Ming Garden architecture, with tiles lining the top of their stone wall. Other gardens in the neighborhood, those without tiles, followed different designs called the Chun or Kui or Jian. Mostly, Tao thought they looked all the same once you were through the gates.

Looking down, the tiles reminded him of his grandfather's worn mah-jongg tiles all lined up in a row. He heard the rooster crow again and smiled, thinking of Auntie Song, who constantly threatened to quiet the bird once and for all by wringing its neck. "Too tough to eat," she told his mother. "But boil it long enough and you might have a decent soup!"

Tao climbed higher. His mother and grandfather would be up soon and he knew the scolding he'd get if he were caught. He could hear his *ma ma*'s raised voice, and see her no-nonsense glare, which stole away all her beauty and made her forehead wrinkle and her dark eyes narrow. He always looked away from her eyes when she was angry at him, and focused on her hands instead, her fingers dancing in front of him. And he could already feel the warmth of his grandfather standing quietly behind him. Then finally, after his tears and apologies, would come the comfort and forgiveness he'd feel when his *ye ye*'s large, wrinkled hands rested lightly on his shoulders.

Tao looked up through the branches to see an immense hazy sky. The morning air was already growing heavier, the warm humidity filtering through the leaves. His shirt clung to his back and he knew the clouds and rain would return by afternoon. He heard the creaks and yawns of the awakening street rise up to where he was perched. His arms and legs were getting tired. He had almost reached the top of the tree and he couldn't wait to see all thirty peaks of White Cloud Mountain, regardless of his punishment. Tao grabbed hold of another branch, but quickly let go when the sharp sting of a thorn caught the fleshy part of his palm. He cried out once just as his foot slipped into air. He felt the strange sensation of floating just above his falling body, watching the branches snap and scrape against his skin, followed by the dull thud of hitting the hard surface thirty feet below. Only then did he reenter his body, consumed by an excruciating pain that traveled from his leg all the way up to his head before everything went dark.

Kai Ying

K AI YING WOULD NEVER FORGET THE SIGHT OF HER pale little boy lying on the courtyard pavement, his leg twisted beneath him. A broken branch, she thought, a crushed leaf. He wasn't moving. At that moment, she realized he might never move again and a feeling of terror overwhelmed her, stopping her abruptly and rooting her in place. Wei, her father-in-law, rushed past her and knelt over Tao. She stood there while her heart raced so fast her whole body shook. *He can't be,* she thought, *he can't.* And try as she might, Kai Ying couldn't think of one tea or soup that could bring the dead back to life. Her father-in-law, who was usually calm and in control, turned back to her, his eyes wide and frantic, his hands waving wildly in the air as he yelled for her to get help from Neighbor Lau, who had the only flatbed pedicab in the neighborhood.

For two hours, Kai Ying sat with her father-in-law in the crowded waiting room of the noisy hospital. She couldn't imagine how anyone could get well in such a frantic place. The air reeked of disinfectant mixed with camphor and menthol, the sharp medicinal odor of tiger balm ointment. With all the hurried comings and goings, it felt more like a train station. Some people crouched or huddled silently, forming a long line down the hallway, their faces pale from distress and illness. Others found ways to pass the time as they waited for their loved ones. She was amazed by how so many people had simply made themselves at home; the woman next to her was peeling an orange, a man who sat across the aisle from them smoked one cigarette after another and talked nonstop to a woman who continued to pick her teeth with a sliver of wood as she listened. Another woman, sitting against the wall, sang softly to herself as she darned a hole in an old black sock. A child's cry floated above the hum of voices. It was a chorus of sounds and movements, and in the middle of it all Kai Ying felt completely paralyzed. She avoided direct eye contact with anyone for fear she'd have to make conversation. As it was, her throat felt so dry she could barely swallow.

She gazed quickly around the room, the air as warm as breath. They had been waiting for so long and there was still no doctor in sight. Across the crowded room hung a large portrait of Chairman Mao glaring down at her, his thin lips pressed tightly together accusingly. *Where were you? How could you have let your only son fall from a tree?*

Asleep, she thought. *I was asleep.*

It was no wonder most of the neighborhood came to her for herbal remedies. Kai Ying wasn't a doctor, but she prided herself on being an observant and efficient herbalist who provided daily maintenance. She took nothing for granted and spent time with each patient; she looked for any signs of illness in the sound of the voice, the pallor of the face or eyes or tongue. She even noted whether particular odors arose from them. Then she reached for their wrists and placed her fingers on their pulse, a small shared intimacy before she discussed the history of their ailments with them. She knew that illnesses could stem from both emotional and physical pain, which then affected different areas of the body and caused an imbalance. Afterward, she would smile reassuringly and select herbs from the rows of jars that lined her kitchen shelves to find the right combination to restore balance, curing everything from insomnia and headaches to constipation and indigestion.

For Kai Ying, the herbal work was both rewarding and life-saving. It was what had brought her in 1947, at nineteen, to Guangzhou from Zhaoqing, a small city a few hours to the northeast, to study herbs with an old family friend, Herbalist Chu. She had planned to stay for only two years, but it was in his cluttered, dusty, sweetly medicinal shop that she first met Sheng, a twenty-three-year-old doctoral student in history who had come in to buy herbs for his mother. Two years later, instead of returning home, they were married, and a year later Tao was born; afterward, her work was limited to dispensing herbs to family and close neighbors who asked for her advice. But last year, when her husband had been arrested for writing that letter to the Premier's Office critical of Mao and the Party, he lost his teaching job, money became tight, and their food coupons were reduced. With what little was left, Kai Ying returned full-time to her work as an herbalist. She'd forgotten how much she enjoyed it, the different smells and textures of the dried chrysanthemums, snow fungus, black moss, and Angelica root that bloomed to life again in her teas and soups, and how fortunate she was to have enough neighborhood business to help them get by.

Sitting in the hospital, she suddenly remembered that Auntie

Song was coming over that morning for more *dangshen* roots to lower her blood pressure. Song had been a good friend of Sheng's mother and was a great help to Kai Ying after her mother-in-law, Liang, had died. She was certain that all the commotion must have awakened her and that when their old neighbor saw the kitchen door closed and everyone gone, she would know something was wrong. She wondered if Song would think something had happened to her father-in-law, for since Sheng's arrest, Wei had rarely strayed far from the house and courtyard. He seemed to grow more lethargic each day, despite all the ginseng soups she fed him. Surely, Song would never imagine Tao had fallen from the kapok tree. Her only consolation came in knowing Song would keep a close watch on the house and tell anyone coming to see her for herbs to return tomorrow. She couldn't afford to lose a patient.

The light in the waiting room shifted as the sky darkened by noon, bathing the room in shadows. Kai Ying wondered if it had begun to rain outside. It had now been over three hours since they'd brought Tao to the hospital and he was rushed to an examining room. Where was he now? Was he going to be all right? The abrupt nurse at the desk wouldn't tell her anything and simply said, "Go sit, the doctor will find you when he's ready," and waved her away.

Kai Ying felt helpless when she returned to the crowded room. She shook her head at Wei and said softly, "Nothing yet." While her father-in-law sat calmly, waiting for the doctor to come to them, she knew if her husband Sheng had been there he would have been pacing the halls, checking with doctors every few minutes, pushing to see where his son was and how well he was being taken care of. Kai Ying found the differences between them all the more glaring at that moment and she longed for Sheng and his impatience. There had been only two letters from him in the past year, the first arriving almost a month after they were told he was being reeducated in Luoyang.

For a while, she worried that Tao would wake up to find he was all alone in a foreign place surrounded by strangers. Then she swallowed her panic and froze at the thought that he might never wake up. She took a deep breath and shifted in the hard chair. First there was her difficult miscarriage three years ago, then Sheng had been taken from her, and now . . . she wouldn't allow herself to think about that. Just then, Kai Ying felt her father-in-law's warm hand cover hers. Wei leaned close and whispered, "Tao will be all right," his calm words grazing her cheek.

Her father-in-law was a retired professor of Chinese art history at Lingnan University, a tall and graceful man with a trimmed goatee and gray hair shaved close to his head. A well-known authority in his field, he had retired at sixty-two after Mao's Chinese Communist Party came into power, almost ten years ago, a time when outspoken scholars and intellectuals like many of his colleagues had fled from China rather than be persecuted and imprisoned by the new government. Wei, who had never been overtly political, and who had never voiced his opinions aloud, had slipped by untouched. Devoted to art and research, he kept to himself, stubbornly refusing to leave Guangzhou, the home of his ancestors. "Here in the South," he once told Kai Ying, "we do things differently from the rest of China." She knew he meant that they spoke Cantonese instead of Mandarin, preferred their food less spicy, and reveled in Guangzhou's long history of open trade with foreigners, which left them less isolated than the Northerners. China's sheer size and lack of communications created vast differences. "Beijing has no idea what we're doing here half the time," he added confidently.

Wei always remained scholarly and soft-spoken, which Kai Ying had realized, early on, was his deliberate way of being heard. His students would have to stop and listen in order not to miss something important. She glanced over to see Wei's long legs were crossed and he sat with his eyes closed so he appeared asleep. But Kai Ying knew he wasn't asleep; he had simply retreated into his own quiet world away from the flurry around him. She'd often found him in this meditative state. It was his way of dealing with the difficulties of life, by going inward. At times, she was envious, wishing she could disappear so easily for a little while. Instead, she was destined to keep her eyes wide open. Her husband, Sheng, was much the same way, but whereas she had always been more a spectator who stood by and watched the world from a safe distance, her husband was more likely to act.

Sheng was also a teacher; he taught history at the Guangzhou High School. After the Communist Party took over and his father retired, Sheng wasn't able to finish his doctorate, but was fortunate to get a teaching position at the nearby high school. Both father and son believed that lessons could be learned from China's history. It didn't take long for Kai Ying to realize that they were both prisoners of the past, though each pursued his desires and preoccupations differently. While Wei's sole interest was in preserving China's past through its art, Sheng believed that if the Chinese were going to forge a stronger nation with a vibrant future, they would have to move past their history and learn from their mistakes.

Sheng never shied away from school politics and student problems, and it was this same concern and impulsiveness that had gotten him into trouble last year. Kai Ying had often heard Wei counsel her headstrong husband, "You should always look for the quiet within the storm, and then you'll find the answers to your questions." Afterward, she watched Sheng turn away from his father with an almost imperceptible shake of his head. She knew what he was really thinking. *No, no, you'll only find the answers to your questions by walking straight into the storm.*

Sheng frightened Kai Ying sometimes. She could feel his discontent, like that very same storm brewing just beneath the surface. She worried their quiet life within the courtyard couldn't contain all his hopes and desires for China to grow and prosper, to be a better place for Tao and future generations. China was at a crossroads, he had said, and it was important that they choose the right path. Growing up back in Zhaoqing, she'd seen her own father's disappointment with the Nationalist government. The Kuomintang government had grown increasingly corrupt under the leadership of Chiang Kai Shek, and while officials and military leaders grew rich, the Chinese people suffered inflation and unemployment. Her father's anger was a disease that spread through his body until all that was left was bitterness. She didn't want to see the same thing happen to Sheng.

"Think of Tao," she had pleaded with Sheng, reminding him there were always consequences to the kind of change he hoped for.

"I am thinking of Tao," he said. She could still hear his voice rise as he continued, "China has to accept change if we expect to move forward! All the Party has done is taken us a step backwards!"

She had wanted to reach out and put her fingers on his lips to quiet him. *Please, please, don't say another word; keep your thoughts to yourself.* No one was safe, she thought. She knew if anyone, even their neighbors, heard what Sheng was saying and reported him to the authorities, he would be in serious trouble. But no matter how he felt, Kai Ying never thought he would go so far as to jeopardize both himself and his family, even if he believed there would be no repercussions. While the Party had ignored Wei as a harmless academic of the old regime, they didn't hesitate to arrest Sheng for writing that letter. The Party had found a way to get to her father-in-law after all, for Sheng's arrest had knocked the wind out of him. Wei had aged in the past year and kept increasingly to himself, spending most of his days reading in the courtyard and looking after Tao.

Kai Ying squirmed in the hard chair and looked down at herself. For the first time she realized she was still dressed in the pale yellow cotton tunic and pants she slept in, having hastily thrown on only an old cotton sweater. Thankfully, she'd had the presence of mind to change into street shoes. Kai Ying couldn't help but think how chaotic she must look. Even in the sticky heat, she felt a chill and pulled her sweater tight across her body. Wei was still wearing the same threadbare brown *mein po,* the silk padded jacket he refused to throw away, even with a new one in his closet. She leaned over and touched the edge of his frayed sleeve, careful not to disturb him. His eyes were still closed, his breathing even. For a moment, she thought he might really have fallen asleep, but she detected the slightest movement of his hand resting on his knee and knew that he was awake. She studied her father-in-law closely, looking for the subtle characteristics that were carried over from father to son. There was a definite resemblance between them around the eyes and in his strong chin. She could already see that Sheng would have the same thick, gray brows when he was older. They were both good-looking men. Sheng wasn't quite as tall but was lean and solidly built, with thick, unusually wavy hair. His real power and grace came through in his passion for his family and his beliefs. It's what had attracted her to him from the very beginning. She sometimes saw the same fearlessness in their son, and when she did, she felt the ache of not knowing when she'd see her husband again.

Kai Ying loved both father and son for their strengths, and despite their weaknesses. She stood between the two, balancing their personalities. The one thing she was certain united them both was their love for Tao. Their differences aside, she saw what wonderful teachers they were in the way they always inspired the boy, keeping Tao interested in the world around him. She couldn't imagine what she'd do if Wei wasn't there at the hospital with her.

Just then, someone coughed and Kai Ying looked up. Across the aisle from them sat a pale young girl watching her. The girl's hair was pulled back in a ponytail and angry red pimples peppered her forehead and cheeks. She wore a soiled, loose-fitting cotton jacket and pants, and her thin hands lay on the rounded bulge of her stomach. She appeared fourteen at most, Kai Ying guessed, just a child. But her watchful eyes seemed older, and there was something about the girl that kept her from turning away. Instead, Kai Ying wanted to lean closer, place her fingers on the girl's wrist to feel her pulse. Just by looking at her, she knew the girl lacked the iron and nutrition needed for the baby's health and growth. She would also need a cleanser of rhubarb, phellodendron, skullcap, and sophora to quiet the heat in her body that was causing the acne. It would also help to prevent any future scarring. Underneath it all, there was a pretty young girl.

Kai Ying was suddenly startled by a woman's scream coming from the hospital corridor, which quickly dissolved into a mournful cry. She sat up straight and her body stiffened as she listened to the consoling voices that followed. *No*, she thought. *No, that won't be me. Tao will be all right.* Fear rose to her throat. She closed her eyes and tried to concentrate on finding tranquillity the way her father-in-law did, but all she heard was a swell of voices rising in confusion all around her.

Wei

WHEN WEI CLOSED HIS EYES, HE FELT COMFORTED by the darkness. If he were patient the noise would soon quiet to a thin whisper and the black shadows moving against his eyelids would gradually fade away. Then the images he carefully conjured up would slowly come into focus. It was similar to the only moving picture he had ever seen, since he'd rarely had the time or inclination for entertainment when he was still teaching and researching. But once he retired, Sheng had finally persuaded him to see a film just before Tao was born. After the Party came into power, only anti-bourgeoisie, pro-Communist movies were allowed to be shown by the new government. Downtown at the Golden Palace Theater, *The White-Haired Girl* was already a well-known favorite, based on the famous opera about a young girl who escapes the cruelties of an evil landlord after her father is killed, and manages to survive in the wilderness against all odds. Several years later, when she's found by the young man who loves her, her hair has turned completely white from all the hardships she has had to face.

Wei had never forgotten how the screen flickered with light before the actors appeared like magic, coming to life before his eyes. As he sat enthralled that afternoon in the darkened theater, he couldn't help but think of Liang, his own white-haired woman. She hadn't faced the same kind of hardships, but her hair did begin to turn prematurely gray not long after Sheng's birth. Yet she refused to color it, or to drink his mother's black moss soup boiled with the immortal herb *He Shou Wu* to help darken it again. Wei had loved her tenacity and independence.

Now, every time Wei closed his eyes, instead of clearing his mind as Kai Ying and Sheng assumed he did in meditation, he waited until the light flickered on in his head and brought Liang back to life. He had met her on a day not unlike this one, gray and wet, with a mist that veiled and softened everything around them on campus. He had been teaching at Lingnan University for three years when he saw Liang walking across the grounds with some other students. It was the way she moved that attracted him at first, floating among them, as if she were in a Pu Ru painting walking through the mist. And there she was, with him once again. He was amazed at how real it felt to see her in his mind's eye, standing there with her hand held out to him, or to imagine her warmth as she leaned toward him and touched his cheek. "You're tired," she said, her voice comforting, her beauty stealing his breath away. It was all he could do to keep himself from smiling, from laughing aloud with happiness to see her again. He never dreamed he would have been so lucky to have met and married someone as remarkable as Liang.

The noise in the waiting room rose and fell around Wei, threatening to drive Liang away as he struggled to hang on to her. He felt his heart beating faster. *I need you,* he thought, *I always have*. He tasted something acidic, the regret of not having shown her just how much. Watching her smile as she slowly faded away, he kept his eyes closed.

Beyond the surrounding turmoil, his grandson was alone some-where in the hospital and there was nothing he could do but wait. Wei wondered if it was some kind of retribution for his years of self-absorption. He had always been too involved in his own work, never taking into consideration how it might affect those around him. Rather than going into business as his father had wished when he graduated from Lingnan University, he concentrated on his art history studies, preoccupied with teach-ing and research. The thought of making money never occurred to him. He was thirty when he finally married Liang, and long after they'd given up on having a child, Sheng came along un-expectedly almost ten years later. Through it all, Wei continued to work long hours, sorting through the evolution of art in each dynasty, cataloguing every artifact or painting, recording each piece of information with the knowledge that this was his small contribution to the long, complicated history of China. What he relished most of all was discovering how the past had brought them to the present. He told himself that his work was a part of all their legacies, but was it? By the time he paused long enough, Wei had missed so much of Sheng's childhood that he had little memory of what his son was like as a boy.

Liang passed away a year after he retired. He lived in quiet despair at having lost Liang just when he could finally have spent more time with her. Each morning, it took all his energy just to get out of bed, and it wasn't until his grandson's birth the following year, in 1951, that he found his footing again. His greatest regret was that Tao never knew Liang, his white-haired grandmother.

Unlike with his son, Wei gave his grandson his full attention. He couldn't imagine life without Tao; the little boy was their beating heart, their future. Wei had taught him to recite the names of the four greatest dynasties before he could string a full sentence together. He could still hear the boy recite *"Han, T'ang, Sung, and Ming"* over and over, like a musical chant. It rang through the courtyard all through the day, becoming the lullaby that put him to bed each night.

Wei had never been so proud.

Even with his eyes closed, Wei felt his daughter-in-law's gaze upon him, a shadow and the warm movement of air as she moved closer. He kept his eyes closed and hung on to his thoughts for a moment longer. Kai Ying was a good woman. Liang had told him as much from the very beginning, even when he felt uncomfortable having a stranger in the house. "She's a young woman with a good heart, quick to learn, and most importantly, she will keep Sheng rooted," his wife had said. By then, Liang hadn't been feeling well, and he realized now that she knew her life was coming to an end. He could only imagine the relief she must have felt entrusting her family to a young woman in whom she felt confident. Almost ten years later, Kai Ying hadn't let her down.

"Lo Yeh, the doctor is here," Kai Ying whispered. Her breath brushed against his ear.

Wei opened his eyes slowly and cleared his throat, waiting a moment for the world to refocus. He glanced over at Kai Ying to see the quiet, desperate look on her face, the tiny lines of fear that crept from the corners of her pursed lips. He wished Liang were there; she would know how to console their daughter-in-law. Sheng took after his mother in that way. He was always the better classroom teacher, involved and well liked by his students. Wei's own inability to say the right words felt like a stubborn knot caught in the middle of his throat. He reached over and put his hand on hers.

Kai Ying

THE DOCTOR WHO FINALLY SPOKE TO THEM WAS clinical and detached. He kept his eyes focused on his clipboard when he told them Tao's right leg had suffered a severe compound fracture. The same height as Kai Ying, he had a serious, careful appearance, from his thick black glasses to his perfectly parted hairline. He appeared slightly anemic, his skin pale and smooth, almost translucent. A prominent blue vein pulsed at his temple. She wondered if he spent any time outdoors in the sun and fresh air, and would have immediately prescribed it if he ever came to her, along with a soup of ginseng, wolfberries, and astragalus roots for energy and blood flow.

He ushered them out to the dank hallway to talk. Black scuff marks traveled along the walls from the gurneys and wheelchairs carelessly knocked against them. From somewhere, Kai Ying felt a slight breeze whispering against the back of her neck. Her throat was parched and she felt her father-in-law standing closely beside her, waiting. While she listened, she couldn't take her eyes off of the brownish stain on the sleeve of the doctor's otherwise white coat. He told them that Tao also had some deep bruising and lacerations and would be watched closely overnight for any signs of head trauma. But it was the leg that was of concern. At Tao's age, it was the growth plate fracture he worried about; it needed to completely heal in order for the bone to continue to grow normally. If it closed as a result of the fracture, it would leave his right leg shorter, causing a limp for the rest of his life. They had already reset the bone, sewn up the outer wound, and put a cast on him. It would be followed by a week to ten days' stay in the hospital. "Your son's very lucky," the doctor added, glancing up for the first time. "His leg took the full impact of the fall. Otherwise, we would be having a different conversation right now. You should be very thankful he's alive."

Kai Ying's mind raced. *Alive*. She swallowed the word as if it were some healing medicine. She immediately thought of the herbs she needed to buy to help Tao's fracture heal while he recuperated. She had the astragalus roots, tienchi ginseng, and tangerine peel, but needed safflower and Eucommia bark from the herb shop, which she wouldn't be able to buy until tomorrow when Tao was awake and would need the soup to strengthen his *qi*, the healing life force that kept the blood flowing from his kidneys to the fractures.

She turned toward her father-in-law, who stared intently at the doctor while he spoke. "We're thankful for the good news," he said.

She heard the edge of relief in Wei's tone.

"May we see him?" she asked, her eyes finally moving from the doctor's sleeve to meet his gaze.

The doctor peered over his clipboard at her for a moment too long, as if noticing her for the first time.

"I want to see him," she said again, louder. Only for Tao could she find the courage to insist.

"Of course," the doctor answered.

As they followed him down the hallway, the doctor assured them Tao was sedated and resting comfortably. He should sleep through to the morning, and the doctor advised them to go home and get some rest. "Tomorrow will be another long day," he reminded them.

She nodded politely, all the while thinking it couldn't possibly be longer than the day she had just lived through.

Tao's room was small and bare. It was dark in the late-afternoon gloom. He seemed to be swallowed up by all the tubes and a machine attached to him that monitored his heart rate with a beeping sound that filled the room. *Alive*, she thought each time it beeped. She stood by the bed and watched the steady rise and fall of his chest. He had always been thin, full of energy and curiosity, a sweet long-limbed boy whose recent spurt in height made him appear older than he was. Now he looked so young and helpless. His bruised and tender body seemed too thin under the white sheet. There was a tube in his left arm, a clear liquid dripping slowly into it, while his other arm was bandaged and resting on a pillow. His right leg was in a cast, propped up and held together in a sling contraption that kept it from moving in any direction. It all looked torturous, but the drugs allowed him to sleep. She hoped he wouldn't wake in the middle of the night frightened and in terrible pain.

A fan whirred in the corner, moving the hot air around. She asked the doctor if she could stay the night with Tao, but he was adamant that she go home and get some rest. "You can return first thing in the morning," he added, his voice softening. In that moment, she knew he was at least capable of understanding her fears, which put her at ease.

"Will he make a full recovery?" her father-in-law suddenly asked. He stood at the other side of the small room by the window and his voice reverberated through the air.

The doctor looked over at him. "We'll know more after we take the cast off," he answered.

Wei cleared his throat in response and turned back to look out the window.

Kai Ying bent over again and kissed Tao lightly on the forehead, her fingers hovering just above the spiderweb of scratches on his cheek and chin. She wished she could make them all disappear. Tao's even breathing made him appear as if he were simply asleep, as when she checked on him every night before going to bed. With his eyes closed, she missed the life that gleamed from his quick, darting eyes. He never missed a thing. She stood quietly and watched him, searching for the same threads of connection that made Sheng and him father and son. Instead, she saw herself in her son's sleeping face; he had her high cheekbones and double-lidded eyes, blended together with Sheng's straight nose, and the Lee family height, for which she was very grateful.

Kai Ying looked down at Tao, his face so uncomplicated in

sleep. He alone had kept her sane during the past year. Every time she looked at him, she was reminded of youth and hope and the joys of pure innocence, even in her darkest moments. Sheng had told her once that his parents had given up hope of ever having a child, and were married for nine years when he was finally conceived. How that moment changed everything. Kai Ying couldn't imagine what her life would be like if there were no Sheng. No Tao.

In the year since Sheng's arrest, life had suddenly shifted for her and Wei. She tried to conceal her misery, but it was impossible for Tao not to feel her constant dread, the thin shadow of fear always standing right behind her. She knew he was curious as to why his father had been taken away, but she and Wei had decided he was too young to fully understand what had happened. They would tell him when he was older, after Sheng returned. Now he only occasionally asked when his *ba ba* was coming home. "Soon," she answered, "when *ba ba* is finished with his work."

For the first few months after Sheng was taken away, Kai Ying went to the public security bureau every day to find out where the police were holding him. Finally, all the authorities would tell her was that he had been sent up north to be reeducated. He would be able to contact her once he was settled. Kai Ying knew that being "reeducated" was like falling down a black hole. Some were never seen again, while others returned defeated, deadened by the experience of hard labor, illness, and starvation. She willed for him to hold on, to return to them. She didn't allow herself to think of what they were going to do if Sheng never returned, if she never heard his voice or felt his touch again.

Even after the doctor had left them alone, her father-in-law continued to gaze out the small, grimy window at the facing building. A narrow alleyway separated the two buildings and the dingy, gray wall across looked dark and ominous. Kai Ying knew Wei loved art and color, and she couldn't imagine why he preferred to stare at the drab wall for so long, rather than hover over his grandson.

Wei finally turned to face her. "I don't suppose there's much sunlight in this room past noon." His voice sounded as if he'd just awoken from a long sleep.

Kai Ying could feel his eyes on her, as if she were one of his students from whom he awaited a response. "No," she answered.

He finally stepped over to the bed and touched Tao's hand, so small and fragile next to his. When she saw Wei's eyes fill with tears, she glanced away and was surprised when he spoke again.

"Tao should have a room that gets plenty of sunlight," he said. "I'll have a talk with the doctor about it."

Like a plant, she thought. *He'll need the sunlight to grow strong again*.

"Yes," she agreed.

Suyin

B Y THE TIME SUYIN LEFT THE HOSPITAL AND WALKED
back toward Dongshan Park, it was nearly dusk. The rain
had stopped and the streets were quieter now, but it remained
hot and sticky and the red rash of pimples on her cheeks both
stung and itched. Out of habit, her hands rested on the hard
sphere of her stomach. Suyin hoped the baby was all right,
tucked away in her dark womb on this airless night. Unlike
other days, she hadn't felt any movement at all. She was seven
months pregnant and it both frightened and amazed her that
she would be giving birth in a few months.

As her time approached, Suyin's only plan was to leave the
baby at the hospital after the birth. She trusted the doctors and
nurses would find the baby a good home. She only wished it
would be with someone like the woman she had sat watching
in the waiting room that afternoon. She recalled the woman's
face, both stricken and beautiful as she sat beside an old man.
From their conversation, she knew the woman's little boy had
been hurt in a fall. Even in distress, Suyin thought she looked
young and vital, completely devoted to her child. The kind of
mother she hoped to be one day. She looked down and stroked
her stomach. At fifteen, she was too young and unprepared to
care for this little being.

Suyin's own mother had been beaten down for so long, she'd
forgotten her ever being young. Her father had disappeared

years ago, leaving her mother struggling to bring up three children alone in a small, two-room apartment in Old Guangzhou. Three years ago, her mother had married her stepfather, a man she disliked from the moment she met him. Suyin had left her family when the baby began to show. She couldn't stay in a neighborhood that was filled with gossiping busybodies. Her mother didn't deserve such shame after working so hard to keep their family together. And she couldn't bring another mouth into the house to feed. Suyin was completely alone now and she would find a way out of this mess by herself.

For the past four months, she'd been living on the streets. By day, she begged near Dongshan Park, away from the Old Guangzhou district where someone might recognize her, and where there was no such thing as empty space as the crowds breathed collectively. Suyin's mother cleaned houses and her real father had been a carpenter who did mostly odd jobs. When she was a little girl, her mother was full of life and had big plans for their family. "One day, we'll have a nice house in the Liwan District," her *ma ma* said, dreaming big. It was where the foreign dignitaries had big, gated houses on wide, tree-lined boulevards much like those in Dongshan. Her mother had once cleaned in one of those grand houses and she'd never forgotten it. She would tell Suyin and her brothers the same story over and over, always ending it with, "This crowded apartment is only temporary, just until your *ba ba* finds steady work." The thought of her mother and brothers brought tears to her eyes.

She remembered being a little girl when her father had taken whatever jobs he could, sometimes going away for weeks or months at a time working on construction jobs in other cities. While he was away, they had to make do on their mother's meager salary, and it seemed that most of the time, they were simply surviving on watery rice soup. In their small apartment, Suyin and her brothers slept in the little alcove off the kitchen on bunk beds her father had built, Suyin in the lower one, her two brothers in the upper. With barely enough room to fit the beds, the ceiling was so low her brothers had to slide in and out of their bunk one at a time. The last time her father went away was eight years ago. He hugged them all good-bye just as he always did and told them to be good. "You help your *ma ma*," he said to her.

She never saw her *ba ba* again.

When it began to rain earlier that afternoon, Suyin had walked into the hospital waiting room and sat down. Her pregnancy gave her an air of legitimacy where no attendant or nurse told her to leave. Weeks earlier, she'd discovered it a safe place off the streets to catch her breath. It was the one place everyone seemed as vulnerable as she was, their faces anxious and unaware of what was going to happen next. Suyin had felt immediately comfortable sitting across from the woman and the old man, as if she were there waiting with them. When they were finally called away to meet with the doctor, she sat in the waiting room until the shadows lengthened and the room emptied, but they never returned.

By night, Suyin slept in the back doorway of a curio shop near the park, where the old woman shopkeeper had taken pity on her. Every morning the woman left a bucket of cold water out for her to wash. She knew she was luckier than most. It was almost completely dark by the time Suyin approached the park, a yellowish glow of lights in the distance. She saw a man standing on the corner smoking a cigarette and wondered if he might give her a few *fen* to buy something to eat. Her stomach rumbled at the thought. "Please," she said as she approached him, holding out her hand, wrapping her cotton jacket tighter around her belly. In the darkness, she could just see the tilt of his head as he looked her up and down.

"Get away," he sneered, and she felt his spittle on the side of her face.

His anger felt like a slap, and Suyin quickly turned away, stung, but not before she regained her voice and said, "You bastard!"

"Come back here and say that to me, you little whore," the man yelled after her.

Suyin kept walking. She rarely approached people for money, and ordinarily waited for someone to take pity on her as she stood outside the park gates among the other beggars, holding an old bean paste can. She usually made enough for a bun or two, occasionally a bowl of noodles. Today she had spent all afternoon in the hospital, hoping the hunger would go away. She wiped the spit off her cheek with the sleeve of her jacket and felt the tears pushing against her eyes. The past few months of begging on the streets had taught her that most people turned away if she approached them. Or worse, they would look right through her as if she were a ghost. But today, the woman in the waiting room had been different. She held on to her gaze for the longest time and for a moment, Suyin felt real again.

Kai Ying

WEI HARDLY SPOKE ON THE WAY HOME FROM THE hospital. It had stopped raining and the air was thick as a blanket. Kai Ying had long since shed her sweater, and her cotton tunic was damp against her body. She had lost weight in the past year, and sometimes felt as if she could actually feel her bones shrinking. The pedicab weaved in and out of the congested streets, the shops and restaurants crowded with people who had just gotten off work, buying something to eat or rushing to catch a pedicab or bus home to their families. Kai Ying wondered how many of them had little boys like Tao, who were happy and healthy, not lying in a hospital bed attached to a machine. In that instant, she felt jealous of all of them.

As they rounded the corner, they passed the Pearl Restaurant, where Sheng had taken her several times. Occasionally, they left Tao home with Wei, or Auntie Song, and had dinner out alone. It could be something as simple as noodles or a plate of rice and vegetables, but it made her feel light and extravagant. Now, as they passed the Pearl, she felt sick to her stomach. At the same time, she remembered they hadn't eaten all day.

"Are you hungry?" she asked.

Wei shook his head.

* * *

When they arrived home, Kai Ying paused in the courtyard to catch her breath as Wei walked quickly into the house. She found herself standing near the spot where Tao had fallen. There was no trace left of where his body had lain that morning. There was no blood, for which she was grateful. Such a stain would be hard to remove, and if it remained, it would always be a reminder of the fall. She didn't want Tao to have nightmares every time he saw it.

Kai Ying looked up at the tree, which she had loved from the first moment she entered the courtyard to join the Lee household. She remembered being stunned by its beauty. It was a constant reminder of her hometown, Zhaoqing. She'd grown up across from a beautiful lake, surrounded by mountain crags and trees. In comparison, Guangzhou was all cold, hard edges. The kapok tree had not only provided its leaves and flowers for medicinal purposes, but seeing it always nearby made her feel less homesick during those early years.

What in the world was Tao thinking, trying to climb the tree? He knew better. She thought of Sheng's impulsiveness and a tinge of anger overcame her fear. The sky was darkening and the courtyard had turned to shadows. The scent of peanut oil filled the air as evening meals were being prepared. Kai Ying was relieved that the villa would be all theirs during this difficult time. Earlier in the week, they'd received word that the Changs, who lived downstairs, were staying in Nanjing through the New Year with their daughter and her new baby. All around her was the buzzing of joyous mosquitoes after the rain. A stray voice, which sounded like Auntie Song, floated through the night from a neighboring villa. It might have been just like any other evening, only it wasn't.

Kai Ying heard Wei rummaging around in the kitchen and wondered what he was looking for. A moment later she saw him walking quickly back toward her and the glint of something shiny in his hand. Before she realized what was happening, Wei raised his arm and swung a meat cleaver at the kapok, with a quick thwacking sound as the sharp, thin blade struck the grayish brown trunk. He grunted and pulled the cleaver out, leaving a three-inch gash. Kai Ying watched the silver blade rise again, then grabbed his arm and held tightly on to it. The kapok not only produced Guangzhou's city flower, but was also the official city tree. China's recent and turbulent history had taught her to avoid any trouble with meddling neighbors who might tell the authorities. Kai Ying wasn't about to let the kapok hurt another member of her family.

"Enough!" she screamed at him. "Enough!" Her voice sounded harsh and foreign as she hung on to his arm.

The courtyard felt airless but for Wei's labored breathing. He murmured something into the dark, but she couldn't quite make out what he had said. Slowly, Wei lowered his arm and she reached for the cleaver and took it away from him. He stood there, arms at his side, his shoulders slumped. She had recognized the months and months of his fear and grief and frustration in the wide swing of the cleaver. Hadn't she felt the very same way herself? She gripped the solid weight of the cleaver in her hand, but she wasn't about to give in now.

As they stood next to each other, Kai Ying was glad she couldn't see her father-in-law's face. She wanted the old Wei back, the man who commanded respect just by walking into a classroom, the man who had sat by the side of his dying wife day after day reading quietly to her, the man who spent hours talking and laughing with his grandson. Instead, she felt only the looming presence of the kapok tree rising above, and the sense that they, too, had fallen.

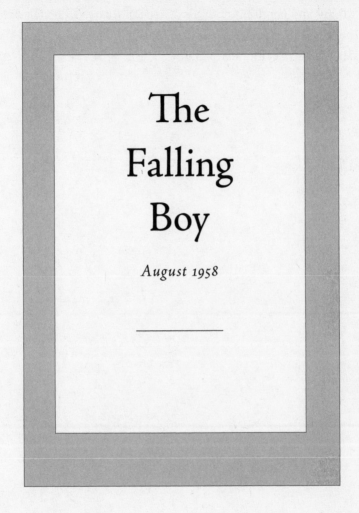

The Falling Boy

August 1958

Tao

ALL TAO REMEMBERED AFTER CLIMBING THE KAPOK tree was waking up in the hospital and crying out for his mother. When he moved, an unbearable pain shot up through his leg into his body. A nurse held him still and spoke kindly to calm him, though he couldn't remember later anything she said. Tao slept most of the time and felt groggy when he awoke, but whenever he peered around the hot and airless room, he glimpsed his mother or his grandfather at his bedside. Then he closed his eyes again.

He hated the hard, heavy cast on his leg. The stone-faced doctor was concerned about the broken bone and its healing process. Now his mother and grandfather were standing out in the hallway and he heard them talking to the doctor about his having a limp for the rest of his life if his bone didn't fuse together correctly. The doctor's voice sounded fuzzy and far away. Tao pretended he was asleep. All he wanted was to go home. And somewhere amidst all the murmuring voices, he wondered whether his *ba ba* knew he'd been hurt and if that might bring him home again.

Song

A UNTIE SONG SAT ON A WOODEN STOOL BESIDE A neatly planted row of *gai lan*, their glossy blue-green leaves hiding the thick, crisp stems of Chinese broccoli she loved. This vegetable garden was Song's favorite place to think, half-hidden by the plants she nurtured from the ground up. With a sharp knife, Song quickly cut at the bottom of the thick stems until a bundle of *gai lan* lay beside her. After almost two weeks in the hospital, Tao was coming home today and she was joining the Lees for dinner that evening.

Song relished the last of her summer crops. Just beyond the *gai lan* rose the bitter melon and her prized long beans, some stalks two feet high and ready to be picked. They grew wildly in the warm, humid climate. It was already August, and next month, she would plant her fall crops of *yu choy*, *choy sum*, and *bak choy*, the green leafy vegetables she enjoyed throughout the winter. But if Tao's leg hadn't healed by then, Song could delay the planting a few weeks. From the time Tao was a toddler, he delighted in watching the vegetables grow, many of the stalks taller than he was. Song had promised him he could help her plant and she wasn't about to go back on her word. What better way for him to heal and gain back his strength?

At sixty-eight, Song still worked in the garden for hours each day. She loved the morning hours, the way the cool earth felt sliding between her fingers as she dug deep into it. She was certain the soil must have some healing powers, and she swore it relieved the arthritis pain in her fingers. Song straightened up, flexed her fingers, and smiled. Even with all the herbs Kai Ying gave her to help alleviate her arthritis pain, or to lower her blood pressure, it was working in the garden that made her feel the healthiest and most alive. Song looked up at the sky and saw the clouds thickening. Neighbor Lau's rooster crowed again and she shook her head. The noisy bird was nothing but a nuisance. She surveyed her thriving garden and felt a flood of joy, recalling a time when such a miracle, this abundance of food, was only a dream.

It was a far cry from the bustling Old Guangzhou district, her home for over fifty-five years; the blocks of weather-beaten three- and four-story Cantonese-style Qilou buildings with shops and restaurants on the street level, known for their arcade-style covered sidewalks that kept out the summer heat and the fierce monsoon rains. She heard once again the high, frantic voices bargaining at the stores downstairs, felt the crowds of people pushing her forward through the cool, dark walkway, breathed in the oily aromas tinged with smoke and sweat, even though just beyond it all, the stink of garbage and urine arose from the narrow alleyways. Upstairs in each Qilou building, several generations of families shared overcrowded quarters. That was where she had spent her childhood, followed by forty years of marriage to Old Hing, her life confined to a small, stifling apartment, a two-story walkup above a fish market and the dim sum restaurant she had worked at as a girl. She smiled to think Old Hing would turn over in his grave to see her now.

* * *

43

When Hing finally died almost twelve years ago, Song's friend Liang had persuaded her to move out of Old Guangzhou and to the villa. "There's plenty of room," she urged. "And you'll have complete privacy." Liang had been her closest friend since elementary school, and was the one person Song would do anything for without question. She felt certain they must have been sisters in a past life. How else could she explain their friendship? Liang was educated and from a good family, while Song had grown up poor and been married off before she finished high school. At sixteen, her father sold her into a marriage with Hing, who was already forty years old and had been married twice before. There were rumors that his first wife had died of fright, so terrorized by Hing that her heart gave out, while his second wife had simply disappeared one night. He told neighbors she had returned to her ancestral village with his blessings, never to be seen again. Six months later, Hing saw Song making dumplings at the restaurant below his apartment and talked her alcoholic father into selling her to him. For a meager sum that would have bought no more than a hundred dumplings, Song became his "hundred dumplings bride," and had remained a virtual prisoner in her marriage to the mean-spirited monster.

After Hing's death, Song had hesitated about moving to the villa, afraid she couldn't adjust to the quiet, once lofty Dong-shan area. It was before the Communists came into power, when all the villas in the area were taken over by the government and divided up among families. She'd visited several times before, but never ventured beyond the kitchen and courtyard. But when Liang led her along the brick path from the courtyard to what used to be the old servants' quarters at the back of the villa, Song stopped short at the sight of the neglected yard. Ever since she was a little girl, she had wished for a garden, which meant freedom to her. To have a garden meant that she'd escaped crowded Old Guangzhou. With her own piece of land, she could plant her seeds and watch them grow. Song couldn't imagine any greater wealth. Within the first month of moving to the villa, Song had cleared most of the yard and readied it for planting.

The Lees were her family now. Song had promised Liang, when her end was near, that she'd watch over Wei, Sheng, and Kai Ying. From that moment on, she treated Wei as a brother, and Sheng and Kai Ying as she would her own children. Tao was their added happiness. The years since she moved to the villa had been kind to her. Even now, it was hard to believe Liang had been gone for nine years. All the joys she had missed in knowing Tao and in seeing what a good daughter-in-law and mother Kai Ying turned out to be were left for Song.

Tao will be all right, Song thought to herself. His fall from the kapok tree had been frightening, and the thought of losing him was a tragedy too great for any of them to bear, especially after Sheng's arrest. Every day she lit incense and prayed to Kuan Yin, the Goddess of Mercy, that Sheng would return home soon. It was still hard for her to believe he'd written that letter to the Premier. She had known Sheng since the day he was born: the long-awaited child who wouldn't have jeopardized his family for any cause.

* * *

Song looked up when she heard the front gate whine open, followed by voices in the courtyard. Tao had arrived! From the corner of her eye, she saw that her Chinese chives were also ready to be harvested. She hurried to gather together the vegetables, stood up, and dusted the dirt from her cotton pants. Along with her long beans and leek flowers, the stir-fried vegetables would provide several tasty additions to their dinner that evening. She carried an armful of vegetables as she made her way to the courtyard to welcome Tao home. There were so many lifetimes in one life, Song thought, as she paused to look back at her beloved garden.

Tao

TAO HAD BEEN HOME FROM THE HOSPITAL FOR TWO days now, and even though he lay in his own bed in his small bedroom, everything felt different to him. In the early-morning light seeping through the thin cotton curtains, all his favorite possessions appeared worn and distant. His faded stuffed tiger flopped on a chair in the corner of the room. The light blue blanket he had slept with as a baby was draped across the foot of the bed untouched. Even his grandfather's wood desk, pushed against the wall just below the window, where Tao sat drawing or practicing his Chinese characters, looked like an old relic. He tried to remember the last time he'd sat down at the desk, and out of habit, run his fingers along the jagged characters of his name, Lee Tao, which he had carved just underneath the right-hand drawer of the battered desk with his penknife. It was his secret. He looked around the room, and it felt as if he'd been away for a very long time and since he had returned, he'd outgrown his childhood.

The curtains were parted just enough for Tao to glimpse the branches of the kapok tree. Already the sky was turning a hazy gray, which meant more thunderstorms by afternoon. When he returned from the hospital and his grandfather carried him into the courtyard, he looked up at the old kapok tree and felt immediately comforted. It was still there. Several times, when he had wakened in the hospital in the middle of the night, it frightened him to think they might have cut it down, leaving a gaping hole where it once stood, all because of him. Tao didn't dare mention his fears to his mother or grandfather. But when he saw the tree still standing in the courtyard, he wrapped his arms tighter around his *ye ye*'s neck. Tao would never blame the kapok for his fall; he'd been the one at fault.

When his *ba ba* returned, Tao would tell him all about his dream and he would understand. He wondered again if his father knew he had fallen, but he hesitated to ask his mother when he saw how happy she was to have him home. Since his *ba ba* left, he'd rarely seen her smile. But, if his father knew he had been hurt, wouldn't he have already rushed home to him? Tao didn't want to think about it.

What Tao would never tell anyone, including his father, was what he really felt the day he fell from the kapok, how for just a moment he was flying instead of falling, and how happy it made him feel. Even now, he envisioned soaring through the gates and beyond the Ming garden wall, high above the narrow, crowded alleyways where he used to run and over the wide, tree-lined streets that led to far-off places he'd never seen. Tao felt so certain that if he had just kept on flying, he'd have reached White Cloud Mountain.

Tao had been having a hard time sleeping since he'd returned home. He dozed in brief spurts and woke up hot and sticky, pushing away the cotton sheet that loosely covered him. August was a month of relentless heat, broken by afternoon thunderstorms and humid, still nights. No matter which way he shifted his body, he wasn't comfortable. His right leg was immobile, cocooned in a heavy, plaster cast that was elevated on a mountain of pillows. His leg itched. He imagined it would look mummified by the time the cast finally came off, like one of his *ye ye*'s artifacts. If he had his penknife with him now, he'd carve what he was really feeling right into the hard plaster. He was miserable, tired of lying in bed all the time, staring up at the water stains on the ceiling, imagining they were far-off constellations. The only good thing to happen the day before he left the hospital was that the bandages had been taken off his arm, so that he could see the raw scrapes had become ugly, drying scabs, but now he could move his arm back and forth with relative ease.

Tao assumed his leg was also getting better each day. The doctor said they would know more when the cast came off. Meanwhile, he would have to spend most of his time in bed. "Try not to move your leg," his mother said over and over, repeating the doctor's instructions. She said it again last night, standing in the doorway. "You told me already," he snapped back, then immediately felt bad. It was the first full sentence he had spoken since returning home. What upset him more was that his *ma ma* looked at him differently now, with the same sadness in her eyes as when his *ba ba* went away.

But Tao wasn't going anywhere.

Plates clattered in the kitchen downstairs. Both his mother and grandfather were early risers. On his bedside table, his mother had left him a piece of buttered toast, sprinkled with sugar on top, along with a glass of soy milk for breakfast. Tao imagined them sitting at the kitchen table drinking tea, his mother eating wedges of orange or papaya, his *ye ye* sipping from a bowl of jook, the rice porridge he ate every morning. He heard the voices of neighbors dropping by to see how he was doing. Tao wished he could be downstairs with them, but, while his mother was busy with her patients, his grandfather kept him company, playing card games or reading to him or telling him stories. He wondered if there'd ever come a time when his *ye ye* would run out of stories to tell.

As he lay in bed, Tao worried about missing school when the term began again in early September. What new characters would they learn to write in his absence? And what was his best friend, Little Shan, up to? He had received some get-well cards from a few of his classmates when he was in the hospital. Since then, he'd heard nothing, even though Little Shan had written he would visit soon. What really upset Tao was the certain drop in his class standing if he didn't return to school at the beginning of the year. He'd always been a bright, attentive student and before his accident, was ranked second in his class. Now, even though they were best friends, it bothered him that Little Shan might jump ahead of him. The only person he knew who was smarter than he was was Ling Ling. She was consistently number one and the prettiest girl in his class. Tao liked her seated first in the class, especially if it meant he was seated behind her and could watch her two pigtails dance back and forth every time she raised her hand to answer a question. Every once in a while, she even turned around and smiled at him when he answered a question correctly. Tao's face flushed warm at the thought. He wanted to be back at school sitting behind Ling Ling, playing Ping-Pong with Little Shan, even doing morning exercises in the crowded noisy yard full of students.

Tao heard the clink of the black iron pot on the fire downstairs and knew his mother was beginning her workday. Every morning since he had come home, even before she went out to unlock the front gate for her patients, she brewed a special tea for him. She held great hope that the herbs would help his body recover from the trauma he had suffered. "It's not just your leg that must heal; your entire body needs to find balance again," she said. People came to her from all over Dongshan believing the same thing.

Tao grimaced. The teas were harder to swallow, simmered down to a dark, potent essence. He preferred her soups, which were easier to drink, herbs and ginseng boiled with a piece of pork or a whole chicken if they had enough food coupons left at the end of the month.

His mother had to cajole him. "Drink this. I know it's bitter, but it will strengthen your blood and help you to grow strong," she urged him each morning as she lifted the bowl to his lips.

The tea tasted acrid all the way down his throat. In the bottom of the bowl, the dark, watery remains resembled a bird's nest of twigs and leaves.

Tao had always liked to watch his mother working in the kitchen, wrinkling his nose at the sharp, pungent smells of the herbs that she slipped into boiling water from brown paper packets. A damp, earthy smell like musk arose, tempered by the sweetness of red dates and dried figs she added to the soup. Entering the steamy kitchen was like stepping into another world where his *ma ma* was a pretty *alchemist,* a new word he'd just read in a book, someone who had the power to transform and enchant. He watched her with her patients, the way she listened and soothed. She knew each person not only by name, but by ailment. *"Here comes Mrs. Yee who suffers from bursitis,"* or *"Young Tan needs more herbs to warm his blood,"* or *"Chong's rheumatism must be flaring up again in this wet weather."* It felt strange to think that he was now one of her patients.

Before his fall, Tao's mother occasionally asked him to deliver herbs to nearby neighbors, which made him feel important. And it was always his job to bring packets of herbs to Auntie Song for her arthritis and high blood pressure. He knew his mother liked Auntie Song for her truthful, no-nonsense ways.

If the courtyard was the domain of his grandfather, all he had to do was follow the brick path that led to the backyard vegetable garden, which belonged to Auntie Song. Tao could usually find her in the garden, or in her small kitchen cleaning and cooking the fresh vegetables she'd just picked. For every packet of herbs he brought to Auntie Song, he carried back three times as many vegetables to his mother in return.

Tao once heard his grandfather say Song had lived through many difficulties in her life, and had been married for a long time to a very bad man, but that she was sturdy and could endure, and that's the way Tao thought of her: someone with strength, not unlike the kapok tree. He liked the way Auntie Song looked. Her face had more wrinkles than he'd ever seen before, but she had only threads of gray in her hair. When she smiled, he could see her missing front tooth, a black hole like a door swung open. She was taller and heavier than his mother, though not fat. Auntie Song liked to keep busy, her hands always in motion, planting or darning or cooking, and he always felt safe around her.

Almost every day after school, Tao helped Auntie Song in her vegetable garden. He pulled weeds, fetched buckets of water, or brought shears and string to tie her long beans together. In early March, she'd taught him to plant his first snow peas, dropping the small seeds into the cool, moist dirt and covering them. "Be careful never to overwater them," Auntie Song had said, hovering over him. "The seeds will rot if they get too wet." He checked them every day, thrilled when the first green shoots emerged from the dirt. His *ye ye* had said they were the best snow peas he'd ever eaten.

Tao wondered what Auntie Song was doing just then, and

how the garden was faring without him. He looked at the thick plaster shell wrapped around his leg and couldn't wait to get it off. He was determined to be completely well by the fall planting.

Outside, the hot wind had picked up, the leaves already beginning to fall from the spiny armed branches of the tree, scratching across the stone pavement. Tao shifted in his bed to get a better look out the window. Every spring, his mother had sent him out to the courtyard to pick up the fallen flower petals from the kapok, which she then dried and later boiled into a tea that calmed fevers. In the fall, he gathered the green kapok leaves to be crushed and rubbed on bruised skin. While he recuperated, his *ma ma* would have to pick up the leaves herself. Tao knew he would forever look upon the tree differently now. Every time he was sent outside to gather the smooth, waxy red petals, or the lance-shaped leaves of the kapok, he would be grateful for their power to heal.

Suyin

S UYIN WOKE WITH A START. A NOISE MADE BY A stalking cat or scurrying rat in the alleyway had entered her dreams and pulled her out of sleep. Sometimes, if she was lucky, she would sleep through the night and forget her gnawing hunger. Suyin lay atop her makeshift bed of the rags and straw she had collected, but it still wasn't enough to ward off the discomfort of the hard ground where she slept tucked away by the back door of the curio shop.

Suyin shifted, the baby a pressing weight. Her back ached and her stomach hurt. If she was hungry, she knew the baby inside her was too, and the thought left her both scared and anxious. She looked around but it was still dark, the moonlight casting the small world around her in shadows. Her tunic was damp with sweat. She never liked the month of August. It was always the most uncomfortable time of the year, the humidity so high her mother had once claimed it made the walls shed tears. Even now, in the dead of night, the air was suffocating, so heavy it felt as if she could actually hold it in her hand.

It was still too early for Suyin to walk over to the main boulevard and rummage through the garbage. She would also have to wait until the marketplace opened, drawing in the morning crowds. The vendors would be more likely to relent and give her something just to get her out of their way, or else they might be too busy to notice her hand reach in from behind their haggling customers to snatch a steamed bun or mango or turnip. She was always cautious, remembering the story of one thief who had his hand cut off by a butcher's cleaver when he tried to steal a chicken. He wasn't much older than she was. Suyin never tried to steal anything more than fruits or vegetables; everything else was too precious to come by, keeping the vendors more attentive.

Suyin rubbed her stomach. "Just wait," she whispered to the baby. "One day we'll feast on shrimp dumplings, green onion pancakes, and buns filled with red bean." They were all of her favorites that she could only dream about, but just the thought of it all now made her stomach clench and she swallowed down the sourness. Suyin leaned back in misery. She reached for some of the dry straw and began to chew on it.

Kai Ying

NOW THAT TAO WAS FINALLY OUT OF THE HOSPITAL, Kai Ying couldn't stop watching him. *He's really home,* she thought. But was he? The more she studied him, the less sure she was that the same Tao had returned to her. The once boisterous and fearless boy she knew had been replaced by a watchful one who lay quietly in bed, his eyes following her every move. She wondered what he was looking at, or what he was looking for, and how she could help him find it.

The small outward signs of his healing were apparent. There were only faint scratches on his face now, and the fading green purplish tint of the ugly bruises on his body, helped by a cream she applied made from the kapok leaves, was almost gone. The irony of it never failed to cross her mind; the tree from which Tao fell was now helping him to heal. But his hair, closely shorn at the hospital, was still a dark shadow on the pale globe of his head. His thin, bony limbs looked as if they could be easily broken if he moved in the wrong way. Kai Ying's heart ached.

What she couldn't say aloud was how Tao reminded her even more of Sheng now, how she imagined her husband with the same shaved head and bony frame at the Luoyang reeducation camp, somewhere in the central plains of China. She treasured his two letters, but she hadn't heard from Sheng again in over six months, and she found herself in a perpetual state of anticipation. Through the heat of summer, she was frozen, waiting to thaw. There were many possible reasons for his silence, but Kai Ying wouldn't allow herself to think of them. If she didn't think of them, they wouldn't be true. She fought hard not to appear sad in front of Tao. As the months went by, she spoke often of Sheng and read Tao snatches from his letters. But since his fall, he hadn't asked her once about his *ba ba*. He hardly said anything at all.

Who was this boy?

After breakfast each morning, Wei went back upstairs. During Tao's first week back, she and her father-in-law had taken on their respective roles in his recovery. While Wei was entertaining him with stories about China's art and history in his calm and steady voice, Kai Ying found it difficult to concentrate on her herb work, which kept her away from Tao most of the day. She listened to her patients and tried to appear concerned and involved, but her mind wandered to her little boy upstairs who had to stay as immobile as possible, held captive by a monstrous cast twice the size of his leg. She didn't want him shadowed by a limp for the rest of his life. Hadn't they gone through enough heartache in the past year?

Kai Ying saw these days as a healing time for her father-in-law, too, whose spirits rose every time he was with his grandson. The morning after the incident with the cleaver, Wei had come down to breakfast and apologized. "I'm sorry," he said, his hands stopping in midair without any other explanation. "I don't know what came over me." Kai Ying saw a slight twitching under his left eye. She couldn't remember his ever apologizing to her, to anyone. "Is everything all right?" she asked. Since Sheng's arrest, she felt him gradually moving further away from them. He paused for just a moment, before he nodded reassuringly and said, "Everything's fine."

The tree had survived. But when they were alone those evenings after they returned from the hospital, she avoided looking directly into his eyes, afraid she would see the look of anguish and defeat in them again. And every time she walked out to the courtyard, she found herself keeping a careful distance from the kapok tree.

As Kai Ying waited for her next patient to arrive, she heard Tao's laughter from upstairs. Wei was with him. It was music, a glorious sound coming from her child that filled her with gratitude. For the first time in almost a month, she allowed herself to relax. It was as if she'd been holding her breath ever since Tao's fall, waiting for what was going to happen next, bracing herself the way Sheng must have to brace himself every morning in order to get through each day.

How proud Sheng would be of Tao. Kai Ying smiled,

reached into her pocket, and touched her husband's two letters; her smile faded. She took one letter out of the envelope as she had a hundred times before, her eyes quickly scanning the all too familiar characters that filled the thin sheets of paper. He spoke sparingly of his life at the camp and the work he was assigned to do there.

Dear Kai Ying,
This is the first letter I've been allowed to write since arriving here in Luoyang almost two weeks ago. There was no way to get word to you sooner, but I'm fine and everything will be all right. I was detained at the public security bureau for weeks until it was decided I would be sent to Henan province for reeducation. Then I was told I could write to you after I arrived.

Kai Ying knew Sheng couldn't write what he was really feeling. His letter would be scrutinized by the authorities before it was sent and he couldn't risk it not being sent to her. In every line, she heard his voice; in each pause were the words he couldn't say. From the moment Sheng was arrested, she knew the police had already found him guilty of being a counter-revolutionary. And of course, the letter he had sent to the Premier's Office was all the evidence they needed. Others had been sentenced for far less. The police were given full power by the Party to carry out administrative detentions without the assistance of lawyers, or the judicial system, for any disruptive acts as long as they weren't criminal. The men and women arrested for any type of nonconformist behavior were almost always sentenced to reeducation through labor.

Sheng had once told her of colleagues he knew who were sent away for years to do manual labor, disappearing from their lives as if they had never been there. "They became shadows," he said. Some were gone for a year or two, while others had still not returned to their families.

The words of the hated poem suddenly returned to Kai Ying, *"Let a hundred flowers bloom; let a hundred schools of thought contend."* She could still hear Sheng's voice that spring afternoon in 1956 when he returned home from teaching, brimming with news. "The Party has just announced they want to hear from all intellectuals and artists on ways to improve China and the Party," he told her, breathless, his face flushed with excitement.

"What are you talking about?" Kai Ying asked. She was in the kitchen, making a soup with lily leaf root for Tao's cough. The steam rose and filled the room.

"Mao is calling it the 'Hundred Flowers Campaign,' in hopes of building a stronger China," he said, unbuttoning his gray Mao jacket. "It's our chance to step forward and let the Party know what we think. If no one does, how will anything change?"

Kai Ying watched his dark eyes come alive. He sounded so hopeful, happier than she'd seen him in a very long time.

"How can you trust them?" she asked, knowing that Mao and his Party had waged an ongoing persecution of all artists and intellectuals during the past decade. During that time, most intellectuals and counterrevolutionaries met secretly and learned to keep to themselves, having cultivated a constant distrust of the People's Party. "It's a trick," she said. "They won't suddenly change." Kai Ying couldn't understand how Sheng could be so easily fooled by Party rhetoric.

"What if it isn't a trick?" he asked. Sheng smiled, refusing to let her dampen his enthusiasm. "What if it's a rare opportunity for change?"

Kai Ying shook her head and remained quiet. She feared that Mao listened only to the sound of his own voice, and she didn't want Sheng to be fooled. He had stepped closer to her and reached for her hand. As if he knew what she was thinking, he promised to be patient, to wait and see what happened before he became involved in anything. Even then, she wished it would all just go away.

For almost a year, caution prevailed, everyone suspicious that the Hundred Flowers Campaign was just another Mao ploy to weed out the nonconformist intellectuals. But in February 1957, the Party made another plea for participation. Not only had Mao approved of this new vision, but Chou En-lai was also calling for constructive criticism, reiterating the belief that the Hundred Flowers Campaign was needed to make China stronger and better. "We might not trust Mao," Sheng told her, "but Chou En-lai has always been a man of reason and humanity." By May, scientists, teachers, and students gradually grew bolder in raising their voices. And what began as careful, guarded steps quickly escalated. Posters by students went up in universities criticizing the Party, their words growing harsher with arrogant confidence as each day passed. "The Privileged Party" was a rallying slogan that sprang up over and over in letters to the newspapers, written accusingly in thick, black strokes on posters, and chanted at gathered forums followed by *The Party grows fat, while the people suffer!*

All of May and June of last year, Kai Ying saw the growing tide as the voices around her rose and anger roiled on both sides. She couldn't help but worry, knowing that Sheng might be one of those voices. *"Don't go! Don't go! Don't go!"* she said to him. He had promised. But he was in and out of a flurry of meetings, even as he was careful never to say anything specific to her about his involvement. Sheng hadn't told her about the letter he'd written to the Premier's Office, and so far the authorities had refused her many requests to see it. Was there even a letter? Why had he signed his name? Did he think they wouldn't find him? Did he really believe some neighbor or colleague or student wouldn't report his clandestine meetings? Sheng had always been headstrong, but never arrogant. How could he do that to her? How dare he? Within weeks, once the criticism turned directly toward the Party members and Mao himself, the Hundred Flowers Campaign was abruptly halted and all the counterrevolutionaries arrested.

Sheng included.

In the end, the Hundred Flowers Campaign had failed miserably and there was only one school of thought, that which belonged to the Party. Kai Ying should have begged Sheng not to do anything stupid. She should have screamed and cried harder until he listened. But deep down she knew it would have done no good. Now all she could think of was: had Sheng become a shadow? Kai Ying pushed the thought out of her mind and looked down at the letter in her hand.

Luoyang is different. The land is wide and flat and with little green to be seen here. I find myself thinking about the kapok tree, having taken it for granted all the years it bloomed in the courtyard. My entire lifetime and I barely noticed. Here, when the wind blows across the endless plains at night, it sounds like a thousand voices crying out. The days are hot and dry now, and I wonder what the winter will bring. Everything about this place feels extreme. I live in a small room with five others. We work twelve to fourteen hour days in a stone quarry and you might not believe how strong I've gotten.

Kai Ying didn't have to be told that such back-breaking work was grueling and dangerous, tons and tons of rock to be blasted from the mountainsides, carried out, and broken up. It was work that Sheng, a teacher and scholar, wasn't used to doing. It was work that no human being should be doing. She worried about the multitude of accidents that could happen that had nothing to do with the other everyday constants, the struggle to stay healthy when there was never enough food or rest or adequate sanitation.

Just writing your name makes me feel better, as if you're somehow closer to me and not all these miles away. Tell my father that I'm well. Tell Tao that I'll be home soon and we'll all finally take that trip to White Cloud Mountain. It's the dream I hang on to each and every day.

The second letter arrived almost four months later, in February of this year, and all signs of enthusiasm had worn away with the news he wouldn't be able to come home for the New Year. It was too far. A lifetime away. She and Wei had sent letters, parcels with dried and canned foods using their allotted food coupons, but never heard whether Sheng had received them. Kai Ying had written to him at once after Tao had fallen. She had naïvely hoped the authorities would allow Sheng to come home for a visit. She had hoped for a reply, just a few words, anything that would let her know he was all right. This was what terrified Kai Ying the most; she knew that if Sheng had heard Tao was hurt, he would have written back to her immediately. During her most difficult moments, Kai Ying resurrected the few personal lines from his letters she had committed to memory. *Don't worry, I'm holding up. I miss you all terribly. Will I recognize Tao when I see him again? Will he recognize me? And you? You.*

She heard the anguish in his voice.

She wasn't going to cry.

Wei

AFTER BREAKFAST, WEI CLIMBED THE STAIRS TO his bedroom for the book of myths he wanted to show Tao. His room was down the hall toward the back of the villa, larger and cooler during the hot, muggy days. It had once been his mother and father's room, and later, the room that he and Liang shared. His mother had been his father's fourth and much younger wife. Even as a boy, Wei thought they looked more like father and daughter than husband and wife. After his father's first wife passed away, wives number two and three, his aunties, stayed in rooms at the other end of the hall. His older half sisters were married by the time he entered school and he had always felt like an only child growing up.

Wei's father often stood on the balcony and watched him playing in the courtyard below when he was a boy, much as he now watched Tao. He was too young then to realize that he had been the much-longed-for son of a seventy-year-old man.

Wei looked for the book for Tao. Every wall was stacked with crowded bookcases. Tao had once said his bedroom resembled a library, which Wei supposed it did, and for which he was grateful. The books reminded him of his office at the university, a place he felt safe.

There had once been a real library downstairs in the villa. Now it was used by Mr. and Mrs. Chang as their bedroom. After Liang's death, the bookcases had been moved up to his room. As a boy, Wei had spent countless hours in his father's library, sitting in his high-back brown leather chair, reading. His father was often away on business and Wei seriously doubted he had spent much time reading any of the hundreds of books that once lined his bookshelves. So Wei took it upon himself to read them. He smiled now to think how little he'd understood of what he read back then.

Just yesterday morning, Tao had asked him if he had really read all the books on his bookshelf. Wei laughed. "Those are only a handful of what I've read," he answered. "You should see all the books I've put away," he said. "Hidden away."

"Hidden?" Tao had asked. "Why?"

Wei smiled and leaned closer. "Well, unlike when I was a boy, the government we have now dislikes certain kinds of books."

"Why would they dislike books?"

"Because all good books are filled with different ideas and truths, and the Party disapproves of books by authors who say something different from what they believe in. They're afraid we'll form our own opinions and no longer listen to them. If they find your *ye ye*'s books, they'll destroy them."

"Are your books bad?"

"No, they're good," he answered. "It's important for us to understand and consider all sides before we make decisions."

"And that's why you're hiding them?"

Wei nodded. "I'm saving them for you. When you're older, you can read them all and make up your own mind about the life you want to live."

"Where have you hidden them?" Tao asked.

He lowered his voice. "It's our secret. When your leg has healed, I'll show you."

As Wei searched his bookshelves, his gaze halted at a slim volume of poetry, given to him on a long-ago birthday by a teenaged Sheng. Wei had written poetry as a young man and once entertained the thought of becoming a poet. The book, by the famous Tang Dynasty poet Tu Fu, was a favorite of his. Reaching for it now, Wei hoped that he'd told Sheng it remained one of his most cherished gifts. Every morning since Sheng had been taken away, Wei read a poem from the book, which somehow made him feel closer to his son. Now he sat down at his desk and flipped through the worn pages, the book opening naturally to the poems where the spine was broken. He read the first stanza of the aptly titled "Thinking of My Boy," written for the poet's favorite son.

Comes spring once more,
Pony Boy, and still we
Cannot be together; I
Comfort myself hoping
You are singing with
The birds in the sunshine . . .

Wei stopped reading, suddenly angered. He knew Sheng wasn't where he could be singing with birds in the sunshine. Just after Sheng was taken away, Kai Ying had pleaded with the police officials to tell her his whereabouts, but to no avail. Two months later, they received word that Sheng had been sent to be reeducated in Luoyang in the western Henan province. As she read the note to Wei, Kai Ying's face turned pale. Luoyang was in the central plains of China, more than a thousand miles away by train, another world away. They had hoped and prayed that Sheng was somewhere closer in Guangdong province. There, at least they could visit, and there was the chance of his returning home for a week's furlough during the New Year holidays. Instead, it would take that long just to travel back and forth from Luoyang.

Wei had once studied artifacts from the region around Luoyang, one of the cradles of Chinese civilization and one of the original Four Great Ancient Capitals of China. Now he could only imagine it as a place of darkness and desolation, where men and women were worked to death or beaten to death or starved to death, a place where even birds never ventured unless they were vultures.

Wei had an old colleague, a Professor Wong from Lingnan, a steadfast and intelligent man who had always been an outspoken critic of Chairman Mao. His family had begged him to leave China before the Communists came into power, but he had refused. Within weeks of the new government, he was seized in the middle of the night by the police and sent to a reeducation camp in Shandong province to work in the mines. Before the sun rose each day, the prisoners were sent deep into dark, dank tunnels, reemerging later into darkness. Did Wong think even the sunlight had abandoned him? He was seventy years old and unfit for hard labor, his body failing even if his indomitable spirit hadn't. The authorities said he had died of natural causes, but Wei knew they had killed him, just as if they'd held a gun to his head.

Wei's eyes filled with tears. He swallowed, the words of the poem tasting bitter in his mouth. He closed the book and placed it on his desk, then unlocked a drawer and pulled out his worn leather-bound journal. In it was a rough copy of the letter he had sent to the Premier's Office. The lines were burned into his memory. *If China is to become a stronger nation, the Party must open its eyes and see that power comes from free expression. What freedom do we have in a Communist society if artists and intellectuals are tortured for following their hearts? What freedom do we have if art and ideas and politics can't be appreciated and openly discussed? How can there be strength in suppression?*

Wei had written his thoughts with such truth and clarity, as if a light had suddenly flooded a long-darkened room. Now those very same ideas had turned to needles pricking his skin, and the truth he'd written had condemned his son to hard labor. After a lifetime of keeping to himself and remaining close-mouthed, what made him write the letter and sign his name? A moment of vanity and conceit, a need to feel important again, which only served to implicate Sheng, who had always been the one active in school forums and politics, and whose given name was also Weisheng, meaning *greatness is born*, each of them the long-awaited sons of their parents. Wei and Liang had called him Sheng since birth, so as not to cause confusion with his own name. So as not to cause confusion. Confusion.

Wei swallowed. He was nothing more than a pompous old fool, sick with regret. The morning the police came for Sheng, he had taken hold of his son's arm in all the commotion, leaned in close and told him, "I wrote the letter. It was me," before they pushed Sheng back and pulled him away. But not before he saw the moment of understanding cross his son's face. Wei had tried to make them listen to him. He grabbed a policeman's arm and said over and over, "It was me, not my son. Take me!" only to be pushed away, hard and firm, as he stumbled back. He heard Kai Ying pleading with the other policemen. "Don't worry," Sheng said to him. "Don't say a word. I'll be all right." His eyes told Wei that he meant it. A look of trust a father would give a son. And then Sheng was gone, and he was the one left helpless and heartbroken.

He couldn't imagine what Liang would think of him now. What kind of father would allow his son to take his place? Wei sat back and closed his eyes, but even Liang wouldn't return to him.

Wei stood in the doorway of Tao's room. He could barely see his grandson behind the cast, but he could feel his growing restlessness each day as he regained his strength. It'd been nearly two weeks since his return from the hospital, and he saw similarities between Sheng and his grandson that hadn't been so apparent before. It was only Tao who gave him moments of solace now. Wei looked around the room, thinking it might be a good change for the boy to be carried downstairs for dinner that evening. Still, it was something he would have to discuss with Kai Ying first. Tao's cast was scheduled to be taken off in a few weeks, and she didn't want him moved, for fear his leg wouldn't heal right and he would always walk with a limp.

Yesterday morning was the first time Kai Ying had looked relaxed around him since he'd taken the cleaver to the tree. Wei had made a feeble apology to her, but how could he tell her that the tree he had always loved had suddenly become his enemy, the only thing he could take his anger out on for hurting his grandson? It sounded like senseless gibberish coming from a crazy old man, when the simple truth was all the pent-up fury was directed at only one person: himself.

* * *

"Is that you, *ye ye*?" Tao asked, straining to look around his elevated cast.

Wei stepped into the room and smiled.

"Yes, it's me."

The book felt solid and heavy in Wei's hands. "Aren't you hungry?" he asked, gesturing toward his grandson's untouched breakfast.

Tao shook his head.

Wei sat down on the chair next to his bed. "Well, maybe eat a little something to keep you going until lunch. You'll need energy to get better."

Tao nodded.

Wei handed him the piece of bread, then tapped on his hard cast. "And how are you feeling?"

"It itches," Tao answered.

Wei leaned over. "Here? Or here?" He scratched several different places down the length of the hard cast until Tao finally smiled. "Ah, I see you're feeling better."

"A little."

"Good," Wei said. "Little by little, and you'll be up and running very soon."

Tao shrugged.

"Look what I brought for you to look at today."

Wei held up the book, which looked similar to the one he had brought the morning before and the day before that. He opened the large leather-bound book slowly and lovingly as Tao remained quiet, watching. "I thought you might like to see these," Wei said, turning the pictures in his direction.

He helped Tao sit up to look at the bright, beautiful paintings of the dragons, tigers, phoenixes, and tortoises. "They're the four creatures of the world," Wei explained.

Tao appeared distracted. He glanced toward the window and Wei rose and pulled the curtains back, letting in more light. "That's better." He sat back down beside him.

"Do you need me to do anything else?" he asked.

Tao shook his head and finished his toast. He looked down at the paintings in the book.

Wei recalled the time one evening when Sheng, not much older than Tao was, stood in the doorway watching him, studying him. He had looked up instinctively from the book he was reading to see his son standing there. "What is it?" he had asked abruptly, distracted, as if Sheng were simply a student waiting to see him. The boy looked at him, slightly embarrassed, lingered shyly for a moment before he finally said, "It's nothing." And then he turned around and was gone. Only now did Wei see it as one of many moments when he should have reached out to his son. "Come talk to me," he should have said. "Come tell me about your day." It all seemed so much easier with Tao.

He looked down at Tao. "Look here," he said, pointing at the paintings. "Each animal represents one of the four directions and one of the four seasons: the Green Dragon, east and spring; the White Tiger, west and summer; the Red Phoenix, south and fall; and the Black Tortoise, north and winter," he said, his voice rising dramatically. He hoped his grandson would be intrigued by the myth, and by the fact they were being guarded by such creatures. "And just what creature do you think is being protected in the very center by the four others?" he asked.

Tao looked intently at the painting, and finally said, "A monkey?"

Wei smiled and shook his head. He saw Tao's eyes light up with interest.

"An ox?"

He shook his head again.

"A horse?"

"No."

"Neighbor Lau's rooster?"

Wei laughed. Tao laughed too, suddenly the little boy he knew again, and it brought a moment of joy. What he couldn't give to his son, he could at least give his grandson.

"It's a snake coiled in the center of the four," he said. "And right now, you're just like that snake being protected by the four creatures of the world until you get better."

Tao smiled. And then he was quiet again in thought. "Will they protect *ba ba,* too?"

Wei hesitated a moment. He looked down at his grandson, who resembled his son so much that it made his heart break. He leaned in closer. "Yes," he said, "they'll protect the both of you."

Tao smiled. Then he reached over and did what Sheng would have never done as a boy, stroked the prickly, gray whiskers on Wei's chin.

Tao

Tao's grandfather carried him down to the kitchen, where he heard his mother and Auntie Song's voices before he saw their familiar, smiling faces.

"Ah, here he is," Auntie Song said, the slightest whistle escaping from the dark window where her tooth had been. She kissed him on the cheek and he could smell the earthy scent of her garden, which made him miss their days outside together. His mother stood back, watching. Tao thought she looked tired and a little nervous, but she stepped forward and reached for his hand and gave it a squeeze.

The kitchen was warm and aromatic with all his favorites: fried rice with scallions and dried shrimp, and long beans and Chinese mushrooms in oyster sauce. Auntie Song returned to her chopping and mincing. The kitchen door stood ajar and Tao looked out into the courtyard. An afternoon thunderstorm had come and gone. Before his grandfather set him down on one of the two chairs facing each other, one for him to sit on, the other arranged with pillows for his leg, Tao leaned close and asked, "Can we go outside for just a little while?"

His grandfather looked over at his mother, and Tao watched one of those silent grown-up conversations between them where decisions were made simply by a look or gesture.

* * *

The courtyard was warm and steamy, fragrant after the thunder-shower. The air felt good after weeks of being pent up in the hospital and then up in his room. The kapok tree stood dark and silent. Was this the same courtyard he had played in since he was just a baby? Tao closed his eyes and opened them again. He looked over at the Ming-tiled wall, the faded red gate, up at the second-floor terrace where he and his *ba ba* used to stand looking for White Cloud Mountain; it was all begin-ning to feel familiar again.

His grandfather walked around slowly, uncharacteristically quiet with him. Tao noticed he carefully avoided the tree and the spot where he had fallen, even when he tried to turn and get a better look at the tree. Since his father left, his *ye ye* had changed. He had once walked in on his father and grandfather arguing about something, their voices sharp and strained. When they saw him standing there, they smiled and lowered their voices, but it was an entire day before they were themselves again. His *ye ye* hadn't been himself for a very long time. He and his mother were sad, but his grandfather's sadness was different, heavier, like a weight pulling him down. Tao just wanted to pull him back up, but he didn't know how. He wondered if his mother had a tea or soup that would help his *ye ye* feel better, and if so, why hadn't she already made it for him.

His grandfather stopped for a moment. He must have been tired of carrying him, the cast itself a heavy burden. Then, as if he knew what Tao was thinking, he strode over to the stone bench and gently sat him down, carefully lowering the cast onto the bench.

"How does it feel?" he asked, rubbing his arm.

"Good," Tao answered. "Am I too heavy?"

"You're helping me build muscles," he said, sitting down beside him. "Let me know when you'd like to go back in."

He nodded, and leaned back against his grandfather. Tao looked around the courtyard and could almost feel his father's presence. If *ba ba* were here, he could easily carry him down to the canal where they'd watch the ducks, even if his mother objected. If he were home again, they would be having a real celebration.

His grandfather drew a deep breath and stretched his long legs out. "It's worth the afternoon rain for this moment afterwards," he said.

Tao took in a big breath, the thick air tasting sweet, like the big magnolia tree blooming down the street. He heard his mother's voice from the kitchen, the sound of oil splattering in the wok. From the distance came other voices. Tao was feeling himself again.

"You ready to go inside?" his grandfather asked. "I'm getting hungry."

He nodded.

His grandfather smiled and picked him up and into his arms with a low grunt. He had just turned around when Tao saw it; the thin, pale gash across the trunk of the kapok. It was no longer than his hand; still, he winced at the thought of the scar it would leave.

Moon
Festival

September 1958

Tao

TAO HEARD THE COURTYARD GATE WHINE OPEN AND quietly close again. The night before, his mother had told him she would be leaving the house early for the marketplace, so he lay in bed listening. Since his return home from the hospital over six weeks ago, she'd rarely been far from his side. Tao could imagine her walking down the street, turning back once before she disappeared around the corner. He already missed her. Still, he knew she wouldn't be gone for too long, and he'd been too excited to sleep knowing he was finally going to have his cast taken off that afternoon. Tao couldn't wait until he was able to freely move around and finally return to school.

It was September and the new school term had started almost two weeks ago. His best friend, Little Shan, had come by last week, bringing with him an air of self-importance at now occupying Tao's second seat. "For now, Ling Ling is still first seat," Little Shan boasted. "You're lucky to be home, we've had to learn at least a dozen new characters so far."

Tao shrugged and acted as if it didn't bother him. "I'll catch up," he said. He was more determined than ever to recapture his place.

"Teacher Eng sweats a lot and always has dark stains under his arms," Little Shan laughed. "Wait until you see him."

Tao smiled and watched as Little Shan rambled on. Not long ago he would have been laughing along with him, lifted out of his loneliness, but he was still reeling from the real surprise that caught him completely off guard. The once short and chubby Little Shan he'd always known had become a taller, thinner version of himself, a growth spurt that had happened over the summer. Tao was relieved to be seated with his leg propped up, but even so, he could easily see that his friend was taller than he was now. It gave Tao a sudden, sharp stomachache to see how much life around him had changed since his fall from the kapok. It was another small blow he tried to ignore after Little Shan left.

Kai Ying

AFTER A SWELTERING AND LETHARGIC AUGUST, September slid in quick and urgent. Kai Ying had canceled all her patients for the day and left the house early. It was still warm and humid in the afternoons, the threat of rain always hovering in the low, gray sky. They'd had a mild summer rainfall but no heavy monsoon storms for the first time in years. She could feel the changing seasons in the air, the arrival of shorter, darker days. Already, the light had a serious, pressing feel to it. Still, Kai Ying was thankful to see the summer end. It had been a demanding one with Tao's fall, which only made Sheng's absence all the more difficult.

It felt good to be outside and simply walking, away from the hot, steamy kitchen and the everyday illnesses Kai Ying treated. The air still held some coolness from the night before and she breathed in deeply, filling her lungs. She'd forgotten how happiness felt. In that moment Kai Ying dared to hope, to believe that Tao's leg would be completely healed when his cast came off that afternoon, and how they would be happily celebrating his recovery along with Moon Festival tomorrow evening.

Kai Ying wanted to get to the marketplace early, before it became too crowded with shoppers vying for the limited chickens or ducks or scant pieces of pork to prepare for their Moon Festival dinner. Since the Party had come into power, there was less and less of everything. They made do with whatever basic necessities they could get with their food coupons and money, supplemented by Auntie Song's vegetable garden. Kai Ying had worked longer hours for the past two months in hopes of buying for dessert a box of the expensive moon cakes, which were Tao's favorite. It was one luxury she hoped the Party hadn't abolished.

Away from the villa, the short distance brought clarity. Kai Ying was free to think and feel everything she'd hidden when she was at home. She had to stay strong and not upset her family any more than they had already been. During Tao's convalescence, their well-meaning neighbors had come by with oranges and starfruit to welcome Tao home. And though she was grateful, Kai Ying just wanted their lives to return to some kind of normalcy. Sometimes, she heard the low murmurs of their neighbors out in the courtyard consoling her father-in-law. "He's a strong boy," they whispered. Still, no one dared to talk about the other small deaths that might remain: the fracture that hadn't set right, the limited use of his right leg, the pronounced limp the doctor said might always stay with him. How would he get along in an already difficult world? Kai Ying had spent many sleepless nights lying in bed worrying. She wasn't alone.

Almost every night, Kai Ying heard her father-in-law's muffled coughing from down the hall and knew he was having a hard time sleeping. He hadn't had a good night's sleep since Sheng was taken away. Sometimes she heard him moving quietly down the hallway, opening the balcony doors and stepping outside. She pictured him staring out into the night as if he could disappear into it. So far, none of the teas or soups she had brewed for him had restored his energy, not even those boiled with the expensive, and more potent, black ginseng. The few times she did try to talk with him, he became distant and uncomfortable around her, much as he was when she and Sheng were first married and she came to live with them.

The smallest details still returned to her, how young and frightened she had been, how her mother-in-law, Liang, had been more than welcoming, while Wei greeted her with a quiet reserve, watching her, scrutinizing. Even if he didn't say a word, Kai Ying felt his disappointment, the thinly veiled knowledge that his son could have married a better educated woman from a wealthier Guangzhou family. She was an outsider and Dong-shan was a world away from where she grew up in Zhaoqing. Her parents were modest and simple dry goods merchants, while the Lee villa was the largest house she'd ever been in. After she entered the household, Wei was always cordial but he seemed awkward and uneasy with her, always surprised when he ran into her in the kitchen or hallway. "He's slow to warm up to people," Sheng reassured her. "Don't worry."

Kai Ying had never forgotten the joy she felt when her father-in-law finally introduced her as his *sun po*, his daughter-in-law, to an old family friend for the first time almost a year after her marriage. Still, in the back of her mind, Kai Ying always wondered if the only reason she was finally accepted by Wei into the family was because of his beloved wife's failing health. The thought still stung.

Over the years, Kai Ying thought she and Wei had found a common ground of support and understanding. But since Sheng's arrest, she felt it gradually slipping away when she needed it most. Did Wei think she knew about the letter Sheng had written? Did he blame her for not stopping him? He'd become distant with everyone except Tao. Now after Tao's accident, her father-in-law had fallen into a new state of distress. She was not only worried about his physical health, but his emotional state as well. Kai Ying heard Sheng's voice telling her once again, *"It takes the same amount of energy to worry about the worst thing that can happen as it does to hope for the best. It's up to you to choose."*

Where was he?

Tao

WHILE HIS MOTHER WAS GONE TAO CONSOLED himself. Not only was his cast coming off, but tomorrow night was Moon Festival, the Mid-Autumn Festival when the moon was at its fullest. It was one of his favorite celebrations of the year. He loved eating the round palm-sized moon cakes filled with sweet bean and lotus seed paste, a hard-boiled egg yolk in the middle, full like the moon. They would begin the celebration with a special dinner and he would help them decorate for Moon Festival by hanging red and gold lanterns in the courtyard. The table would be set extravagantly with his grandmother's good blue and white bowls with the rice pattern around the edge. His *ye ye* told him the blue and white colors in porcelain vases and bowls had become popular during the Yuan Dynasty, when artists began to express themselves freely instead of following the orders of the emperor and his court. They were his grandmother's favorite dishes. And next to the bowls would be their ivory chopsticks instead of their old wooden ones.

And just before it turned dark, he and his grandfather would go outside to the courtyard where his *ye ye* would tell him the legend of Houyi, the archer, and his wife the beautiful maiden Chang'e, the Moon Goddess of Immortality. While they always remained the central characters, his grandfather explained, there were several versions of the same myth, and each year he told Tao a different one.

The beginning of the story always remained the same: Houyi was commanded by the Emperor Yao to use his archery skills to shoot down nine of the ten suns to keep the earth from burning up. Upon completing his task, the emperor gave the famed archer a pill that granted him eternal life. Knowing its value, Houyi left the pill at home with Chang'e when he was sent away on another mission for the emperor. From there, the story of why Chang'e swallowed the pill of immortality splintered off into different versions. So far, Tao's favorite account was Chang'e having to protect the pill from Peng, one of Houyi's apprentice archers, who forcefully tried to take the pill from her. Knowing that she was unable to fight him off, her only choice was to swallow the pill herself. Afterward, Chang'e escaped and flew up into the sky. When Houyi returned home to find his wife gone, he tried to follow her but was forced to turn back when Chang'e reached the moon, where she discovered she could never return to earth and to her husband. Houyi eventually settled on the sun and was able to visit his beloved wife only once a year on the night of Moon Festival.

Tao wondered if his father would return and visit them tomorrow night. Even once a year was better than nothing. He knew the first thing he would do when he gazed up at the full moon was to close his eyes and wish that his *ba ba* could be guided home again by the moon's bright light.

Tao heard his grandfather downstairs and hurried to eat his piece of bread and drink his soy milk. Outside the window he watched as the leaves of the kapok tree moved back and forth as if they were waving to him.

Tomorrow at this time, everything would return to normal. He'd be downstairs in the kitchen eating breakfast with his mother and *ye ye*. The cast would be off and Tao would be as light as Houyi the archer flying through the sky. He would grow taller and learn two dozen characters and see his friends again. His classmates would gather around him in the yard and he would tell them the story of his falling from the tree, exaggerating small details just as his grandfather, who was the best storyteller in Guangzhou, often did. Tao would add just a few feet to the height from which he had fallen, or tell them he'd seen the peaks of White Cloud Mountain right before he slipped. *Weren't you scared?* they would ask. *Didn't it hurt?* He would look his classmates straight in the eyes, but he wouldn't tell them that he didn't remember anything after hitting the ground. There wasn't time to be scared, he'd tell them. It had all happened so quickly. But he knew if it were a myth his grandfather was telling them, he'd have flown up into the sky like Chang'e and Houyi, and would now be living on the moon or the sun.

Kai Ying

A S KAI YING APPROACHED THE MARKETPLACE, IT appeared as if all of Dongshan had made an early start shopping for Moon Festival. The stalls were crowded three or four persons deep as bargaining voices filled the air. In stacked wooden cages, the live chickens clucked frantically, growing more anxious with all the noise. Kai Ying had worn a lightweight gray cotton tunic and pants and still found she was perspiring in the humidity. She longed for the cooler days of winter. Instead of entering into the throng to fight for what little there was, she quickly turned the corner to avoid the pushing crowds. She still had a piece of salted fish at home and decided to take her chances. Kai Ying kept walking farther downtown until she was a few streets away from the bustling market and could walk briskly down the street and toward the Dai On herb shop. She would pick up a few herbs she needed first, then double back to buy a box of moon cakes from Mr. Lam's shop before returning to the marketplace to see what was left.

The scent of roasting chestnuts on the street reminded Kai Ying of the first day she stepped out of the train station, having just arrived in Guangzhou to study with Herbalist Chu. Her hometown of Zhaoqing was another world away. Kai

Ying had grown up surrounded by natural beauty, a gift she never realized until she arrived in Guangzhou and was confronted by the incessant noise and the congestion of so many people, buildings, and streets. She found the city suffocating and everyone unfriendly. The bicycles and pedicabs whizzed around her as if she were just an obstacle in the way. Kai Ying felt as if she were constantly stumbling those early days in Guangzhou. She never ventured far from Herbalist Chu's shop, feeling safe within its narrow and crowded rooms. She was terribly homesick, that first month in Guangzhou, missing her family and the mountains and lakes of Zhaoqing. There wasn't a day she didn't want to get on a train to return home.

The Dai On herb shop seemed frozen in time. Kai Ying paused a moment before she entered the old building, the faded sign above the door buckled with age. It appeared as it must have for generations of Herbalist Chu's family, and just as it did when she first stepped in the door at nineteen. She was immediately confronted by the familiar smell of mold and musk from the mushrooms, tinged with the sweetly medicinal scent from the herbs, berries, and dried dates. It took a moment for her eyes to adjust to the dimness of the room, her gaze resting on the wall of narrow drawers behind the dark wood counter that held the hundreds of herbs she'd come to know so well. Kai Ying felt immediately comforted, as if she were falling into the familiar embrace of an old friend.

The past returned to Kai Ying every time she stepped into the herb shop. She was that young woman again, overwhelmed by the sheer number of different herbs each drawer held. There were six hundred commonly used herbs and thousands more that weren't used on a regular basis. And while each herb possessed a singular quality, it took a combination of several herbs working together to balance the five major organs: the liver, heart, spleen, lungs, and kidneys. Herbalist Chu told her that the really expensive, hard-to-get herbs and the good-quality ginseng were locked away in the back room. It was where he also kept the high-priced ground deer antlers that could "make a man young again," he once said, and winked at her, revealing the powdery substance that left a brownish film in the palm of his hand. At the time, Kai Ying couldn't imagine how she would remember every herb and she was in constant doubt of her effectiveness and intelligence to succeed as an herbalist, or a healer of any kind.

As Kai Ying looked around the shop now, she wondered if Herbalist Chu had hidden away all the expensive herbs before the Communist takeover. On the wall opposite the drawers were shelves of large glass jars, which once contained dried deer tail, shark's fin, dried scallops, fish maw, and bird's nest. The floor was still cluttered with large wooden barrels no longer brimming with dried *Lingzhi,* or spiritual mushrooms, citrus peels, dried fruits, cinnamon bark, wild yam root, and poor man's ginseng. Still, it was one of the best herb stores in all of Guangzhou.

Kai Ying looked up at the top row of drawers. They were so high up she'd had to climb a ladder to get to them. The third drawer from the left once held her favorite secret of all, the small, translucent white and pink pearls that Herbalist Chu ground into a fine powder and mixed into a cream that kept skin young and smooth. At the time, women came from all over to buy the expensive cream, the smaller the pearls, the greater their value. There were handfuls of tiny pearls in the drawer and Kai Ying liked to hold their lightness in the palm of her hand, knowing only the wealthy could afford such an extravagance. Each month she slipped a small pearl into her pocket, one for every month she had to stay and study in Guangzhou. Kai Ying knew it was wrong, but she told herself it wasn't really stealing because she intended to put them all back in the drawer before she left. If Herbalist Chu knew, he never said a word. She kept the pearls hidden away in a small cotton pouch in her upstairs bureau, each one a reminder that she was closer to returning home.

At the time, Kai Ying believed the cluttered rooms of the herb shop were all that a small-town girl needed until she returned home to Zhaoqing. But then she met Sheng and married into a family of scholars, and remained in a city she had only meant to visit.

After Kai Ying bought the herbs and moon cakes, she made her way back to the market, where the crowds seemed only to have swelled with the heat. Shoppers laden with bags quickly surrounded her. Street dogs roamed the area, sniffing at the bags, whining for scraps until they were pushed or kicked away. The exuberance Kai Ying felt just an hour ago was now gone. She bought oranges and taro, which grew heavy and cumbersome as she pushed her way from one stall to another. All she wanted at the moment was to go home and see how Tao was doing.

Kai Ying quickly turned around when she heard her name called. It was one of their neighbors, Mrs. Sai, who approached her complaining about yet another ailment she hoped Kai Ling would have a remedy for. Her illnesses changed day by day.

"I have a terrible cough," she said, before she'd even said hello. "I barely slept last night I was coughing so much." She turned and coughed weakly.

"Come see me tomorrow," Kai Ying said, and smiled. "I'll be away this afternoon."

"But what am I to do tonight? What if I cough so much I can't sleep again? Can't you give me something today?"

"I'm not working today," she said.

"Not even for me?" Mrs. Sai persisted. "With Sheng gone, it must be difficult to keep up financially. And now with Tao . . ."

"We're fine," Kai Ying interrupted. It was too hot to stand there listening to a know-it-all neighbor. The woman was a nuisance, but it was true, Kai Ying was in no position to turn down business. "Come to the house in an hour."

Mrs. Sai smiled broadly. "You're so good to me," she said, hurrying off to finish her shopping.

Kai Ying watched Mrs. Sai leave. It was simple enough. She would give her some figwort root, dried monkey root, and dates for a soup to suppress her coughing and increase her yin, and then send her quickly on her way. For now, she still had to buy barley and a chicken, or maybe even a duck, courtesy of Mrs. Sai's cough.

Kai Ying made her way to another stall when, out of the

corner of her eye, she recognized the girl walking past her. It took her a moment to realize where she'd seen her before, the way the girl's hands rested on the sphere of her protruding belly. But by the time Kai Ying turned around, the pregnant girl from the hospital waiting room had been swallowed up by the swarming crowd.

Suyin

SUYIN NEVER EXPECTED TO SEE THE WOMAN FROM the hospital again. Guangzhou was a big sprawling city and people from all over Guangdong province came to the hospital. Still, she immediately recognized the woman. In that fleeting moment, Suyin hoped the woman had remembered her, too. It was what her mother would have said was an omen, and whether good or bad, fate had brought them together once more. She needed something to pull her out of this misery.

During the past week Suyin had felt terrible. Her feet and hands were swollen and every sip of water gave her heartburn. She woke up all night having to urinate. She wanted to go to the hospital, but she was afraid they would make her leave and never return. It was the only place she felt safe. Instead, she suffered through each night, her back aching from the hard ground, her belly so tight and heavy she thought it might explode. Once, the idea of giving birth was her worst nightmare. Now Suyin prayed that the baby would come as soon as possible. She preferred an immediate, searing pain that would come to an end, compared to the ongoing discomfort she was feeling each day.

It was too difficult for Suyin to stand and beg for long periods of time anymore, so she began walking to the marketplace every morning, trusting someone would take pity on her. She was too slow and noticeable now to try to steal anything, and usually, some vendor, seeing that she was so young and pregnant, relented and slipped her some wilting vegetables or a piece of fruit. The other day, one woman had given her a pomelo, a fruit she'd loved since she was a little girl. As hungry as she was, Suyin held it in her hands for a moment before she peeled through the thick, spongy skin, exposing the pieces of fruit inside, larger and sweeter than the sections of a grapefruit. She quickly ate the entire pomelo at one sitting, only to regret it when her stomach was upset for the rest of the night. Still, it was the best thing she'd eaten in months. Usually, if she had any energy left, she returned to the market before it closed in hopes of finding something left behind. Wasn't there always something forgotten? She prowled around the empty stalls, the garbage piled high and abandoned, realizing there wasn't much the world had to offer her or her baby.

Suyin knew she wouldn't be able to keep it up much longer. She was exhausted. She hadn't felt the baby kick in the past few days and worried that something was wrong. What if the baby was already dead? What if they both were to die in childbirth? Her heart began to race in fear. She leaned over and breathed in and out slowly until she was calm again.

Most days Suyin longed to be back at home, wedged in a bunk bed below her two brothers in their hot, small apartment, the voices of their neighbors seeping through the thin walls as if they were right there in the room with them. Or even back in school, the noisy, damp-smelling classroom where she had been almost invisible, except during the week before she left school. Suyin had made the mistake of telling a girl she thought she could trust that she might be pregnant. The next day at school, her classmates followed her every move and taunted her relentlessly with *Suyin has come down with the nine-month flu*. While school had become intolerable, she knew now the world was an even uglier place.

Suyin almost didn't go to the marketplace that morning, but her hunger finally outweighed her discomfort. She stood amongst the crowd and glanced back to see the woman had turned around, as if remembering something too late. Was she looking for her? Suyin felt a shiver up her back. She watched the woman through the swarm of pushing bodies when she felt a sudden, sharp kick from the baby again. It was a good omen. The woman hesitated before she turned around and walked away. *I'm here*, Suyin wanted to call out. *I'm right here*. Instead, she waited a moment longer before she followed the woman from a safe distance.

Wei

WEI PAUSED ON THE BRICK PATH THAT LED BACK to Song's rooms, deciding whether to continue. Kai Ying had come home from the market and was preparing Tao for his return to the hospital. Wei hadn't planned on visiting Song; he'd stepped out to the courtyard and found himself moving naturally toward the path, just as he had done so many times in the past. Before Sheng was taken away, he and Song often sat together reminiscing about Liang and the old days. She never minced words and he enjoyed spending time with her. As different as they were, Song was the only one who understood that the past was still very much present for him.

Wei missed their conversations, but he couldn't bring himself to confide in her about his part in Sheng's arrest. His shame still felt like an open wound. But even more so, Wei knew if he looked directly into Song's eyes, she would know something was terribly wrong and ask questions. And then what would he say? It seemed much easier for him to avoid her.

But something had changed since Tao's fall—his loneliness had gradually come to outweigh his shame. He awoke this morning from a disturbed sleep with the sudden need to talk to Song. He had no idea what he was going to say to her. She would never forgive his deception, but she might understand how something like this could have happened. It was all he hoped for.

Wei knew he would find her in or around her garden, and there she was.

"Just in time," Song called out, waving him over to where she stood near a cleared patch of earth.

As he approached, Wei smelled the bucket of manure before he saw it sitting beside her, waiting to be worked into the soil. No one could make vegetables grow like Song did.

"I don't have the time to help right now," he said. "We're on our way to the hospital. I just came over to see how you're doing." And then he added, "It seems like a long time."

"You never did like to get your hands dirty," Song said, and then laughed.

She was still the strongest, most productive person he knew. All the years when he'd been hiding within the university walls cataloguing artifacts, she had been living through life's everyday struggles.

"And if it seems like a long time since you've visited, it's because it *has* been a long time," she added.

Wei smiled and reached out for her arm as Song walked toward him. Her height always surprised him; she was a good half a head taller than Liang.

"Time at least for a cup of tea?" she asked.

He nodded and followed her.

Song looked up at the sky. "It looks like the weather's changing."

Song had put on a little weight during the past few years, but Wei thought it suited her, softened her hard edges now that she was older. Song couldn't have been more opposite in appearance and in manner from Liang. Her emotions rose to the surface at a moment's notice, whereas his wife was always calm and steady. Right after Liang passed away, Wei couldn't walk down the street without seeing women his wife's age who were alive and well. Inwardly, he despised them. Why were they alive while Liang wasn't? It was a spitefulness he hadn't known he possessed. And yet, he never felt that way about Song. It wasn't until Liang had died that Wei realized how similar Song and his wife were in heart and mind, and how their mutual grief had opened the door to their friendship.

Wei looked down at his clothes and couldn't imagine how he must look to Song now. When he was teaching, he always kept up his appearance as a professor and scholar. Now, he saw it all as just one more weakness. Wasn't it because of his vanity that Sheng had been arrested? During the past year, Wei had lost weight, his flesh fallen away so that his clothes hung loosely on his stooped shoulders. His cheekbones protruded, leaving dark hollows under his eyes that made him appear constantly exhausted. Anyone who hadn't seen him in a while would take one look and think he was in the midst of battling some great illness. And Wei supposed he was.

He followed Song through the doorway of her dim apartment. He closed his eyes for a moment, allowing them to adjust. During the hot summer days, Wei always found her back rooms cooler than the main house. In winter, she always wore two padded jackets against the cold, damp air. And in March and April, during the misty, wet season of the plum rains, he thought of her apartment as a warm, dark cave. In any season, there was no direct sunlight until the sun set in the late afternoon, which meant her door was almost always open, a plume of daylight leading to the kitchen. If his daughter-in-law's kitchen smelled of medicinal herbs, Song's kitchen was filled with the rich aromas of food that never failed to make his mouth water.

Wei stepped inside.

Song poured him a cup of tea and he glanced up and nodded in thanks. When she parted her lips and smiled, he glimpsed the dark space where one of her teeth had been. He once mentioned to her that she could have her tooth replaced if she wanted to. Song shook her head and had said, "What for? I'm too old for it to matter anymore. At least this way, it's a reminder of all the battles I've fought to get here." She made it a point then to part her lips, showing the empty space like a badge of honor. Song never told him how she lost the tooth, and if Liang had, it was just one more thing he hadn't heard or didn't remember, lost in his own world.

"What have you been doing with yourself?" Song asked. She put a plate of custard tarts down on the table and sat down across from him.

"Telling stories to Tao," he answered. He stared down at his cup of tea.

"He's going to be just fine," she said.

"Yes, he will be."

"And so will Sheng," she added.

Wei remained silent. "What makes you so sure?" he finally asked. He could feel her gaze upon him.

She reached over and patted his hand, her touch warm and dry. "He's a strong young man," she said. "And he has all of you to return to."

The words rose to the tip of his tongue and this time, he didn't swallow them back down. "I've been a foolish old man. I've made a terrible mistake," he said quietly.

"What mistake?" Song asked. She inhaled. Her voice had softened to a quiet, serious tone, one a mother would use with a child when she knew something was wrong.

He heard the steam rising from a pot she had on the burner, the soft whistle of air flowing upward, the lid clattering. What was she cooking? he wondered. The sound filled his head and made everything around him feel cloudy and far away. The soft whistling sound in his head grew stronger and louder. Wei brought the teacup up to his lips and drank down his tea. He looked up and into her eyes. It was the least he could do: accept responsibility with what little dignity he had left. The hot liquid burned his tongue all the way down his throat. It wasn't enough to make up for what he had done, but it was a start.

"What mistake?" he heard Song ask again.

He looked up and he was there in her kitchen as she refilled his teacup and set it down on the table in front of him. Nothing had changed. He was still an old fool. Song had no idea what was going on with him and he didn't have the energy to start at the beginning.

"Are you feeling all right?" Song asked. He saw the look of concern that now clouded her face. "You haven't been yourself for the longest time."

Song didn't know how wrong she was. He was exactly himself, a coward who didn't deserve her friendship. Instead, Wei cleared his throat and glanced up at her.

"I'm fine," he said.

Tao

TAO SMELLED SMOKE. JUST LIKE AFTER A STRING OF firecrackers had gone off during New Year's, the smoke rising, the burning scent lingering in the air. His mother stood to the side of the hospital table where he lay and squeezed his hand tighter as the high shrill of the saw sheared through the length of the cast. He glanced down at his leg to see the white powdery residue of the plaster spring up and float through the air. The room was small and his grandfather had to wait outside for them in the hallway. The doctor told him to relax and they would have the cast off in a short time. Tao held tightly on to his mother's hand.

Tao closed his eyes for a moment, his thoughts drifting elsewhere. The sound of the saw blurred into the buzzing of a thousand bees. His mother's thumb stroked the back of his hand, telling him everything was all right. It's almost over. He would never forget the time his hand slipped from his mother's in a busy downtown area. He was four years old and was suddenly lost in a crowd of people with his *ma ma* nowhere in sight. He remembered feeling as if he'd fallen into a well, looking up and seeing only a small piece of the sky as he struggled to catch his breath and keep up the pace. Soon, he felt as if he couldn't breathe. *"No, no, no!"* He suddenly stopped and screamed at the top of his lungs. Bodies jostled him to and fro, until a hand grabbed him by the back of the collar and pulled him to the side. His mother had backtracked and was calling his name over and over again when the man waved her over. Tao was crying by then, and when he saw her hurrying toward him, he began to cry even harder until she had picked him up and he was in her arms again. *"I'm here, I'm here,"* she repeated, stroking his back. It was a memory that still haunted him.

The buzzing stopped. Tao opened his eyes and his mother was still there holding on to his hand.

"There we are," the doctor said. He looked up and smiled for the very first time.

The cast was split open like a perfectly divided pea pod, but instead of peas, his pale, thin leg wrapped in gauze was the prize in the middle. The doctor lifted his leg carefully, slowly unwinding the gauze to unleash the sourness of the enclosed plaster and unwashed leg, examining it thoroughly. "I want you to be careful," he added, looking at Tao and addressing him for the very first time. "No more climbing trees."

Tao nodded. No climbing the kapok or getting lost in a big crowd, he thought, where he wouldn't be able to keep up with his weak leg. He imagined struggling against the wave of people pushing him forward, only this time he could see himself pushing back.

"You'll need to make sure he doesn't exert himself when he gets home. The leg is still weak and he needs to take it slowly," the doctor said to his mother. "We'll get him a pair of crutches to use until his leg gains back its strength."

Tao watched as she moistened her lips with her tongue. His *ma ma* took care of people every day, he wanted to tell the doctor. She knew what to do.

"Yes, of course," his mother said, still holding tightly on to his hand.

It began to rain on the afternoon of Moon Festival; the clapping sound of water falling from the branches of the kapok tree and off the tiles of the courtyard wall filled the house. That evening at dinner, Tao stood up from the table, and without using his crutches, slowly limped to the window. His leg felt weak and naked and he was afraid to put too much weight on it. Why couldn't he walk like before, he thought, after all those weeks trapped in a cast? At the window, he stared out at the darkness, the moon completely obscured by the clouds.

"Do you want to hear the story of Houyi and Chang'e now?" his grandfather asked.

Tao turned around and shook his head. "There's no moon," he answered.

"There's still the story."

"It's not the same without the moon."

His grandfather stroked his whiskers. "But we know the moon is still up there, beyond the rain and the clouds."

What good was the moon if you couldn't see it? Tao thought. If it wasn't there to help his *ba ba* to find his way home again? But, he nodded and limped back to the table and sat down, no longer caring which version of the myth his grandfather was going to tell him.

Kai Ying

IT RAINED THROUGHOUT THE NIGHT OF MOON FESTIval and continued into the next morning. The winds increased, howling through the courtyard and rattling around the house. Kai Ying, in the kitchen waiting for her first patient of the day, took down several jars of herbs from the shelf and set them on the counter. She hoped she still had some Teasel root and Eucommia bark to add to the soup she was brewing to help strengthen Tao's leg. On the burner, steam rose from a boiling pot of water, the kitchen warm and humid.

Kai Ying had had trouble sleeping last night. She could still feel Tao's disappointment at not glimpsing the full moon. It had been a difficult day for him in other ways. From the moment his cast came off, she felt his frustration at being unable to walk normally. His leg was thin and sickly looking, the muscle slack.

The doctor had given him a list of exercises to do every day to regain its strength and flexibility. Tao also disliked using the crutches and she watched how hard he was trying to adjust to walking without them. He was like a toddler again, taking slow, tentative steps while always remaining in close proximity to a wall he could lean against or a chair he could grab. He was too young to understand his leg would take time to heal. Patience came with age and experience, something she herself had been forced to learn in the past year.

Kai Ying wished she could do more to help Tao's leg heal faster. She wondered what Sheng would say to make him feel better, and suddenly, the realization that she might never know swept over her, as if his voice had slipped away. She remembered it low and calm, punctuated by a strong, deep laugh, but why couldn't she hear it? And just as unexpectedly, Kai Ying's cheeks were wet with tears. She never cried during the day. She quickly wiped her tears away with the back of her sleeve.

"Are you all right?"

Kai Ying looked up to see Auntie Song quickly closing the kitchen door against the wind and the rain. She looked away, embarrassed, and wiped her face again with her sleeve. "The steam," she said, though sure Song wouldn't believe her. Her own voice sounded foreign to her. She cleared her throat and pretended to be busy with the herbs. "I'm fine," she said, wiping her cheek again. She was relieved it was Auntie Song and not an early patient.

"There's nothing like a good cry to clear the way," Auntie Song said. She stood there, tall and imposing, wearing a cotton tunic and pants damp from the rain and muddied from her early morning work around the garden. Outside, the rain began to fall harder, playing a concert against the rooftop. "Looks like I made it just in time," she said.

"I'm just getting your herbs ready," Kai Ying said. "I was going to bring them over to you when the rain let up."

"No hurry," Song said. "Besides, I wanted to come by and see how Tao is doing this morning."

"He's still upstairs," Kai Ying said. She put a pot of water on to boil for tea.

"I'm just beginning to plant. I was hoping Tao could come over and see the garden today," Auntie Song said, listening to the falling rain. "It looks as if we'll have to wait for another day."

"He loves your garden," Kai Ying said. "*Lo Yeh* is upstairs with him now. It's still difficult for him. The doctor doesn't want him to put too much stress on his leg for a few more weeks. But now that his cast is off, he doesn't understand why he can't simply go back to school and walk and run around like he did before."

"Any boy his age would think the same thing," Auntie Song said. She smiled reassuringly and sat down at the table. "My brothers couldn't sit still for a minute, always getting into mischief. Tao has been laid up for a good two months," she added. "Don't worry, in a few weeks his leg will have gained back its strength and he'll be able to return to school. He'll get through this."

Kai Ying nodded. She took a deep breath and kept her hands busy measuring out the herbs. On a square of paper, she divided equal parts of *tang-kuei*, cinnamon, astragalus, peony, and ginseng for a tea to ease Auntie Song's arthritis.

"I know it's a mother's burden to worry," Song said. "It doesn't end with each day, does it?"

"No, no it doesn't," Kai Ying answered. "And neither do a wife's burdens." She stopped herself and poured a cup of tea for Auntie Song. Sheng's long silence was a heavy weight on all of them.

"I'm sure there's a good explanation as to why Sheng hasn't written," Song said.

"Yes, I know. It's just that . . ."

"What?"

"The only reason he wouldn't write was if something was wrong . . . and he couldn't write."

"There could be all kinds of explanations," Auntie Song said. "You know nothing is ever so simple. We can't begin to guess what he's going through, so it doesn't help to second-guess. You'll just drive yourself crazy with worry. I may not have been blessed with children," Auntie Song said, and sipped her tea, "but I've had my share of a wife's burdens."

Kai Ying stopped what she was doing. She didn't know what she would do without Auntie Song always there to help her through the difficult moments. "Enough burdens for two lifetimes," she said.

"Three!" Song added.

They both laughed, and Kai Ying felt better.

Besides Liang, Kai Ying was the only person Song had ever confided in about her own past. Song's marriage to Old Hing had provided her with nothing but sorrows. Kai Ying knew how fortunate she was to have married a man like Sheng, who carried the best traits of both of his parents: Liang's compassion and Wei's intelligence. She prayed to the gods that he was all right, and that he would return to them soon. But lately, hope only brought her misery at the end of each day.

Upstairs they heard a burst of laughter from Tao and Wei, but they remained silent. Outside, the storm gathered strength. Kai Ying removed the pot of hot water from the fire and refilled their tea, then continued to wrap the rest of Auntie Song's herbs.

Song

OVER THE YEARS, KAI YING HAD BECOME THE daughter she never had. Song watched her in the kitchen now, thin and tired; her eyes still puffy from crying. The shine of youth had just rounded the corner and was disappearing into the serious, dark side of life. Song wished she could ease Kai Ying's pain, just as Kai Ying had once done for her.

"Do you remember the afternoon we first met?" Song asked, breaking their silence.

"Yes, of course," Kai Ying said.

"You were such a big help to me."

"Fate brought you to the herb shop."

"Fate brought me to you that day."

Kai Ying smiled.

"I never told you why I went to the herb shop that afternoon."

"Wasn't it to get something for the pain?"

Song shook her head. "I was hoping Herbalist Chu would help me to end my life."

Kai Ying stopped wrapping the herbs and stared at her in surprise. "What are you saying?" She stepped toward the table and sat down across from Song.

Song cleared her throat. "I really believed that Old Hing was the devil himself. And how can you win with the devil? I'd given up and was hoping Herbalist Chu would take pity on me, slip me something that would put an end to it all, a touch of dried toad venom or cinnabar or crushed oleander leaves. I was too weak to do it on my own." Song paused to drink down the rest of her tea. "I found you there instead."

Song would never forget that late afternoon in 1947. It was cold outside and she wore a scarf that covered her swollen cheek, while an excruciating pain pulsated from her mouth to the top of her head. There were no other customers in the Dai On herb shop when she walked in. Song had never seen the young woman sitting behind the counter before, her head down, studying a book in front of her. Of all days, where was he? Where was Chu? She would later find out that the old herbalist was out running errands and had left Kai Ying, his young apprentice, who had arrived in Guangzhou less than a month before, to fill orders.

Herbalist Chu had always been a sympathetic friend. He had detested Old Hing long before Song was married to him.

He knew most of his customers by name and by their medical histories. Song trusted him. She thought about leaving the shop and returning later, or waiting for Chu to come back, but it meant enduring the throbbing pain in her mouth, which had grown so unbearable she couldn't wait. Song approached the counter slowly.

Kai Ying looked up. "Can I help you?" she asked.

"I need," Song began, though it sounded as if her tongue were stuck to the roof of her mouth. The young woman leaned forward, trying to understand what she was saying. "I need," Song tried again.

Kai Ying closed the book she was reading. "What is it? What do you need?" she asked.

It was the tone of her voice, a tenderness that made Song look up and stare at the young woman for a moment. She was just a girl, Song thought. What could she possibly know? Still, without saying another word, Song pulled down her scarf, exposing the swollen right side of her face that left her eye barely able to open.

Kai Ying led Song to a back room and poured her a cup of tea while she tried to assess where the swelling originated. Song strained to open her mouth as wide as she could. She was in too much pain to worry about anything else. An awful smell of decay filled the small room. Kai Ying quickly sterilized a needle and drained the swollen cavity of pus from the abscessed wound where Song's front tooth had been. Then she cleaned it out, and made up a poultice of jasmine leaves and herbs to stop the bleeding.

"Why did you wait so long?" Kai Ying asked when she had finished. "You must have been in agony for days."

"I couldn't get away," Auntie Song whispered.

"Why?"

It was a small word for such a difficult explanation. After the bleeding stopped, they sat quietly at the table. Outside, the wind whistled through the old building. Song sucked on a poultice, her strong, large-knuckled fingers wrapped tightly around the warmth of the untouched cup of tea. And for a moment, she thought it might burst between her hands.

This young woman had eased her pain, made her feel human again. Then, for the first time, Song told a perfect stranger about her husband, Old Hing, calling him a violent monster, an angry pig, a festering tumor. Once Song began to talk, she couldn't stop, even with the pain. A few nights ago, when he didn't like what she'd made for dinner, he had knocked her tooth out during a beating. The wound had festered when part of the tooth remained in the cavity, and the pain became so unbearable she'd crept out when he'd fallen asleep. Their marriage had been filled with arguments and fights that were of neighborhood legend, escalating into battles that brought out the entire community. Her neighbors often had to hold Hing back, fearing that it was just a matter of time before he would kill her.

No one was sorry when Old Hing died of natural causes just six months later.

A year later, fate intervened again when Song learned that Liang's son wanted to marry the young herbalist who had been so kind to her. After Liang's death, when Wei was grief-stricken and inconsolable, Song was grateful to have been there to help guide Kai Ying through her first few years in the Lee household. It made Liang's absence more bearable for her, too.

And so through the years, Song had learned there were many ways to heal.

Song remembered that day as both the beginning of their friendship and the start of Kai Ying's career as an herbalist. Almost twelve years later, Song was grateful to be alive and sitting across from Kai Ying once again.

"You never told me of your intent that afternoon." Kai Ying reached across the table and poured Song another cup of tea.

"You were so young and just beginning your career," Song said. "You were there learning to heal, not to end lives. I decided to wait for Chu to return."

"And when he did?"

"We're all given burdens," Song said, reflecting back. "But somehow, mine felt lightened after that afternoon with you. When I returned to see Chu, I wasn't ready to leave this world just yet." Song had finally realized Old Hing had become the festering wound in her life and she wasn't going to let him win, at any cost.

"I'm very thankful for that," Kai Ying said.

Outside the wind and rain had grown stronger. The first real monsoon of the season had finally arrived. Song was relieved she hadn't really begun to plant yet. They both looked up when they heard the whine of the courtyard gate as it slammed open and banged against the wall.

Kai Ying

KAI YING STOOD UP AND LOOKED TOWARD THE COURT-yard. "The wind? Or could it be a patient?" she said to Auntie Song. "It must be something serious for someone to venture out in this storm."

She quickly drank down the rest of her tea and opened the kitchen door. As much as Kai Ying loved the herb work, there were days she longed to have more time for herself. This wet, windy morning was one of them.

"I'll just go upstairs and say hello to Tao," Auntie Song said. She stood, reached over, and tucked the packets of herbs Kai Ying had put together for her into her tunic pocket.

A moment later, a high, piercing cry was carried in with the wind from the courtyard. Without a word, Kai Ying rushed outside to see a girl doubled over in pain near the kapok tree, not far from where Tao had fallen. She was holding her belly, and Kai Ying recognized the pregnant girl from the hospital. When she reached her, the girl was frantic. "Something just happened," she said, panting. "I felt something. The baby . . ."

"You're going to be all right," Kai Ying said. "Come with me." She helped the girl walk toward the house, the wind pushing them forward. The monsoon was going to usher this baby in. "Just breathe slowly and stay calm. It won't be long now."

"I can't," the girl said, her face tight with pain as she squeezed Kai Ying's hand.

"Just a few more steps," she said, urging her forward.

But the girl's legs buckled under her and Kai Ying lowered her slowly to the wet ground and knelt beside her, the rain whipping against them. With the palm of her hand, Kai Ying cushioned the girl's head against the hard ground and repeated, "Breathe slowly, in and out."

The girl looked frightened, but she listened.

"Can I help?" Auntie Song asked, suddenly there, hovering over Kai Ying.

Kai Ying didn't take her eyes off the girl. "She's about to have her baby. I think her water's broken," she told Auntie Song, raising her voice above the tumult. "Quick, go get *Lo Yeh;* we need to get her into the house right away."

Song scrambled away and she heard her calling for Wei in the distance. The girl squeezed her hand tighter and cried out for her mother. The rain was driven sideways now by the winds, slapping Kai Ying in the face, the leaves from the kapok littering the courtyard all around them. Kai Ying shifted her body to shield the girl from the rain. "You'll be all right, I promise."

Tao's birth had been quick; a dull ache which grew in intensity, followed by the searing pain of those last few pushes and then it was over. But she knew every case was different; some women spent hours and hours in labor, or died in childbirth. She once heard about a classmate of hers whose baby had been dead inside of her for weeks, and when it was finally delivered the poisons had already spread through her.

Kai Ying looked down at the girl who was gaunt and thin all over except for the baby bulge. Her clothes were filthy and Kai Ying couldn't begin to guess when she'd last had a decent meal. How did she get all the way here to Dongshan? And how was she able to find her?

"I can't, I can't do this," the girl cried out. She moaned and writhed.

Kai Ying held on to her tightly. She wondered if the baby would have a fighting chance. She quickly cleared her mind of such thoughts. She hadn't lost a patient yet and she wasn't about to now.

"You can, you can do it," Kai Ying reassured her. "I'll be right here with you."

The girl cried out again and Kai Ying leaned in closer to protect her from the storm, and it felt as if they were in a vacuum, separated from the rest of the world.

"What's your name? Tell me your name," Kai Ying asked, hoping to calm her.

Between her quick, labored breaths the girl finally answered, "Suyin. My name's Suyin."

Wei

EVEN SO, THE WORLD INTRUDES. THE LINE HAD suddenly come to Wei when they had finally carried the girl into the house and laid her down on the sitting room floor. He started a fire in the stone fireplace and they placed blankets underneath the girl. It was there she would have to give birth, all of them soaked to the bone. Outside, the monsoon grew stronger, thundering down on them, fierce winds rattling the windows. It bothered him that he couldn't remember where the line came from.

Wei watched Kai Ying's face turn serious. It was going to be a difficult birth, she whispered. The girl was already weak and exhausted, the baby pushing against her thin frame. Kai Ying brushed back her wet hair and he saw a quick breath of fear fill her, something he'd rarely seen in his daughter-in-law in all her years of herbal work.

"What can I do?" he asked.

Kai Ying took another breath and looked nervously out at the rain before she said, "Can you bring back the midwife, Mrs. Lu, as quickly as possible?"

Wei felt suddenly vigorous and confident again as he hurried off to fetch Mrs. Lu. As he fought against the wind and rain, slowly making his way down the street, the line had returned to him again, *Even so, the world intrudes*. It must have been a line from some famous Tang dynasty poem he had long ago memorized. It bothered him even more that he couldn't remember the lines that followed. When Wei returned home, he would scour his books of poetry until he found the poem. He'd spent most of his life avoiding the world, but ironically, it had landed right there at their doorstep.

By the time he returned with Mrs. Lu, the baby had already come into the world.

Kai Ying

AFTER THREE DAYS, THE RAIN FINALLY STOPPED. Kai Ying lay awake in bed and listened for the baby's cries. Suyin had hardly moved since delivering the baby, stirring only to nurse the child or sip from the bowls of black chicken and fish stomach soup Kai Ying made for her, sweetened with dates and wolfberries to help build up her strength. Suyin had lost a great deal of blood during the birth and had little strength left to push when the baby finally arrived. Kai Ying had never delivered a baby before and was terrified when Suyin's contractions came closer together and *Lo Yeh* hadn't returned with Mrs. Lu. Auntie Song had gone upstairs to check on Tao. Still, she wasn't about to let the girl or her baby die. Now when Kai Ying thought about the multitude of things that could have gone wrong during the birth, the death of one or both of them, her whole body trembled.

Exhausted, Suyin slept. Kai Ying couldn't imagine how long it had been since Suyin had had a good night's sleep. All she and Auntie Song were able to find out from the girl was that she'd been living and begging on the streets to survive. She never mentioned any family.

Kai Ying drifted off, only to be awakened a short time later by the soft whining sounds that were so similar to the cries Tao had once made as a baby. Kai Ying hurried down the hall.

The room was dark and stuffy. A stale smell enveloped Kai Ying as soon as she opened the door and she paused a moment, allowing her eyes to adjust. Suyin was a dark shape in the middle of the bed. The baby girl, who slept in Tao's old bassinet to one side of the room, was whimpering now. Kai Ying picked up the baby. She felt so small and light. She was underweight and a red rash blotted both of her cheeks and her stomach, but her lungs were strong and she appeared alert. Kai Ying hadn't realized how much she missed holding a baby in her arms, and couldn't help but wonder what Sheng would think of all of this. It was almost nine months since she'd heard from him, the same time it took to create the life she held.

Be alive, she thought. *Please be alive.*

The baby squirmed in her arms and Kai Ying relaxed her hold on her. When Tao was born, Kai Ying was nervous all the time, afraid that something would happen to him. The world around them had become filled with menace. This little baby was different; she was already resilient in the face of all her mother had gone through before, and during, her birth. She had even survived the monsoon. The baby girl stopped crying and stared up at her, her arms flailing. She had a full head of downy black hair and her mother's eyes, open and inquisitive, with long, dark lashes. She stared a moment longer at Kai Ying before she whimpered and began to cry again.

"Quiet now, you'll wake your *ma ma*," Kai Ying whispered. She held the baby close and checked to see if she was wet before taking her downstairs. It didn't appear the girl had enough milk to breastfeed right now, so Kai Ying supplemented with soy milk until she could find a wet nurse with the help of Mrs. Lu.

Suyin would need a few more weeks to recuperate before

she was strong enough to take care of herself, much less take care of a crying, hungry baby. Meanwhile, even without all the formal festivities of a red egg and ginger baby party to announce her birth, they would do their best to welcome this little girl into the world. Kai Ying would begin by giving her a customary first bath that afternoon, three days after her birth.

There were so many details to think about. Kai Ying knew it was bad luck to call a baby by its given name for the first month after birth, in order to ward off the bad spirits who might return and take the child away. They had called Tao *little monkey* for the first month of his life, choosing an animal so he'd be unwanted by the spirits. Kai Ying often followed all the old Chinese traditions taught to her by her own mother. But when she looked down at this baby, she thought differently. This little girl had already made it over the first hurdle of surviving her birth. Until Suyin was well enough to name the baby, Kai Ying would secretly name her.

"You must be hungry, Meizhen, let's go downstairs," she whispered. It meant *beautiful pearl* and was the name she would have chosen for her own daughter.

On their way downstairs, Kai Ying stopped by the balcony. She opened the door quietly and stepped out into the fresh air. The night felt calm after the storm, and the baby had fallen asleep again in her arms. Kai Ying gazed up at the moon, bright and magnificent in the dark sky, although it had already waned. They had missed their chance to see it on Moon Festival. Unlike Houyi and Chang'e, her dreams of a reunion would have to wait for another year.

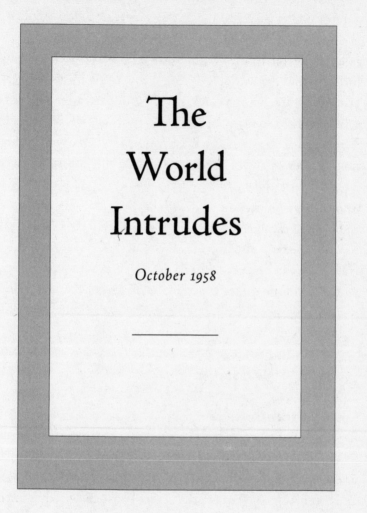

The
World
Intrudes

October 1958

———

Tao

TAO WAS FINALLY RETURNING TO SCHOOL TOMOR-
row, two weeks after his cast had been removed, and he
could barely sleep in his excitement. It was still early, a weak
October light just seeping into his room, and he willed it to
hurry, hurry so that the day would begin. He closed his eyes
and opened them again, breathing in and out, filling his lungs
with air. His *ba ba* once told him that if he paid attention, he
could actually smell, even taste the seasons. He had begun to
notice that the powerful scent of the kapok flower meant it was
late March, or the sweet, sticky taste of mangoes and pine-
apples which came in the fall, while the worst part of summer
brought the stinky smell of the durian fruit, which made him
gag just to think of it. Next month in November there would be
the orangey citrus scents of winter, followed by Chinese New
Year in January or February. He lay in bed and wondered if his
father could smell the same things wherever he was.

Tao pushed his covers away and sat up in bed. The morning
light brightened and filled the room. His right leg still looked
as pale and thin as a toothpick, as if the cast had sucked all the

life out of it. Tao refused to use the crutches anymore, but his leg was still weak and unsteady and he was constantly afraid that if he put too much weight on it, it would break again. Snap and crack. He winced at the thought.

He knew he should get up and walk. It was the only way his leg would regain the muscle and strength needed to keep up with his classmates. Why did it feel like he had to learn how to walk all over again? "Don't worry so much," his grandfather told him. "It won't be long before you're back to running faster than all your classmates."

He was tired of waiting.

Tao walked from the window to the doorway of his room. One, two, three, four . . . he kept track of each step he took. His father had often paced back and forth across the courtyard when something was bothering him, or he needed to clear his thoughts. From his bedroom window, Tao had watched him walk from the kitchen door, past the kapok tree to the front gate, and back again. Once, when his parents had argued about something, he counted while his father walked back and forth fifty-two times before he paused, and then returned to the kitchen to talk to his mother. Compared to his *ba ba*, Tao's steps were still slow and hesitant. He opened his door and peeked out into the hallway. Sometimes his grandfather woke up early and came to check on him, but it was all quiet this morning.

Tao turned around and took another step, leading with his stronger left leg, his right following, stiff and unbending. He wanted to be rid of the limp when he returned to school, but everything was taking so much longer than he hoped. It upset him to think his classmates would see him differently now, as a cripple. He would have to prove them wrong. Tao rubbed his leg gently to get the blood circulating the way his mother had taught him before he limped back toward the window. The sun had finally risen through the branches of the kapok tree, and a moment later, Neighbor Lau's rooster crowed again to announce its arrival. He listened for any sounds of the house awakening, but there was only silence.

On his desk were his schoolbooks, which he had studied diligently every day. Little Shan brought by his assignments so he wouldn't fall too far behind. There was a stack of papers in which he practiced writing all the new characters. Tao had them all memorized and would make up the weekly exams when he returned. He was determined to be sitting behind Ling Ling again as soon as possible.

Tao leaned against the desk and suddenly his entire body felt tired. All night he had drifted in and out of sleep, waking when he heard his mother get up every time that baby cried. At first he thought the high whining sounds came from stray cats in the courtyard. Then his *ma ma* told him that a patient had had a difficult birth, and that the girl, Suyin, and her baby would be staying with them until she regained her strength. Tao had heard her screams and moans the morning the girl had the baby downstairs. He'd stood on the stairs, not knowing what to do until Auntie Song brought him back upstairs, telling him not to be afraid, his mother was helping a patient deliver her baby. Why wasn't she staying at her own house? he had asked his mother. "Because she doesn't have a home," she said. He wondered if it would take as long for her to get her strength back as it did for his leg to heal.

Tao felt funny knowing a girl and her baby were staying in the room next to his. He'd glimpsed the girl only a few times from the doorway. He hadn't really seen the baby yet. Was it sick too? The room used to belong to his great-grandfather's second wife, Great-Auntie Shu. The room was always dark and smelled old like mothballs. He once heard Auntie Song say that Great-Auntie Shu liked her plum wine and kept her room dark because of her headaches in the morning. His own room once belonged to his great-grandfather's first wife, but by the time it became his, she'd been dead for a very long time. Great-Auntie Shu had been much younger than the first wife, and his *ye ye*'s mother, younger still. Tao couldn't understand why his great-grandfather would want so many wives. When he asked his mother, she smiled and said, "Well, if he didn't have three wives, there wouldn't be *ye ye* or *ba ba* or you. And then where would I be?" He thought about that for a long time. Tao imagined his *ma ma* would still be living in Zhaoqing, married to someone else with another little boy who wasn't him. Afterward, whenever he looked at the portrait of his great-grandfather, he always remembered to thank him for marrying so many wives.

Tao stopped and listened, but the room next door was quiet, except for the baby's crying. What Tao couldn't understand was that if the girl slept in the same room as her baby, why didn't she take care of it? "Because," his mother answered, "she's still very weak after the birth, and a baby needs full-time care."

Tao glared out the window. He was no crying little baby needing full-time care from anyone. He was well enough now to go to school all by himself.

* * *

"You're up so early," his mother said. She stood in the open doorway of his room, as if his thoughts had conjured her up. Usually her hair was tied back or pinned up in a bun, but he liked it hanging down loose, which always made her appear younger.

"I'm exercising," he said, using the same tone the doctor used when he discussed the need for him to *exercise to strengthen the leg*. Tao walked toward her, trying not to limp. His mother smiled and he saw how happy it made her to see him walking again, and how pretty she looked on the rare occasions she did smile now.

"Very good, *sai-lo,* I'm so proud of you," she said, opening her arms to him.

Little man. It was what his father called him, a nickname he hadn't heard since his *ba ba* was taken away. Tao had just reached her and barely felt her arms wrap around him when the baby began to cry in the next room. His mother gave him a quick squeeze and a kiss atop his head before she pulled away and was gone.

Wei

WEI WAS UNEASY WITH A STRANGER IN THE HOUSE. He found himself listening throughout the night for unexpected movements. There had been too many distractions already. He had never been adaptable as a young man, why should he be now at the end of his life? How did Kai Ying know they could trust the girl? They knew nothing about her. She had simply wandered in off the street and into their lives. And where was the baby's father?

When he had voiced his concerns to Kai Ying once or twice, she'd finally said, "What would you have me do, throw her out on the street after she just had a baby? She's only a child herself," she added. The girl must have come from somewhere, he thought, she could go back there when she was stronger. Until then, he would wait and keep a watchful eye on her.

Wei hadn't seen the girl since she moved into his auntie Shu's room. Although the room was at the far end of the hall, he often heard the high whine of the baby crying in the night. A moment later, he would hear Kai Ying answering her call. He couldn't help thinking that if his daughter-in-law was meant to have another child, she wouldn't have had a miscarriage. He also knew if Liang were there, she would be angry with him for having such thoughts.

Wei shook his head. He understood this younger generation even less than that of his parents. In the mirror above the sink he saw that his reflection resembled his father more and more as he aged. He wasn't much older now than his father had been when Wei was born. He wondered what it was like to have a youthful father like Sheng was to Tao. Might he have been a different person if his father had more time and energy to spend with him, or if his mother had been less distant? Would he have been less self-absorbed and distrustful of the world around him? As a boy he had been curious about his parents. He once asked his *amah*, Ching, who had also looked after his half sisters before him, if his mother loved his father.

She looked at him and smiled, pausing a long time before she answered, "It's about duty, not love."

"She doesn't love *ba ba*?" he asked, confused.

"Your *ma ma*'s family made a very good arrangement. And your *ma ma* and *ba ba* love you very much."

Wei still didn't grasp what she was saying. Of course they loved him. But how could they love him and not each other? It all seemed too complicated, and the confusion must have shown on his face.

"Don't worry," his *amah* laughed. "Love isn't always found where it should be. You'll understand when you grow up."

Two decades would pass before Wei would recall what his *amah* had said. By the time he was in his late twenties, when most men had settled down, Wei was more interested in his research; thoughts of marriage or having a family were distant. His father had died many years before, never knowing whether the Lee family name would be carried on. His mother and half sisters had given up trying to find him a wife. "Wei will never marry," they teased. "He'll never find any woman as beautiful as his precious artifacts!" He paid little attention to them, until, less than a year later, he saw Liang for the first time. It was Liang who made him understand what his parents never had, and it was she who gave him happiness for almost thirty-five years. And then she was gone.

Wei looked in the mirror and saw an old man. He splashed his face with cold water and thought he heard the baby crying. He pushed the unpleasant thoughts out of his mind and dressed. After all, this was the morning they'd all been looking forward to. Kai Ying had her patients to tend to and the baby to look after, so Wei would be walking with Tao on his first day back to school.

Wei waited at the courtyard gate as Kai Ying hugged Tao, dressed in his pressed blue school uniform, and whispered words of encouragement to him. "Now, take it slowly," she said. "You don't have to do everything on your first day back."

Tao nodded and hugged her again, then limped over to the kapok tree and reached up to touch the scar on its trunk before he limped back over to Wei.

"What was that for?" Wei asked, pointing at the kapok. He wanted to forget he was the one responsible for having put the gash there.

"So it'll feel better," Tao said.

Wei looked down at his grandson. Until that moment, he had forgotten telling him that trees were living entities. He'd forgotten so much.

"You're a good boy," he said.

* * *

It was October and a calm breeze blew. Wei was relieved to feel milder temperatures were finally coming. Outside the front gate and all along the boulevard, scattered leaves of magnolia, kapok, and maple thickly blanketed the sidewalk. He wondered if it would make walking more difficult for his grandson.

"Why don't we take a pedicab on your first day back to school?" Wei suggested.

They stood for a moment in silence while he waited for Tao to decide. Very early that morning he had watched his grandson walking back and forth in the courtyard, trying to appear as if everything were normal, though it would take months at least for him to walk without a limp.

"Let's walk," Tao finally said.

Wei smiled and let his hand rest on his grandson's shoulder. "I expect Little Shan will be thrilled to have you back."

Tao nodded. "But he won't be happy when I take back my seat," he said.

Even walking at a slower pace than usual, they arrived at the school early. He waited with Tao at the front gate until an older man came out to unlock it. Then, as if the simple act of swinging open the gate had also rung some invisible bell, other students began to arrive. The yard quickly filled with the high shrill of voices, boys and girls in their blue uniforms swinging their book bags as they walked in gathering groups.

"You can go if you want," Tao said.

He watched his grandson glance toward the yard nervously.

"Do you mind if I wait here a little longer with you?" he asked.

Tao nodded, but let go of his hand.

A moment later, they heard Little Shan calling Tao's name from across the yard. His grandson's face lit up.

"There he is," Wei said, and smiled. "I'll go now. I'll be waiting right here when school's over." He placed his hand atop his grandson's head. "Don't overdo it on your first day back."

"I won't," Tao said, already moving slowly and steadily away from Wei toward his friends.

Kai Ying

WHEN KAI YING ROUNDED THE CORNER, SHE SAW the ugly, three-story brick building that housed the public security bureau administrative offices. She hadn't been back in months, but with Tao's return to school that morning, she had asked Auntie Song to watch Suyin and the baby, using the excuse of visiting a patient. Since Tao's fall, she was more determined than ever to find out if Sheng was in Luoyang, and more important, if he was still all right. Kai Ying needed to know something; anything was better than not knowing.

She waited, hot and nervous, in a spare, colorless room for what felt like hours before an unsmiling pigtailed young woman in an olive drab uniform ushered her into another room. Kai Ying hated to think of all the herb business she was missing while she waited yet another hour before she was finally called in to see a Comrade Cheng. He was a very busy man, the girl informed her, and could see her for only a few minutes.

Comrade Cheng's office was small and crowded, the air thick with cigarette smoke. A large photo of Mao dominated one wall and against the opposite wall stood a row of bulging black file cabinets. Atop a stack of files on one cabinet, a portable fan wobbled as it droned on with a clicking sound, like pebbles being tossed against glass. It was all Kai Ying could do to keep herself from getting up to steady the fan. There was no window, and during the summer, she imagined the office must be stifling.

Comrade Cheng was a heavyset, balding man with a thin sheen of sweat he constantly wiped away from his forehead and neck with a dark blue handkerchief. After their initial pleasantries, he poured her a cup of tepid tea, lit a cigarette, and leaned back in his chair, observing her in a way that made Kai Ying uncomfortable.

"How can I help you?" he asked. He exhaled and a stream of smoke caught in the whirl of the fan.

Kai Ying cleared her throat, her mouth dry. She glimpsed a small photo of his family on his cluttered desk, which gave her hope. At least he was a family man. "I'm here about my husband," she said. "His name is Lee Weisheng and I was told he was sent to Luoyang for reeducation."

"And how is it that I can help you?" he asked again.

His smile disappeared into a serious gaze that she couldn't really read. It made her feel even more anxious.

"I haven't heard from him in nine months. Please, Comrade

Cheng, is there any way I can find out if he's still at Luoyang? Or if he might not be well?"

Cheng snubbed out his cigarette in the already overflowing ashtray. "Hundreds of men are sent to Luoyang every day. It would take time for me to track down your husband, Mrs. Lee, and I simply don't have the time."

"Might you try?" she asked. She felt her heart banging against her chest even as she tried to remain calm.

He waved his arm toward the file cabinets. "You see what I'm up against."

"Please," she said. She sipped the tea, which tasted like dirty water.

"What was he charged with?" Cheng asked, lighting another cigarette.

"He was accused of writing a letter to the Premier during the Hundred Flowers Campaign. I never saw the letter. If there was one, it was written with the intent of making China a stronger and better country, just as Chairman Mao had asked. My husband is a good man."

She had to remind herself to slow down and take a breath. Pleading would show weakness.

Cheng leaned back in his chair and wiped the back of his neck with his handkerchief. "I'm afraid there's little I can do from here. I'm sorry."

"I see you're a family man," she said, gesturing to the photo on his desk. "You must understand how difficult it is, not only for me, but for our son."

"Ah yes, my family is very important to me," Cheng said, agreeing. "Your husband should have thought more about his family before he wrote that letter. Now, please, Mrs. Lee, I really don't have the time." He stood up abruptly to let her know their meeting was over.

Kai Ying stood and felt his gaze move across her body, which sent a chill through her. At the risk of angering him, she persisted, "Whether my husband was right or wrong, wouldn't you do as much as you could for your own family?"

Cheng paused for a moment and looked her up and down. "Your husband is a lucky man to have a wife so devoted to him. Of course, I too am a family man, and I hate to think of your son upset. You must be very lonely with your husband gone; perhaps we can find a way to make this situation work, while helping each other at the same time?"

It took a moment for Kai Ying to understand what he was saying, his eyes locked onto hers. She felt sick to her stomach and wanted nothing more than to run out of the hot, suffocating room. Instead, Kai Ying steadied herself and ignored his question. She held out a red envelope, which contained a hundred yuan she had saved. She knew it was the way things were done, and hoped it would be enough for this vile man. "Please, if you should find out anything . . ." she said.

His gaze shifted from her tunic front to the red envelope and he licked his lips. "Of course, of course," he said. "Just remember, my offer to help is always open." He reached across the desk and took the envelope from her hand.

Song

WHEN THE BABY HAD BEGUN TO CRY, SONG HAD picked her up and she had fallen asleep again. Now she sat in the chair by the bassinet, afraid that if she put her down, the baby would start crying. Song hadn't held a baby since Tao was born. The soft bundle in her arms felt new to her, warm and alive. She smiled to think she'd grown winter melons that were heavier than this baby was. She sat in the darkened room while the girl slept and slept, having promised Kai Ying she would watch the baby while she was out visiting a patient.

There was a time when Song had longed for a moment such as this. Her marriage to Old Hing was another lifetime ago, and much of her anger had faded. Still, once in a while that bitter taste rose up to her mouth. It did again now as she held the baby. Almost fifty years later, she still remembered the searing pain in her abdomen where Old Hing had punched her. She should have known better than to provoke him, though it never took much to stir up his rage: a wayward look or the tone of her voice. He was like a piece of cinder; Song never knew when he would flare up. Her pregnancy had lulled her into a false sense of security. She began to hope and plan. Old Hing had left her alone the first half of her pregnancy, so she'd made the mistake of becoming complacent, thinking he wouldn't hit her while she was carrying his child. Even now, Song wondered if she might have done something differently. She should have turned and run when he came after her, rather than raise her arms to shield her face. She should have protected her baby more or fought back harder. She accepted her responsibility, too. But Old Hing only became more infuriated and hit her harder. Song miscarried in her sixth month. Her dead baby was a little girl. For years after, Song consoled herself knowing that at least her child would never have to know Old Hing as her father.

"Who are you?"

The girl's voice startled Song. She looked across the room at the girl lying in the bed watching her. Usually the girl slept while Song watched the baby.

"My name's Song," she answered. "I live here with Kai Ying, the woman who delivered your baby, and her family."

"I'm Suyin."

Song smiled. "You told us your name, just before you had the baby."

"My baby?"

"Right here." Song stood up and brought the baby over to the girl.

"I don't remember if it's a girl or a boy."

"A little girl," Song said, placing the baby into Suyin's arms. There was a sour odor coming from the girl and her hair was oily and pressed down on one side of her head from sleep.

Suyin held the baby awkwardly in her arms and stared down at her. Almost immediately the baby woke up and began to cry. The girl shifted positions, trying to comfort the baby, but it didn't seem to matter. Her crying grew more frantic and so did Suyin's rocking movements. "Take her, take her back," she implored.

The girl had so much to learn about becoming a mother, Song thought, as she leaned over and reached for the baby.

Tao

EVERYTHING HAD CHANGED AT SCHOOL, DIFFERENT from the first moment Tao limped into the dimly lit, chalky-aired classroom to find his seat one row over and several chairs behind Little Shan and Ling Ling. He had expected to sit right behind his friend, or at most, one or two seats behind him. The fact that so many other students had also surpassed him came as a surprise. Teacher Eng's voice droned on and on and Tao had a hard time concentrating. By the end of the first day, his leg felt weak and sore from trying to keep up, and when he saw his grandfather standing at the gate waiting for him, he took a deep breath and tried to smile.

"How was your first day back?" his *ye ye* asked.

"It was all right."

"How's your leg feeling?"

"A little tired." He pulled at the collar of his shirt. The sky was clear, the sun shining.

His grandfather took his book bag from him. "It's going to take a little while, but everything will become normal again."

Tao remained quiet.

"Don't you think so?" his grandfather asked.

Tao knew it was rude not to answer his *ye ye* a second time, but he couldn't bring himself to say anything for fear he might start crying. He wasn't a baby. But he knew now that nothing would ever be the same, not since his *ba ba* was taken away. Instead, he looked up at his grandfather and nodded before he reached over and took his hand.

Tao was welcomed home by his mother and Auntie Song with his favorite coconut tarts. They asked him question after question he didn't feel like answering, but did, so they wouldn't see how unhappy he was. Each day was harder than the one before, and by the end of the following week, Tao didn't care if he ever returned to school again. Little Shan had found new friends while he was gone, and as much as he tried to fit in, he couldn't understand why Little Shan would like the same obnoxious boys who used to pick on them for being "scared little girls" and the "teacher's pets." It seemed everything about his friend had changed, not just his appearance. Now that Tao was back, he could only hope Little Shan would see what a mistake he was making and return to the way things were.

Each morning Tao struggled down the stairs, his leg still stiff. He leaned up against the banister for support, hoping his mother would tell him to stay at home and take a day off to rest his leg.

But she never did. Instead, she seemed to care more about the strange girl and her baby. He'd hardly seen the girl in the weeks she'd been there. She didn't come downstairs in the morning until after he'd left for school, and spent most of the evenings in Great-Auntie Shu's room. The first time he did meet Suyin, he thought she looked just like any young school-girl and couldn't imagine her having a baby. She was pale and thin, as if she hadn't eaten in a very long time. Her skin was bumpy and her eyes looked cloudy, although she greeted him pleasantly enough when they were introduced. Still, he looked hard for any small thing about her that he could immediately dislike.

For one thing, Suyin was selfish, whether she knew it or not; she took up so much of his mother's time. Every morning his *ma ma* was coming or going to the market or herb shop for something to make the girl a tea or soup. This morning when he came downstairs, she was in the kitchen rinsing pigs' feet, she said, to add to the black vinegar and ginger soup. Women were supposed to drink it for two weeks after they'd given birth. "It has plenty of nutrients she needs now," his mother added. He watched her drop all the ingredients into a pot, a sour, tangy smell rising with the steam. When he didn't say anything, his mother finally looked up.

"Is everything all right?" she asked.

Tao looked up at her, and before he could say anything, he felt all the tears he'd been holding back rise to the surface and flow freely down his cheeks.

"What is it, what's the matter? Is it your leg?"

He wanted to tell his mother that he hated school, he hated

the girl living in their house, he hated walking with a limp, but it was one of his classmates, Lai Hing, he hated most of all. They'd never gotten along, but had always chosen to stay out of each other's way. But now Little Shan followed him around like a starving dog, and there was nothing he could do. The day after Tao returned to school, Lai Hing had yelled, "Are you crippled for life?" across the classroom for all his classmates to hear. Tao felt his face grow hot and it took him too long to answer. By the time he did say something, it was lost in the laughter and voices of his classmates.

And then yesterday, while they were in the yard, Lai Hing had asked, "Where's your father?"

"He's away working," Tao answered.

"My father said he was sent away because he's a traitor and not a true comrade of the Party."

Lai Hing wasn't much taller than he was, but he was big-boned and stocky. He reminded Tao of a little bull.

Tao stepped forward, his anger rising to the surface. "What does your father know?"

"He knows plenty, that's what. My father works at the public security bureau's administrative offices, and he says your *ba ba* was sent really far away to a work camp for traitors who speak against the Party."

"You're a liar!" Tao yelled.

He could feel the blood rushing to his head. In the distance he could see Teacher Eng at the other side of the yard. Without thinking, he balled his fist and swung at Lai, missing by a foot. *Never let your anger rule your actions*, his grandfather had once told him. He didn't quite understand him then, but he did now. Lai pushed him hard and Tao fell backward, his tailbone hitting the pavement first. He felt a sharp pain shoot all the way up his back. Instead of defending his *ba ba*, he had only let him down.

When Tao tried to get up, he felt a twinge of pain in his leg. He heard Lai Hing and his friends laughing at him. *Take a breath. Be calm*, he thought to himself. *There's no hurry.* Tao slowly stood up, straightened, and waited a moment until he swung again, this time hitting Lai Hing hard and squarely in the stomach. The boy doubled over. The laughing had stopped, and in the next moment, Tao was shoved away by one of the other boys, who threatened to hit him. *Hit me! Break my leg again*, Tao thought, *both of them if you like!* This time he wouldn't mind staying home forever.

Instead, Little Shan stepped in between them and steered Tao away from the others. For the moment it felt as if his old friend had returned to him.

"What are you doing?" Little Shan asked. "Lai Hing will knock you out with one punch."

"He's a liar," Tao repeated. "I don't like him."

Little Shan took a step back and stood easily a few inches taller than Tao. He paused a moment before he said, "Well, I do."

The memory made Tao cry harder now. Little Shan could do whatever he wanted, he didn't care. The bruise on his tailbone would go away. Through his tears he saw his mother coming toward him and he quickly stepped just out of her reach; he was still angry at her for ignoring him. What he really wanted to know lay hard and bitter on the tip of his tongue. The tart smell of the soup made him feel queasy. He took a breath and wiped his nose with his sleeve. "Tell me . . ." He choked down another sob. "Tell me why the police came and took *ba ba* away."

Wei

EVEN BEFORE WEI ENTERED THE KITCHEN, HE FELT an edge of panic rise in him. Tao was distraught. The boy was crying, pulling away from Kai Ying and refusing to go to school.

"What is it?" he asked. "Tao?" Looking at his grandson, he saw misery. The vinegary scent of Kai Ying's boiling soup hung heavily in the air.

Tao was crying so hard he hadn't heard him. Kai Ying held on to him, looking tired and pale. She'd lost even more weight in the past month.

"He wants to know why his *ba ba* went away," Kai Ying said. "Something happened at school . . ." she started to say, but the words caught in her throat and she didn't finish the sentence.

Wei wished he could start the day all over again. The irony

was that he had awoken that morning feeling better than he had in a long time. It was a beautiful day, clear and bright, a rare morning in which the heaviness in his heart and mind felt lighter. Wei knew the truth was always there waiting to show itself, he just hadn't expected it to surface this morning. He should have known better.

Wei felt as if he couldn't breathe in the hot, steamy kitchen. The door facing the courtyard was open, and every so often, a cool breeze blew in a whisper of relief. He swallowed his fear and steadied himself against the table, then reached out and touched his daughter-in-law's arm so that she stepped aside.

"What's the matter?" Wei asked. His voice was surprisingly calm. He seated his grandson at the table and sat down next to him. Tao looked at him and tried to stop crying, his hiccupping breaths calming.

"I don't want to go school," Tao answered.

"Just last week you couldn't wait to return to school."

"It's different now."

"What about Little Shan?"

"I hate Little Shan."

"Best friends are hard to come by."

"He isn't my best friend."

"Then what's this about your *ba ba*?"

Wei knew he would never be able to turn back now. He wondered if Sheng would ever forgive him for what he'd done to his family.

"There's a boy in my class who said *ba ba* was a traitor, and that's why he was sent away."

"Is that what you believe?"

Tao shook his head.

"That's good, because your *ba ba* did nothing wrong," Wei explained. "The authorities accused him of writing a letter criticizing the Party, when in fact, he never wrote such a letter."

Wei glanced up at Kai Ying, who had reached over for his empty teacup, listening.

"How do you know?" Tao asked.

Wei had never lied to his grandson before. He might have embellished a story here and there, but the only secrets he kept were the ones the boy was too young to know. Wei had never outright lied to him and he knew he couldn't now. He glanced out to the courtyard and at the kapok tree. When he turned back to Tao, he saw Sheng again at the same age, always so formal and closemouthed around him. He remembered all the times he heard Sheng talking to Liang, joking and laughing, but as soon as he entered the room, it was as if the air had changed. He and Sheng hadn't learned to be friends until late in his life. Now he only wanted his son home again.

"I know . . ." Wei began, realizing the words that followed would change all of their lives forever. "I know because it was *me*. I was the one to write the letter, not your *ba ba*."

Wei felt as if he'd been falling for the past year and had finally hit the ground. He stared down at the table and couldn't look at either Kai Ying or Tao. He suddenly felt exhausted and wanted only to lie down and close his eyes. The kitchen was suddenly quiet, as if everything had stopped. For a moment, he wasn't even sure if he'd really said the words aloud.

"It was *you*?" Kai Ying finally said. Her words reverberated against the walls and returned to him. He felt her standing just behind him.

He looked at Tao. "Your *ba ba* had nothing to do with it,"

he said again. "He's a good and courageous son who assumed my blame. His only fault is having a coward as a father."

"I don't understand. Why? Why would *you* have written the Premier a letter?" Kai Ying asked, her voice rising with each word. "You never paid any attention to politics before. How many times did you tell Sheng to mind his own business and to stay out of trouble?"

Wei shook his head as if that were an answer. He stood up and turned to face Kai Ying, who stood stone-still holding his teacup.

"Kai Ying, I'm so sorry," he said, trying to explain what couldn't be explained. "I don't know what possessed me to write the letter. I don't know why. Sheng seemed so certain that the Party wouldn't do anything this time, and I thought . . ."

"You thought?" Kai Ying interrupted. "You thought?" Her eyes narrowed as her voice rose with fury, edged with a hard, cold precision. "You thought you wouldn't be touched because you're the great Professor Lee from Lingnan University. You thought you were smarter and better than everyone else. That's what you thought!" Kai Ying shouted. She stepped back and hurled the teacup, shattering it against the wall, startling them all.

Kai Ying's angry words hung heavily in the thick air. She had always been the peacemaker in the family. Wei pulled at his tunic collar and felt the room spinning, but he didn't look away from Kai Ying, a small vein pulsing angrily on the side of her forehead, her entire body trembling. Her dark eyes were unrecognizable, filled with something worse than anger: disappointment. Every little sound suddenly seemed magnified, the soft bubbling of the soup boiling, the clock ticking, the pumping of his thin, warm blood from his heart to his brain. And for just a moment, Wei wondered if it were possible to drown from the inside out.

Outside came the singsong voice of the fruit peddler calling out *"Bananas! Oranges! Mangoes!"* Every morning he went up and down the street, carrying two heavy baskets of fruit balanced on a wooden pole across his back and shoulders. Wei thought he had the best lichee and mangoes of anyone at the marketplace. He wanted to run out and buy all the fruit in the peddler's baskets as an offering, although he knew even the sweetest fruits in all of Guangzhou couldn't buy him forgiveness.

When the baby's cries suddenly drifted down from upstairs, Kai Ying looked away, and just as quickly she rushed out of the kitchen.

Tao had stayed seated at the table. His grandson was no longer crying, but watching him with the distant gaze of a stranger. Wei hoped the boy would understand that he never meant for any of this to happen. But before he could say anything, Tao scraped back his chair and stood up.

"Tao, I'm sorry," Wei said.

"You made *ba ba* go away."

"I didn't know."

"I hate you," Tao said, "I hate you."

After

October 1958

———————

Kai Ying

I T TOOK ALL KAI YING'S STRENGTH TO PRETEND nothing had changed, when in fact, their entire world had. Even the air she breathed seemed tinged with bitterness. There *was* a letter and Wei had written it. Kai Ying's thoughts simmered as she put on the rice and washed the mustard greens Auntie Song had brought over. She sliced a small piece of pork and the lotus roots and scallions and then minced the garlic. She lit the fire and poured peanut oil into the wok and waited for it to get hot. Her hands moved without any thought as to what they were doing. They had to eat, didn't they? They had to find a way to live with this truth, didn't they?

Kai Ying saw it all so clearly now, the guilt that had to be consuming Wei each day as he retreated more and more into himself. As difficult as it was, Kai Ying understood why Sheng had taken her father-in-law's place when the police came; Wei would have never been able to survive outside of the villa, much less at a reeducation facility. But why hadn't Wei told her the truth? Why did he allow her to suffer for over a year, not knowing if there really was a letter, letting her believe that

Sheng was the one to jeopardize everything they had? And how was she ever going to forgive a man who would let his pride betray his family?

Kai Ying quickly threw the garlic and scallions into the wok, followed by the pork and lotus roots and black bean paste, frying everything quickly together, her long wooden chopsticks stirring it all evenly as the hot oil splattered and the warm, inviting fragrance filled the kitchen, masking the acrimony which lay just underneath. It was one of Sheng's favorite dishes and the thought brought another kind of sorrow.

Tao

TAO HARDLY SPOKE TO HIS GRANDFATHER. HIS one-word answers came only after his mother had gotten angry at him for not responding to his grandfather at dinner. "Tao, your *ye ye* is speaking to you," she said, her voice laced with a sharpness he rarely heard directed at him.

In his room that night, she was still distant and stern when she told him she never wanted to see him disrespect his grandfather, or any other adult, again. It wasn't the kind of person she raised him to be. "Do you understand?" she asked. Tao chewed on the inside of his cheek and nodded. What he couldn't understand was how she could speak to his grandfather after what he did, but Tao knew better than to ask. "That's not an answer," she said. "Yes," he said, "I understand." He chewed on his cheek again until he tasted blood.

Song

SONG CUT THE STEMS OF *YU CHOY* AND *BAK CHOY* and washed the dirt off in a wooden bucket by her side before shaking off the excess water and laying them in her basket. Harvesting her vegetables was usually a task that gave her great pleasure, but today she moved through the motions absentmindedly. She glanced up when she heard a noise come from the courtyard, the glare of the midday sun blinding her for a moment. In the bright light, she thought there was a shadow in the distance moving toward her. Song hoped it was Wei coming to see her, but when she raised her hand against the glare, there was no one there.

Just two days ago, Song listened in disbelief when Kai Ying, shaken and on the verge of tears, told her that it was *Lo Yeh* who had written the letter. "That's impossible, Wei has no interest . . ." she said, only to suddenly remember the day last month when he'd visited her, realizing now what he must have been trying to tell her. What was Wei thinking to have written that letter? In all the years she'd known him, he had always refused to accompany Sheng to any kind of political gathering, calling it a waste of good time. His life began and ended with his family and his work at the university.

Since then, Song had been desperate to know how he was doing. She'd seen him only once in the courtyard and he appeared so old and frail that it frightened her. He'd lost so much weight his clothes hung loosely from his tall, thin frame. Why hadn't she seen what had been right in front of her? He avoided her pleas to sit down and talk to her.

"What's there to talk about?" he said. "What's done now has to be undone."

"You made a mistake."

"I've been such a fool," he said, his voice barely a whisper.

"My father used to say that the only fool is the man who can't admit he's one," Song said. "Can't you see Sheng knew what he was doing? It was his choice."

"And my weakness," Wei said. "I stood by and allowed him to be taken away in my place."

"He knew what he was doing," she repeated.

"I should have never put him in that position!"

"You know nothing about your own son," Song said, her voice rising. "And that should be your biggest regret. You've lived in the past for so long you can't see what's right in front of you. You made a mistake, an unintentional mistake. Who in this life hasn't crossed that bridge?" she asked, her voice falling. "Sheng would have never allowed them to take you. He's young and strong, he'll survive."

Wei looked away from her. Song wondered if he'd heard anything she'd said. When he turned back to her, she saw the same despair and sadness in his eyes as when Liang had died.

She hadn't seen him since.

Suyin

SUYIN LAY IN BED UNABLE TO SLEEP. AFTER MONTHS of living on the streets in a constant state of exhaustion, she spent the first two weeks after giving birth oblivious to the world around her. It was as if she'd fallen into an endless dream, the bed a safe and warm place she never wanted to leave. Suyin could hardly keep her eyes open and awoke just long enough to sip some soup or nurse the baby. But it all felt distant and hazy, and before any other thought came to her mind, she'd fallen back into a deep sleep.

Now Suyin stared up at the high ceiling, wide-awake in the dark. Her baby was nearly a month old, and she was no longer in the grip of exhaustion and was thinking clearly again. After following Kai Ying home from the market, she began walking to the Dongshan district at least twice a week. Suyin liked the wide, clean streets lined with shady trees where she could move slowly and undisturbed, daydreaming of what it would be like to live in one of the grand old villas her mother had always talked about, safe from the outside world behind their tall walls. Suyin remembered it had been raining hard the morning she felt her first strong contraction, a searing pain that made her stop and double over. *Not yet, not yet, not yet,* she chanted. She took several deep breaths. When the pain finally subsided, she kept walking. She was only a few blocks away from where Kai Ying lived and Suyin willed herself to keep moving. When the second contraction came, she had just pushed open the courtyard gate.

Suyin wondered how much longer she'd be able to stay at the villa. Just last week she heard Kai Ying and the old professor downstairs in the kitchen quarreling, though she couldn't quite make out what they were saying. They'd hardly spoken since. Suyin couldn't help but wonder if they'd been arguing about her. How could she blame them; she had wandered off the street and into their lives from nowhere.

Several nights since, Suyin had slipped downstairs to the kitchen, looking for any kind of food that she might store away, just enough, she thought to herself, so that her theft wouldn't be noticed. She needed to be prepared if she was asked to leave; dried plums, green peanuts, biscuits, anything that might keep her going until she figured out what to do next. Suyin knew that the hunger would never go away, and it wasn't just her now, she had the baby to worry about too.

She looked around the dark room at the shadowy pieces of furniture, the bassinet to one side of the bed, the baby asleep in it. It was still hard to believe that she'd given birth and the baby was alive and well in the room with her. The darkness no longer frightened her like it did when she was a child. The old ghosts she imagined lurking in the shadows were nothing compared to what she saw in the light of day. Suyin turned onto her side and felt a sudden pressing tension at the back of her neck as her thoughts returned to that afternoon.

Suyin's stepfather never came home during the day. She remembered hearing the door opening, thinking her two brothers had returned early, only to see his oily smile appear instead. Why was he home? He usually didn't return until dinner, or even later, most nights smelling of alcohol. Not until that afternoon did he ever really pay any attention to her. "You're growing up," he said. Suyin didn't think anything about it and poured him a cup of tea, even though she could smell the rice wine on his breath. "Why aren't you at work?" she dared to ask. "Because I'm done for the day," he said. He looked at her strangely and she wished her brothers would return. When Suyin turned around, she could feel him standing behind her. When she told him she had to run an errand, he blocked the door and wouldn't let her leave the apartment. He wouldn't let her leave and she felt her heart race and her mouth go dry. She had schoolwork to finish and the boys would be back any minute, she said. He looked at her again and she felt something heavy in the middle of her stomach. And then the terrible stink of his breath was on her. "You're all grown up now," he said, his hand over her mouth, his body pressing against her even as she tried to push him away. "You're such a pretty girl." When he had finished, he left her there on the floor and wouldn't even look at her. Suyin lay there paralyzed until she heard her brothers coming back and she prayed for the feeling to return to her limbs again.

Suyin sat up in bed, her heart pounding at the memory. The baby whimpered and began to cry, at first softly, and then louder. Just as quickly Suyin was at the bassinet and picking her up. At first, the baby was so small and soft in her hands, she was afraid to hurt her. But Auntie Song had taught her always to support the baby's head and neck and everything would be fine. Since then, Suyin had relaxed and held her constantly, even after she'd fallen back to sleep. She stroked her daughter's dark tufts of hair. "Quiet, quiet," she whispered, nuzzling her neck. She would never think of her as his. Never.

Suyin returned to bed, missing the warmth of the baby against her body, and wondered what would become of them. She touched the red, itchy pimples on her cheek and tried not to scratch, like Kai Ying told her. She longed to see her mother and brothers, but that was impossible now. Suyin felt her heart racing with each thought. She took a deep breath and closed her eyes. She wanted to sleep and sleep and never wake up.

Wei

WEI LEFT THE HOUSE EARLY EACH MORNING AND began to walk. He had no particular direction in mind, but the walking brought him solace. He wasn't sleeping much, his words turning over and over in his mind. *It was me. I wrote the letter.* Almost immediately after saying them, it felt as if a weight had been lifted off his shoulders, only to be replaced by another one, heavier and more nebulous. How could he ever make things right again with Kai Ying and Tao?

Wei would never forget the look in Kai Ying's eyes, how diminished he suddenly appeared in them. He wasn't the revered professor everyone held him up to be, she'd said. And she was right. Now he wondered if he ever really was. So many times he'd wanted to tell Kai Ying that he'd written the letter, but there was always something, something that stopped him, the words balanced anxiously on his tongue. And now it turned out exactly as he'd feared; everything he had spent a lifetime building was meaningless.

Kai Ying had gracefully pretended nothing had changed that evening at dinner, even as their food congealed in their bowls and Tao refused to look at him and he willed the baby to cry again to break the silence.

*   *   *

The day was just dawning, the air still fresh from the night before. Wei avoided the crowded main boulevards, instead turning onto the smaller side streets as he walked in and out of the narrow alleyways. He found himself following the same route he had walked for over forty years of teaching at Lingnan University. Old habits were a way of life for him. He knew the maze of intimate streets by heart and couldn't bear the large crowds and bicyclists that used to push him along in directions he didn't want to go. Wei was never comfortable being around too many people outside of the classroom, and over the years, he'd found ways to avoid them and move along at his own pace while remaining as inconspicuous as possible.

As he approached the Pearl River, the water was flat and murky, boats tethered to the edge rocking calmly from side to side. He heard faint laughter and took a detour, walking slowly along the crowded bank where scrawny dogs chased each other, old men and women sat on the benches gossiping or dozing, and still other early risers were exercising. A dedicated group was doing *tai chi;* the slow, deliberate, swaying movements of their hands and legs were like poetry. A man waved at him, and asked if he wanted to join the group. "Come, come!" he said, but Wei shook his head, waved back, and walked on.

When Wei came to the darkened walkway under a bridge, he stopped to watch a lone middle-aged woman practicing some sort of dance. Unlike everyone else, who was dressed in the drab gray or green tunics of the Party, she wore a bright red flowing outfit, lifting her leg high into the air and sharply snapping a red fan open in perfect unison. The fan snapped closed again when her leg came down. She could have easily been arrested for such suggestive behavior. Still, Wei was intrigued with her precise movements, her total concentration; the effectiveness of the red fan as it opened and closed in unison. She paused once and glanced in his direction before she began the next set. Wei watched with admiration and wondered what it must feel like to be that agile, to move with such ease and grace through life, unafraid to perform a dance she loved, a remnant of bourgeoisie decadence. Wei walked on, only to look back when heard the slap of the fan echo through the tunnel.

Suyin

SUYIN COULDN'T SLEEP AGAIN. SHE SLIPPED SOUND-lessly out of the room without waking the baby. At the bottom of the stairs she turned toward the living room instead of the kitchen, where her baby had been born. She'd been curious as to what the rest of the villa looked like. Kai Ying had mentioned that another family lived downstairs, although they were away visiting their daughter. *Just a quick look*, Suyin thought to herself, *I won't touch a thing*. She wished she had a candle or an oil lamp. Fortunately, there was enough moonlight to allow her to find her way. Living on the streets, she'd always felt better when the moon was full, the darkness less consuming.

Suyin opened the door to the sitting room and lingered on the threshold before stepping in. All she saw were shadows at first, which slowly began to take on shapes. They had carried her in here and pushed the sofa back, laying her on blankets on the rug before the stone fireplace. Above the fireplace she remembered there was a painting of a man. She couldn't see his features clearly, not then through the pain, or now, in the darkness, although she had felt him hovering over her throughout the birth. Suyin reached out to touch the fabric of the sofa, stroking the smooth and silky material. She couldn't imagine ever sitting on something so beautiful.

"What are you doing in here?"

The voice came out of nowhere, abrupt and accusing. What *was* she doing wandering around the house in the dark? It appeared exactly the way she didn't want it to. She swallowed and turned around slowly, her heart pounding in fear. What if she'd been in the kitchen looking through the cabinets? The old professor was standing behind her, waiting for just this moment to validate all his suspicions about her.

"I wanted to see the house," she answered, her voice small and hesitant.

"In the dark?"

Suyin didn't know what to say.

His tall, shadowy figure stood waiting for an explanation. Most of the time the old professor seemed lost in his own world, sitting in the courtyard with his eyes closed when Tao was away at school. Still, she always felt his gaze on her when she was downstairs with them, watching and waiting for her to misstep, watching and waiting for this very moment.

"I wasn't able to sleep," she finally said, almost in a whisper. She braced herself for what would come next, expecting him to call her the thief she was, or order her to leave the house immediately with the baby.

Instead, he watched her for a long moment before he cleared his throat, and said quietly, "Neither could I."

He walked toward her and turned on an oil lamp. Suddenly the room appeared before her eyes.

"It helps to see with the lights on," he said.

"I should go back upstairs," she said.

"Didn't you say you wanted to see the house?"

Suyin stepped away from the sofa and quickly looked around the sparse room. She imagined it was once very grand, filled with beautiful furniture and paintings, but now, in the yellow glare of the light, she saw there was only the single faded sofa with its worn armrests and sagging cushions, the threadbare rug underneath it where she had given birth. The stone fireplace looked abandoned, darkened with soot. Suyin's gaze traveled to the painting hanging above it. The man looked distinguished in a long silk gown and gray hair. When she turned to face the old professor she saw the resemblance.

"My father," he said.

"You look a lot like him."

"More so as I've gotten older," he said. "We were very different in every other way."

The old professor's voice wasn't angry at all. Instead, he sounded weary and sad, much like what she felt about the room.

"I think all children say that about their parents," she said.

He almost smiled. "Yes, I suppose you're right. If we're

fortunate, we reach a point in our lives when we begin to meet halfway. Before then, we spend all our time going in different directions. And sometimes," he added, "it's too late to find your way back."

Suyin didn't quite know what he was talking about. She suddenly felt exposed in her thin cotton tunic and pants. When the professor paused, she said, "I better go back upstairs, the baby might need me."

He nodded. "Yes, of course," he said. "Goodnight."

"Goodnight."

"There used to be a library," he suddenly said, "down the hall and to the left. I spent a great deal of my childhood in there."

"You've always lived here?" she asked.

He nodded.

Her eyes wandered around the room again. "It must have been wonderful to have grown up here."

"It was," he said, and then he did smile.

Suyin wanted to see the library, but didn't dare to ask. "I should go," she said, not knowing what to say next.

"Yes, of course," he said, and nothing else.

Suyin edged past him and hurried out of the room. The old professor wasn't so bad after all. She could almost see him standing in front of his students, tall and engaging, teaching them about the world. Suyin wondered if she'd ever be able to return to school. At one time she wanted to become a teacher, which felt like a child's dream now. She turned back once to see if the old professor was following, but as soon as she had left the room, the light flickered off and it was dark again.

Wei

WEI HADN'T EXPECTED TO SEE THE GIRL, SUYIN, roaming around the house in the middle of the night. He'd been waiting to catch her at something, but strangely, instead of being angry at finding her in the living room, he was relieved to find someone in the house who didn't know about the letter. At first, surprised at finding her there, he'd spoken sharply, but when he saw how young and frightened she appeared, he wondered if he'd misjudged the girl, and tried to put her at ease. Was this the same effect he had on most people? Surely his students must have been afraid of him, too, always distant and self-absorbed. Perhaps this was like all the other mistakes he'd made lately, and her finding Kai Ying had simply been an act of fate. She appeared intelligent enough, simply curious and interested in everything he'd long taken for granted.

Wei left the house early again the next morning. He was reminded of his childhood, when his *amah* Ching walked him to school each morning. It was a time when Guangzhou was still an intimate city, famous for its large harbor that drew ships in from all over the world. Sometimes after school, Ching took him down to the port to watch the ships come in, their colorful flags of origin flying atop each one. He heard languages from all over the world and tried to guess which country they were sailing from. He memorized each flag so he could go home and look them up in his father's library. America, Spain, the Netherlands.

It was a memory of breadth and distances crossed that filled him with an unexpected joy.

Wei again walked toward the Pearl River, choppy and murky in the morning breeze. He followed the river's path until he flagged down a pedicab to take him down to the harbor. As they approached the streets leading to the port, the pedicab passed the burgeoning crowds of early-morning shoppers and street vendors. Wei smelled the salt fish air, the roasting chestnuts, and the long, greasy donuts frying in their large open woks and eaten with rice porridge. Wei was excited being there again, watching the big ships enter the Guangzhou harbor from the Pearl River, which was once called the "Silk Road on the Sea" during the Ming and Qing dynasties. What courage it must have taken for men to leave their homes and families for months, even years at a time, sailing on the vast open seas with only the dreams of adventure, along with the lingering threat of never making it back home to their loved ones again.

Wei paid the pedicab driver and walked down to the old wooden harbor where Ching used to take him. He stood looking out to the Pearl River, murky and roiling, which connected with the Dong, Bei, and Xi rivers moving throughout China. They would never change, no matter how much Guangzhou had since his childhood. The rivers would always flow at their own will and for that he was grateful. They were once China's main arteries to and from the rest of the world. He could only imagine how many of the artifacts he'd studied at Lingnan were brought down the rivers from other parts of China on large cargo ships. He wished Tao were there, so he could explain to him just how powerful China once was, and how everything had changed since Mao and his Party came into power. All the vibrancy and color had been drained from the city of his childhood. Times were more difficult and opportunities slim, all restricted under Party control. Was that why he'd written the letter, to reclaim his past? What did it matter now, if he didn't have his family to share it with?

Wei had spent his entire life hiding behind walls, first at the university and then at the villa. It was time to step forward and do something other than wait defeated, day after day, hoping to hear from Sheng. He needed to know if his son was still alive. The authorities had told them nothing. If he could just see Sheng, it wouldn't change the situation, but it might at least give Kai Ying some peace of mind. It was the very least he could do after all the hurt he'd caused. Wei suddenly recalled an old proverb from his childhood: *an ant may well destroy a whole dam*. And a father may well find his son, he thought.

As Wei watched the ships move in and out of the harbor, it was the first time in a year he felt an inkling of peace. He closed his eyes against the glare of the sun and felt Liang standing beside him. It had been weeks since he had sensed her presence, and his heart raced, thinking she had finally returned to him. He wasn't alone anymore. *I'll make everything right again*, he whispered to her. *What were you thinking?* He could hear her questioning him, though her tone wasn't angry. Then he saw her smile and felt the warmth of her hand taking his.

At that moment, Wei was certain of what he had to do.

Song

S ONG CUT ANOTHER STEM OF *BAK CHOY* FROM HER garden for Kai Ying before she stood up. She heard a noise coming from the courtyard and walked toward it, stopping at the end of the brick path where she'd seen Wei leaving from the front gate, just hours earlier. He left the house early every morning now and walked, he told her, to clear his head. Song was just about to call out his name when something stopped her. He seemed in a hurry to get somewhere and her first thought was not to disturb him. Song was tempted to follow him, to see where he was off to every morning, until she looked down at the mud-splattered clothes she was wearing. It was only after the gate closed behind him that she realized he was carrying something that looked like his old leather work satchel.

Again she heard footsteps. Song covered her eyes against the sun's glare to see Kai Ying hurrying toward her. Song's smile disappeared when she saw the anxiousness in her eyes.

"What's happened? Is everything all right?" Song asked.

"*Lo Yeh*'s gone."

"No, no, he's out walking. I saw him leave the house this morning . . ."

"No, he has gone to Luoyang," Kai Ying said, her voice anxious. She handed Song a piece of paper. "He left this note."

Song put down her basket of vegetables and looked at Wei's fluid characters. She remembered what Liang had once said to her. *In another life, Wei must have been an Imperial scribe.* It was true, in his beautiful script he had written: *I've gone to Luoyang to find Sheng.*

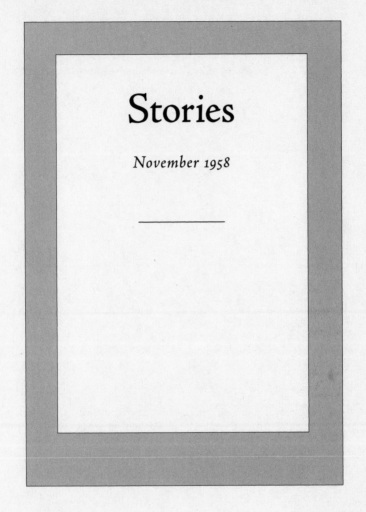

Stories

November 1958

———————

Wei

THE LAST DAY OF OCTOBER BROUGHT COOLER AND milder temperatures, the sky overcast and gray. Wei left the house early, just as he had been doing for the past few weeks so his absence wouldn't warrant suspicion. He'd left a letter for Kai Ying on the kitchen table, and was almost approached by Song, but he hurried out of the front gate before she could talk to him. There was nothing left to say, and he didn't want to explain why he was carrying his old leather satchel with him, bulging with a pair of pants, a few shirts, and a woolen sweater for Sheng. He was also wearing his new *mein po*. It would be cold and dry in Luoyang, a flat region surrounded by mountainous terrain that was so different from Guangzhou.

Ever since he visited the harbor two weeks ago, Wei had been planning this trip. He checked his pocket once again for his money as he walked to the bus station. There were so many unanswered questions that worried him, but he avoided them now and hoped to find the answers along the way. Nothing was going to detour him from seeing Sheng. After years of remaining stagnant Wei had a purpose; he was no longer standing still and gathering dust.

⁕

As Wei approached the bus station, the sun broke through the clouds. It was a good sign. He shifted the satchel he carried to his other hand and could already smell the bus fumes from a half block away. Taking the bus would be slower, but he assumed it was also cheaper. He had no idea how long it would take to see Sheng. Until then, he'd have to use his savings sparingly. During his last years at Lingnan, Wei had set a little money aside, hidden among his books. Before he left, he divided the money into two envelopes, one in the inside pocket of his *mein po,* the other tucked in between the clothes in his satchel.

Wei hadn't eaten much before he left the house and his stomach rumbled. He stopped to buy a bag of dry plums and some biscuits in a tin to tide him over for the first leg of the trip. He could buy more when they reached the next city.

Wei hurried, anxious now. The last time he'd been away from Guangzhou was more than twenty-five years ago when he caught the train to Shanghai to give a lecture on Sung Dynasty art. Then, his satchel was filled with notes on the complicated dynasty that was divided into two distinct periods; the first defined by art, philosophy, growth, and stability, while the latter half was characterized by war, brutality, and displacement. It all came back to him now. He had also brought along color reproductions of the misty, ethereal paintings of that period, which reflected the conflicting moods of the time. How could he have once been so confident, so sure of himself standing in front of an audience of hundreds of faculty and students, while he'd spent the past ten years hiding away behind the walls of the villa? Wei saw it now as the conflicting halves of his own life. How was it he could know so much and so little?

Wei paused for a moment to catch his breath. The city was awakening. He began to see more people walking down the streets, clutching their bags and possessions as bicyclists skillfully weaved in and out, carrying everything from cages filled with chickens to a pig carcass wobbling precariously on the backs of their bicycles. But what amused Wei most was the sight of two riders, pedaling side by side in perfect sync as they transported a set of straw mattresses tied across the backs of both bikes. Such simplicity somehow agreed with him, entire lives flitting by on the backs of bicycles.

Wei grew warmer as he continued down the street. He unbuttoned the collar of his tunic, but kept his *mein po* on rather than carry it, even as the sooty air became more oppressive as he approached the station.

The Guangzhou Long-Distance Bus Station shared the same building as the Guangzhou Railway Station. Within the cavernous structure was a world of its own as people arrived and departed from all over China. Walking through the train station, Wei was immediately surrounded by a crush of rushing bodies and the high, singsong voices of merchants selling everything from kites to pots and pans. Sweaters and silk pajamas were stacked high in all sizes, vibrant silk scarves, umbrellas, and Parker pens in every color—the shrill, frantic voices calling from every direction and vying for his attention. *"Right here, right here, the best quality in town at the lowest prices!*" It had been a long time since he was in the midst of so many people moving so quickly.

Wei pushed his way through the crowds and walked to the far end of the building, which housed the quieter bus station. A few passengers sat on wooden benches waiting for their buses to arrive or depart, and an older woman directed him to the bus schedule; a large black board with changing white names and numbers. When he didn't see Luoyang on the board, he approached a young man sitting behind the counter reading a magazine.

"Can you tell me if there's a bus that goes directly to Luoyang?" Wei asked.

"Luoyang?"

"In the Henan province," he added.

Wei watched the young man flip through a blue book, his finger moving down the columns line by line until he had found Luoyang. He wondered how he'd gotten the job when he had no idea where Luoyang was.

"There's a bus that leaves in an hour, but it's a very long trip. It looks as if there are about twenty-two stops in between," the young man finally said.

"How long will it take?"

"Three or four days," he said. "Maybe more."

"That long?" Wei asked. He was aware that Luoyang was far away, but hearing that it took days on a bus left him feeling suddenly defeated.

The young man looked up at Wei for the first time. "You might want to take a train instead. It's faster and should take half the time to reach Luoyang. And even the most inexpensive seat would be more comfortable."

Wei smiled and thought the young man looked faintly like a student he once had, though he thought that of so many young people he saw. "Do you know what the cost would be?"

"You'll have to ask at the train station." The young man gestured in the direction he'd just come from.

Wei nodded. "Thank you," he said, turning away.

Wei looked around, trying to find a place to buy a cup of tea and something to eat. He felt dizzy in the noisy, crowded building, with the trapped stink of cigarette smoke, sweat, and the acidic edge of urine. He leaned against a concrete wall and for a moment he thought he might pass out, a sourness rising to his mouth, which he quickly swallowed back down again. He wasn't about to pass out before the trip had even started. Wei rooted through his jacket pocket until he found his bag of *mui*, the salty dried plums, and sucked on them until his queasiness subsided and he felt better again. It was what his mother always gave him as a child when he had bouts of motion sickness, and one of the many childhood habits that had stayed with him.

Unlike the young man at the bus station, the thin, short-haired woman at the train station was terse and abrupt in her green drab uniform. "Buy a ticket or stand aside!" she snapped at him as he tried to explain himself. Wei would never have been spoken to so rudely at the university. The thought left him indignant and gave him courage. "Let them wait," he snapped back. He stood there and calculated everything in his head.

Even if he bought the lowest fare train ticket, a quarter of his savings would be gone before he even left Guangzhou, but the trip would be much faster and less arduous. "One ticket to Luoyang," he reluctantly said. Then he sat down and waited for the train to depart.

Kai Ying

B Y THE TIME SHE AND AUNTIE SONG HAD TAKEN A pedicab to the train station, the train for Luoyang had already left and Wei was nowhere in sight. For a moment, Kai Ying stood in the middle of the bustling train station feeling completely lost. It was Song who whispered in her ear, "Let's go, Wei will find his own way," and led her back out into the sunlight and fresh air where she could breathe again.

Since returning home, Kai Ying tried not to show her distress, but her emotions swung from fear to anger. What was Wei thinking to go so far on his own? How would he be able to find his way? With all his education and intelligence, Wei was an innocent out in the world, a place he always took so little interest in. He'd spent a lifetime in a world of his own making, and now Kai Ying couldn't imagine how he would survive outside of Guangzhou, where he had no control. There was no telling where he was, or how he was, as the train traveled farther and farther away from Guangzhou to a part of China that might as well be another country.

Kai Ying couldn't imagine losing Wei, too.

At dinner that night, Kai Ying told Tao his grandfather had gone away for a short time. Suyin ate with them every night now, and watched quietly from the other side of the table.

"Where did he go?" Tao asked.

Kai Ying had decided to tell Tao the truth. "He went to Luoyang, hoping to see *ba ba*."

Tao looked up at her. "Why didn't you tell me?"

"I am telling you."

"I could have gone with him."

She heard the whine in his voice and knew he was upset. "It's a very long way from here and you have school. Anyway, this is something *ye ye* has to do on his own. He's a smart man and he knows how to take good care of himself," she said with a quiet finality.

"How far away is it?"

"Over a thousand miles. It'll take him two days or more by train just to get there," she said, her voice quieting as if she were talking more to herself than to him.

"He'll come back soon?"

"Of course he will. He just needs . . ." She paused and looked down at him. "He just needs to see if he can visit your *ba ba* to make sure everything is all right."

"Have you ever been that far away?"

"No."

"When is he coming back?"

"I'm not certain," she answered. "It depends."

"Depends on what?" Tao asked.

Kai Ying paused and took a breath. She suddenly wanted to get up and walk away from all her son's questions.

"One day I hope to see all of China," Suyin suddenly said. "I'd go to Beijing and Shanghai first," she added.

Tao turned to her. "What about your baby?"

Suyin's voice was a welcome surprise. Kai Ying smiled at her gratefully.

"She'll go with me," Suyin said. "Or maybe I'll have to wait until she's older."

Kai Ying watched them talk. They could be brother and sister. Their voices filled the room, while she caught her breath. Now that Suyin was rested and had put some weight back on, she was quite a sweet-looking girl. There was only one matter of concern; Kai Ying had discovered food suddenly disappearing during the past week. She hoped that she wasn't wrong about the girl, who, in her serious, industrious way was also becoming a big help to Kai Ying. They'd fallen into a comfortable routine; Suyin was learning to take care of the baby while also helping around the house and running errands to the market or the herb shop for her.

Suyin also seemed particularly interested in her herb work, asking questions and watching her closely, which pleased Kai Ying, who had begun teaching her the qualities and characteristics of each herb and how they worked together to strengthen and heal the body from the inside out. Just the other afternoon, Kai Ying laid out the basic herbs used as the core ingredients of any restorative soup: red dates, Chinese wolfberries, goji berries, ginseng, and astragalus roots, much to the girl's delight.

Suyin had remained closemouthed about her own family and Kai Ying didn't push. Her story would emerge when the time was right. The baby had just turned six weeks old and neither of them had mentioned a name for the child or what lay ahead. Kai Ying was certain of only one thing; she didn't want to see anyone else leaving the house unexpectedly.

Wei

THE TRAIN HAD LEFT THE STATION JUST BEFORE nine in the morning, his car no more than half full. There was a strong smell of camphor and menthol; the distinct medicinal odor of Tiger Balm ointment that mingled with the stale smoke-scented air. Wei glanced at all the passengers, deciding that the Tiger Balm emanated from one, or both of the two older ladies who sat toward the front of the car. The familiar scent brought back memories. His father had rubbed the ointment on his neck and shoulders whenever his rheumatism flared up, while his mother preferred *Hua Tuo Luo Li* oil. Kai Ying had made him a special liniment for his occasional back pains, which was just one more thing he'd forgotten to bring with him.

Wei had chosen to sit toward the middle of the car, where several rows of seats in front and behind him remained empty.

Cigarette butts and spittle littered the floor. The seats were hard and thinly cushioned but they would do. With his satchel secure in the rack above, Wei sat by the window and watched engrossed as the train moved slowly out of the station. Outside, the rain had stopped, and the crowded city streets flickered before him as the train picked up speed at the outskirts of Guangzhou. Soon the landscape changed to that of open land and trees. Wei sat back, but not before he quickly observed all the other passengers who were on their way to Shaoguan or Chenzhou, or any of the many small cities along the way to Luoyang. Besides the two older women who sat up front, a thin man in his thirties sat deep in thought across the aisle from him, smoking one cigarette after another. There were a handful of middle-aged women traveling with each other, and a large, boisterous group of men toward the back of the car, all dressed in the casual work clothes of day laborers. They had talked and laughed continuously since the train had left the station; their boxes and bags tied together with twine were stuffed up in the racks. Wei wondered if they lived in Shaoguan and worked in Guangzhou, or vice versa. If they worked the night shift, they would be going home right about now. He imagined every day was like a small party for them during these train rides, this kind of camaraderie a good part of their lives. He'd had few close friends in his life; Song and his family made up his small world and even that he'd managed to destroy.

Wei looked out the window and closed his eyes for a moment. He'd slept even less the past week leading up to the trip, a mix of nerves and anticipation, and opened his eyes again only when he realized someone was speaking to him. Wei turned from the window and caught the last word of the question meant for him. ". . . Luoyang?"

"I'm sorry?" he said.

The thin man across the aisle leaned toward him. He cleared his throat and asked Wei again, "Are you traveling all the way to Luoyang?"

Wei nodded.

"Your first time?" A cigarette burned between his fingers as he watched Wei.

"Yes. Is it that obvious?" he asked.

"Just the way you're watching everything like you haven't seen it before."

Wei cleared his throat. "I haven't."

The train clattered on with an occasional shriek of the wheels grinding against the rails, and the constant rumbling of the cars whose swaying motions made Wei's stomach upset. The man turned and sat sideways so that he now faced Wei. He wore a loose-fitting blue tunic and a pair of cotton pants and sandals. His hair was neatly cut and just beginning to gray. He was a handsome man, his face younger than Wei first thought. He wasn't much older than Sheng, and he didn't appear like a day laborer or a retiree who had the time to ride a long-distance train across China. The man crossed his legs in the aisle and offered him a cigarette. When Wei declined, he inhaled deeply, the smoke drifting out his mouth and nose.

"I know Luoyang well," he said. "I used to travel back and forth from Guangzhou to Luoyang all the time. This is my first trip back in many years."

Wei watched the cigarette burn between the man's long, tapered fingers and knew he wanted to strike up a conversation.

He supposed it did make the hours pass faster. Still, Wei simply nodded, hoping to be left alone. The train rattled on and the laborers in the back of the car had quieted down.

"My name is Tian," the man said, and reached over to extend his hand.

"Lee Wei," he said, taking the man's hand. There was little chance he'd be left alone now.

"Are you visiting someone in Luoyang, or are you going to see the sights?" Tian asked.

Wei weighed the question. It made the actual trip real to him now. Up until that moment, it was still something distant and imagined to him. He had never entertained the thought of sightseeing in Luoyang. "There's someone I hope to see there," he finally answered.

"A friend?" Tian asked, and smiled.

Wei shook his head.

"My son," he answered.

The train suddenly slowed, lurched forward, and then picked up speed again as they passed small farms in the distance, water buffalo peppering the fields. Tian smiled thoughtfully and sucked on his cigarette. "Does your son live in Luoyang?"

"Temporarily," Wei answered.

Tian nodded. "I lived there for a short time, but Guangzhou will always be my home. For one thing, the climate is much more agreeable to me."

"You said you used to travel to Luoyang and back all the time. Do you have family there?" Wei asked. He hoped to steer the conversation away from Sheng.

"Oh no, my family's from the southern Fukien area. I was raised in Guangzhou." Tian dropped the butt of his cigarette onto the floor, carefully putting it out with the heel of his sandal. "Before, my trips to Luoyang had to do with a girl I was seeing at the time. This trip is more of a pilgrimage."

He watched the man's simple, graceful movements. There was something about him that inspired curiosity. Luoyang was a long way to travel if there wasn't someone, or something, waiting on the other end.

"Does she still live there?" Wei said. "I hope you don't mind my asking."

Tian looked directly into his eyes, and Wei saw a hint of sadness, something that was long settled deep within him. "I wish I knew," Tian finally said.

Wei sat back. There were worse things that could happen during a long trip than to listen to a man's tale of love. "You moved there to be with her?"

Tian lit another cigarette, letting it burn between his fingers. The smoke rose toward the roof of the car and lingered.

"It wasn't more than a few months," he said regretfully. "We were young then."

Wei watched Tian with interest. Why was this man returning to Luoyang after so many years if he was no longer with this woman? And why did his words still feel edged with urgency? "What happened?" he asked.

Tian shook his head. "It's a long story," he answered.

Before he said anything else, the train abruptly braked; wheels shrieking against the rails as the car jerked roughly to a stop, throwing Wei forward. His shoulder hit the seat in front of him. From the corner of his eye, he saw Tian's cigarette fly out of his hand as he grabbed on to his seat's armrest to avoid falling into the aisle. A passenger screamed and the raised voices of the others filled the car as the train slowed down to a crawl.

"Are you all right?" Tian asked.

"I'm fine," Wei answered, rubbing his shoulder.

The truth was he hadn't thought about all the unforeseen accidents that could happen at his age on such a long trip. Still, Wei couldn't remember when he'd felt so alive. By the time he looked out the window for the cause of their abrupt stop, the train had picked up speed and was on its way again.

Wei

THE TRAIN SLOWED DOWN AS THEY ENTERED THE outskirts of Shaoguan. The noise from the men at the back of the car picked up again in anticipation of their arrival, a hum of activity filling the car as possessions were put away and bags retrieved. On the outskirts of the city, plain two-story, whitewashed brick buildings lined the streets. People lingered in front of small businesses selling everything from vegetables to clothing to bicycle tires, while scattered groups of bicyclists rode toward the city center.

"The train stops here for half an hour. I suggest we get off and buy something to eat and drink," Tian said. "We won't reach Chenzhou until late afternoon."

When the train came to a full stop, Wei stood up, his shoulder sore, his back already stiff as he stretched and reached for his satchel. He followed Tian off the train and down a dusty, narrow street near the train station that opened up to a crowded, bustling marketplace. Wei felt fortunate to have been befriended by Tian, who knew exactly what to do, and in whose guidance he felt safe. For the first time since leaving Guangzhou that morning, he faced the cold reality of having left behind everything secure and comfortable. With each stop, Wei was moving farther away from those he loved and closer to place he knew nothing about.

They bought noodles and dumplings from a market stall and quickly ate standing, the bowl hot in his hands, the soup scalding his tongue. Wei had forgotten how hungry he was and would have bought another bowl of noodles if they hadn't had to rush back to the train. Tian stopped at another stall and bought two bottles of rice liquor while Wei waited. Before he knew what was happening, Wei was pushed from behind and fell hard to the ground. A young man helped him up, muttering apologies as he patted away the dust from his jacket. Wei stood shakily, rubbing his elbow, the sleeve of his new *mein po* torn.

"Are you all right?" Tian asked, rushing over.

The man who had knocked him down had quickly disappeared into the crowd. Wei nodded, fiddling with the small rip in his sleeve, which hurt more than his elbow.

"This will help to make you feel better," Tian said, and smiled, holding up his bottles.

Wei nodded again. "I imagine it will," he said.

He'd never been much of a drinking man and couldn't recall the last time he'd had the fermented rice liquor. Sheng, on the other hand, often returned from seeing friends or from school meetings when he was young, flushed, and smelling of the sharp, cheap liquor. Before he married Kai Ying, Wei was afraid he'd taken to drinking a bit too much, but after settling down and the birth of Tao, Sheng drank only on special occasions.

When they boarded the train again, the group of laborers who sat in the back had disembarked in Shaoguan. Without their boisterous voices, their already empty car felt even more so. Wei noticed all the women who had boarded in Guangzhou had remained, while a younger man and woman boarded just ahead of them for the next leg of the trip. Wei sat down and closely examined the tear on his sleeve. He felt better knowing Song or Kai Ying could mend it when he returned. Only then did he realize something else was wrong. He checked the inner pocket of his jacket, his heart pounding against his chest, only to confirm what he already knew: his envelope of money was gone. Wei stood up, but the train was already moving at full speed and the man at the marketplace was long gone.

The alcohol burned going down Wei's throat but he liked the immediate warmth that spread through his body with each swallow. It even dulled the sting of being pickpocketed. Wei was down to half of his money and he hadn't even reached Luoyang. Thankfully, he had bought his train ticket and kept the other half in his satchel. There was nothing he could do now, and so Wei focused on what was right in front of him. It felt colder since they left Shaoguan, the air clear and brisk as he buttoned up his *mein po*. His feet were cold and he wished he'd brought more socks than the two extra pairs tucked in his satchel.

Outside the window he saw more farmers working the land. Everything appeared to be moving in slow motion as they sped by. Wei glanced at his watch, nearly three in the afternoon, and he suddenly realized Tao would be getting out of school just about then. Was Kai Ying or Song there to greet him? What was he doing on this train heading to who knows where when he would normally be waiting for Tao and walking him home? His heart ached to recall his grandson's unhappiness and to know that he was the cause of it. Of everything that had happened, it was losing Tao's love and respect that stung the most.

"Another drink," Tian said, thrusting the bottle of liquor his way. "It warms the heart."

Wei swallowed another mouthful, wincing as it went down his throat. He hoped it would numb the heart too.

Tian laughed. "I see it's already working."

"I'm afraid I'm not much of a drinker," he said. Wei handed the bottle back to him.

"You will be by the time this train arrives in Luoyang," Tian said.

Wei woke with a start, frightened. It took him a moment to realize where he was, the sharp pain in his back and neck reminding him of the hard train seat and the awkward way his head was slumped against the window. His elbow ached with a dull throb. He remembered Tian had been saying something to him when he felt suddenly dizzy from the rice liquor and needed to close his eyes. Now Wei awoke slowly, not allowing the hollow rattle of the car or the stale air to intrude, not ready to step back into the real world of the train just yet. He glanced down at his watch, surprised to see he'd been asleep for almost two hours.

Across the aisle, Tian was reading a newspaper, the half-filled bottle of rice wine lying in the seat next to him. Outside, the sky had darkened with low, gray clouds. Slowly Wei was rocked back into the enclosed world of the train car. In another hour they would reach Chenzhou so he closed his eyes again until then.

The train had stopped for a shorter time in Chenzhou, only enough time for Tian to dash off to buy them something to eat from the vendors at the station. As he watched Tian bargaining with the food vendors from the train window, he thought again of how swiftly they'd developed an alliance. While it was something that came naturally to Liang, it was the first time he'd warmed up to a stranger so quickly. There was something about the man that gave the impression of both calm and intelligence. And something more, a sadness that Wei could identify with, as if they were two lost souls traveling to an unknown landscape. Or so it would be if it were a story he were telling to Tao.

Tian bought two bottles of beer and some *zong*, the fist-sized sticky rice filled with salted pork, cooked peanuts, and a bit of salted duck eggs, all wrapped in bamboo leaves. There were many variations and costs; Wei's favorite was made every year by Song during the Dragon Boat Festival, which always included Chinese sausage or dried shrimp and Chinese black mushrooms for added flavors. For dessert, Tian bought coconut milk and shredded coconut gelatin. As simple as it was, he hadn't enjoyed a meal so much in a long time. Wei turned to thank Tian again. He had refused to accept his money, so it was agreed Wei would buy their next meal.

By the time they'd finished eating, it was dark outside and a weak yellowish light filled the car, the dark window reflecting a tired old man back at Wei. Ironically, it was the first time he had felt so energetic in the past year. The rumbling sounds of the train deepened with the night. The rest of the passengers had already begun to prepare for the night ahead, extracting pillows and blankets from their bags. Only then did Wei realize how unprepared he was for the long trip. The next handful of stations would be quick stops as the train continued on through the night until they reached Linxiang early in the morning. By Wei's calculations, they would have traveled over five hundred miles by then.

Kai Ying

KAI YING COULDN'T SLEEP. IN THE DARK, ALL OF her anger had now turned to concern for Wei. She imagined his equally sleepless nights on the train. His back must be bothering him, as it always did when he sat for too long without moving. She wondered if he'd brought the bottle of ginger and sesame oil liniment she'd made for him, and if he had enough clothes to keep warm. Kai Ying thought about checking Wei's room to see what he had brought with him, but it somehow felt like an intrusion and so she told herself tomorrow, tomorrow she would check.

Since her father-in-law had retired, his room had become his office and library and sanctuary where she usually found him sitting at his desk, head down, reading some book. As soon as Kai Ying entered, she immediately felt hesitant and unsure of herself, as if she'd somehow become small and insignificant among his things. Even Sheng and Tao always knocked before they entered.

The house creaked and Kai Ying thought she heard footsteps. Before Tao was born, one of the first stories Wei had told her was about the two ghosts roaming the villa. "You needn't be afraid of them," he said. "Who are they?" she had asked. Wei explained that when he was a boy, his family had three full-time servants who lived at the villa. His *amah*, Ching, was his nursemaid who slept in the small alcove off of his room. Their cook,

Sun, and their housekeeper, Moon, lived in the back rooms which now belonged to Auntie Song.

Kai Ying tried to imagine what it must have been like to have servants doing all the things that now filled her days. It was the bourgeoisie lifestyle Mao and the Communist Party had despised and fought against, declaring victory for the people. And yet, why was there never enough rice or oil or coal for the people?

Wei told her Sun and Moon had worked for his family ever since they were young women. Before then, they'd been silk workers from the village of Shun-de. When Wei was a boy of nine or ten, Sun and Moon were already middle-aged, and had been working for his family for over twenty years. "They were as different as the sun and the moon," her father-in-law said, and laughed. "There was hardly a time when they didn't disagree about something. They would have argued about the time of day if they'd had the time!"

When Wei was not yet fifteen, Moon fell ill. Sun devoted herself to taking care of her until she died, six months later. Afterward, Sun stayed on until she became too old, but she was never the same. She passed away just after Wei graduated from Lingnan. Had he seen their ghosts? Kai Ying asked. Her father-in-law shook his head. "They've only shown themselves to the women in the household," he said. A few years after Sun's death, his mother occasionally saw Moon carrying fresh sheets to one of the bedrooms, or Sun, moving in and out of the kitchen. While he had never seen them, he'd felt them. He remembered feeling a cold wind blowing through the hallway in the middle of a hot August day. "I knew it was them," he said. The villa had been their only real home and he couldn't imagine them anywhere else. Kai Ying had thought the same thing about him. She heard another creak. Could it be Sun and Moon returning to the villa wondering where Wei had gone?

Kai Ying yawned and tried to clear her mind. Instead, it was Tao's innocent question that returned to her thoughts. *Have you been there?* She'd never been farther away from Guangzhou than her hometown of Zhaoqing, never needed to see more of the world than what was in front of her. She turned on her side and closed her eyes, but still the underlying thought lingered, why hadn't she been brave enough to have boarded the train to Luoyang to find Sheng?

Wei

WEI STARED OUT THE TRAIN WINDOW INTO BLACKNESS. He imagined all the farmers he'd seen in the countryside were indoors now with their families, eating together or telling stories about their day or preparing for bed. He looked past his reflection at the poorly lit train car he sat in. Everything appeared sad and dull in the dingy light as the train rattled on into the night and most of the other passengers slept. Wei suddenly felt homesick. Heartsick. He was no longer tired and wished he hadn't napped earlier so that he might sleep now to pass the time. Instead, there was nothing but the long night ahead of him. He looked over at Tian to find him still awake with a book in his hands, though he didn't seem to be turning the pages.

Wei shifted over to the aisle seat and closer to Tian. "You're not going to sleep yet?" he asked.

Tian turned toward him and said, "I find I don't need very much sleep."

"You never finished your story," Wei said.

"What story is that?" he asked.

"What happened to the woman who lived in Luoyang?"

Tian put his book down. "Ah, yes, that story," he said. When he reached for the bottle of rice wine, Wei saw a slight tremor in his hand. "That calls for a bit of liquid courage."

Wei declined when he held the bottle toward him. Tian took a swallow, then lit a cigarette and let it burn between his fingers.

"I'm sorry," Wei finally said. "You don't have to tell me if it's too difficult."

"Her name was Ai-li," Tian said, leaning closer to Wei. It was clear by the glint in his eyes that he'd made the decision to tell his story. "We were together for five years. She was from Luoyang, where she'd remained living and working in an office during our courtship. I took the train back to Luoyang every two or three months to see her. When we had saved enough money, we were going to marry and Ai-li was going to move to Guangzhou. Our plan was to buy a small apartment, and later a bigger place. Her dream in the beginning was to have a house and a child." Tian smiled at the memory. "At that age, dreams feel more tangible than reality. You can see and taste the happiness right in front of you. I was simply happy to be with her."

"How did you meet?"

"We met in Guangzhou where I was going to school. Ai-li was the friend of a friend, and she was visiting her in Guangzhou when we met at a gathering. It was early 1946, a challenging time for all of us students. The World War had just ended and our civil war was escalating again. We were all filled with concern and hope and the raw energy that comes with youth."

Wei recalled many of his students over the years at Lingnan. They must have gathered together outside of class in their rooms or restaurants, small dramas occurring daily. He felt strangely close to them at that moment, many of who would be Tian's age or older, now. There had been so much confusion and upheaval at the university at the time and it was such a vulnerable age, filled with daring. He'd never stopped to ponder just how many of his students lived and died for the Communist or Nationalist causes back then. How could he have been so oblivious? Wei suddenly wondered if Tian had been a student at Lingnan.

"Were you in college then?" he asked.

Tian nodded. "I never went to a university. I was studying at a technical college when I first met Ai-li. You?"

Wei nodded. "I'm retired now. I was a teacher," he said, and no more.

"I could have guessed." Tian laughed. "You have the eyes of a teacher."

"And how's that?"

"An intellectual curiosity."

"Ah, a nice excuse for prying," Wei said, and laughed. "So I might as well ask you how this woman Ai-li came to steal your heart."

"That's exactly what I would expect," Tian said. He took another drink. "She was barely nineteen, with long flowing black hair, full lips, and a shy expression that soon relaxed as the evening wore on. From the first moment I saw her, I wanted to kiss those lips. She had stolen my heart. It sounds terribly unoriginal, but it did happen to me."

Wei thought of Liang. "I believe it happens more often than we think."

"Our first year together was perfect," Tian continued. "The fighting between the Kuomintung and the Communists made it more difficult for us to travel back and forth to see each other, but our courtship from a distance was somehow made more precious by the challenge. Even from afar, we were completely happy together. Strangely, I never worried she might find someone else. I would have married Ai-li within the first month of knowing her if I could have," he said, his voice softening. "I should have."

"You were both very young."

Tian nodded. "There seemed to be all the time in the world, and then suddenly there wasn't."

"What happened?" Wei asked. "Did she meet someone?"

"In a way," Tian said. He took another drink from the bottle and put out his cigarette. "After I finished college, while the Party fervor continued to build, I moved to Luoyang to be with Ai-li. I rented a small room there. I'm embarrassed to say that I didn't adapt very well to Luoyang. Ai-li was away working all day, while I was having trouble finding any work. Before I moved to Luoyang, Ai-li hadn't told me she'd begun attending Party meetings in the evenings. She'd become friends with a young woman in her office who had persuaded her to attend a meeting with her. Ironically, it was Ai-li who returned week after week, while her friend lost interest. Her pro-Communist beliefs increased with each of my visits. It was early 1949, and as you well know, all of China was teeming with revolution, but I had no idea Ai-li was becoming so involved with the Party in Luoyang. The more she talked about the Party, the more I began to resent that it was becoming such a big part of her life. Thinking back, I carry some of the blame. I wasn't very easy to be with at the time," Tian said, looking over at Wei. "Visiting Luoyang had been fine, but when faced with a hot and arid climate for months on end with no job prospects, and Ai-li spending more and more time at her Party meetings, I missed my family and friends in Guangzhou. We had the usual small arguments, but nothing out of the ordinary for a young couple finding their way."

Wei nodded. He thought of Liang and how she always kept his life calm and balanced so he could concentrate on his work. How much did she have to put aside in order to appease him? He'd been so blind to the life he had.

"Months later," Tian continued, "when I returned to Guangzhou to visit my family and friends, I was offered a job working at a family friend's paper company. I had fully intended to return to Luoyang and make a life there. But I had just turned twenty-three, and the job offered more money than I'd ever made. I was elated to think that Ai-li and I could finally get married and live in Guangzhou, but instead of being happy when I returned to Luoyang with the news, she was clearly upset by it."

Tian stopped talking and rubbed his eyes.

"I should also mention," he continued, "that Ai-li's entire appearance had changed gradually during the last two years we were together. By the time the Party had declared victory in 1949, she had stopped using any kind of makeup and disdained all the false propaganda that represented a bourgeoisie society. When I returned from Guangzhou, I was shocked to see she had cut her beautiful long hair, which she knew I had always loved, to a short and blunt cut like so many of the other female Party members. If a haircut could express anger, it was hers. I was upset but tried not to show it.

"I kept telling her, 'You'll get another job and make new friends in Guangzhou. With my salary, we'll be able to marry and start a life of our own, just like we always hoped.' She only smiled distantly. Any person who wasn't half as much in love could have seen that she no longer believed in that life."

"Did she say anything to you before then?" Wei asked.

"Our disagreements had mainly to do with politics," he answered.

Tian stopped and looked around the car, as if to make sure no one else was listening before he continued.

"When I first moved to Luoyang, Ai-li implored me to go with her to a Party meeting. 'You'll see how right it all is,' she said. 'Our life together will only gain strength through our dedication,' she went on. But I would have none of it. 'Aren't I good enough for you? Why do you need the Communist Party to make you happy?' I asked. 'Because the world is bigger than us,' she said. Ai-li spoke of regretting all of our foolish talk, and viewing our hopes and dreams as nothing more than bourgeoisie ideals held by silly children."

Tian stopped to take a drink.

Wei didn't know when, but the dim lights in the car had gone off, leaving them in shadows. The car was now illuminated only by Tian's weak reading light spilling sadly upon him, making it appear as if he were being interrogated.

"You don't have to go on," Wei said.

"It's all right," he said softly. He cleared his throat and continued. "After a very difficult week, Ai-li suddenly relaxed as if all the fight had seeped out of her. For the first time in a year, I saw traces of the old Ai-li return. She stopped going to Party meetings in the evenings and came to see me instead. For the next week of my stay, it was as if we had found our way back to each other. Slowly, quietly, we discussed our plans again, and it was finally agreed that I would return to Guangzhou first to begin my new job and Ai-li would follow in a month or two, after she'd settled everything in Luoyang, to begin our life together."

Tian looked over at Wei. "You think me foolish to believe her, but at the time, I needed to believe her. Wouldn't I have known if she were lying? It was so much easier to see what I wanted. Ai-li seemed herself again, excited about the move, and I was relieved to be able to stay put in Guangzhou and work, eager to show her more of the city and how wonderful it would be for us living there."

Wei reached over for the bottle of liquor in Tian's hands, swallowed a mouthful, and handed it back to him. But instead of taking a drink, Tian simply cradled the bottle in his hands.

"It was closer to three months by the time Ai-li was ready to come to Guangzhou," he continued. "On the Friday she was to arrive, I left work early and hurried to the train station to wait. I still remember the feeling of anticipation that raced through my body. When the train arrived, I searched for her in each window and then waited and watched as each passenger stepped off, thinking surely she would be next. But she never was."

"What happened?" Wei asked, although he already knew Ai-li had never boarded a train.

"My first thought was that she must have missed the train. I contacted her work but no one had seen her. She had few really close friends except for those in the Party. Her family lived far away in the countryside, near Fuzhou, and I had only met a cousin of hers in all the time we were together. Ai-li often said she didn't really belong anywhere. But she belonged with me. I waited for the next train to arrive, thinking she might have transferred along the way and was coming in on another train. It was dark when the last train arrived, and Ai-li wasn't on it."

Tian shook his head as if he still couldn't believe it. He dropped the cigarette butt to the floor and stamped it out with his sandal.

"What did you do?" Wei asked.

"By then I was frantic. I returned to my room, half out of my mind with worry, believing that something must have happened to her. I remember it being so hot that night; the room seemed to suck all the breath from me. I lay on my bed sweating, just waiting to catch the first train that left the following morning for Luoyang. The last time I saw her, everything between us had seemed fine again. She had dropped the Party façade and was the same sweet, gentle young woman she always was. During our last week together, she was happy and filled with plans to make the move to Guangzhou. I've replayed every moment of our time together and there's only one detail that keeps on returning even after all these years. When Ai-li left me at the train station, she didn't look back as she always did. She walked straight down the steps, turned the corner, and was gone."

Tian stopped talking. He looked past Wei and out the window as if he were still searching for her.

Wei sat back and rubbed his shoulder, feeling the dull throb of his scraped elbow. Hadn't he felt the same fierce desperation? The raw, frenzied emptiness of having his son simply vanish. Ai-li had most likely chosen to disappear; Sheng wasn't given a choice. Why hadn't they heard from him in such a long time? Wei wondered if Luoyang was a city of ghosts. He glanced across the aisle to see that Tian had closed his eyes. Was he dreaming of seeing Ai-li again? It was her memory that he still loved. Wei, of all people, knew what a strong hold that could have. He leaned back and pulled his *mein po* tighter around him. The world was a harsh place for brokenhearted men.

Kai Ying

KAI YING QUIETLY MADE HER WAY DOWNSTAIRS. She heard movement down in the kitchen and thought for a moment that Wei might have returned, but instead, when she turned on an oil lamp, she saw Suyin rifling through the cabinets.

"If you need something, all you have to do is ask," Kai Ying said, her voice even and firm.

The girl turned, startled, the light catching the surprise and fear in her eyes. "I didn't mean . . ." she began.

"I need you to promise me that it stops here and now," Kai Ying said.

"I was afraid . . ."

"Promise me," she repeated.

Suyin looked as if she wanted to cry. "I promise," she said softly.

Without another word, Kai Ying turned around and went back upstairs.

Kai Ying tossed and turned in bed, unable to sleep. She was upset, disappointed rather than angry at Suyin. She liked the girl, but if Suyin was going to stay in the house any longer, Kai Ying needed to be able to trust her from this night forward. Kai

Ying hoped she'd made the right decision in giving her another chance, but she couldn't imagine what would become of a fifteen-year-old girl and her baby, alone, and out on the streets again.

Song

EVEN SONG'S GARDEN COULDN'T PROVIDE SOLACE. The day was just beginning, the dirt still damp and cold as she dug up old roots and turned over the soil with thoughts of her spring planting already in mind, but even visions of long beans and *gai lan* couldn't ease her mind or alleviate her restlessness. She hadn't felt this nervous churning in her stomach for a long time, not since the days of Old Hing, when she never knew if he was going to flare up and find fault where there wasn't any. Song always felt as if she were standing on thin ice, ready to take the plunge into the icy depths at any moment, the frigid water filling her body, coursing through her veins, and stealing the last of her breath. She had to do something to take back her life before it was too late.

Song had never told anyone, not even Liang. It would remain her burden. She did return to see Herbalist Chu during those difficult days after she met Kai Ying, only it wasn't about a way to end her own life. "A rat problem, I suppose," Herbalist

Chu had said. He looked at her knowingly, and then asked her if she was sure of what she was doing. "Yes," Song said, without a moment's hesitation. She had never been so sure of anything in her life.

It all happened much quicker than she had expected, a bit of *chuan wu* in Old Hing's food, and by the second day he was bedridden with difficulties breathing, struggling for air as his heartbeat slowed, and by the third day—stopping altogether. Only once, after he had lost his voice, did she see him watching her, his gasping breaths filling the room. She could see him wondering if she'd had the courage to end his life, his dark, angry pupils revealing all, coming to the conclusion that she was too weak, too stupid to have poisoned him. She could read his thoughts. *"Yes, yes it was me,"* she said, leaning close to his ear and making sure that he had heard her.

He died that evening.

Old Hing was nearing eighty-five years old and most of their neighbors chose to believe he'd died of natural causes. A lucky man, they told her, to have gone so quickly, although she knew some wondered how such a vile man could be taken so simply in his sleep and without suffering. Song had waited, ready to take whatever punishment came her way, but weeks and then months went by before she quietly assumed her new role as a widow.

Song had compartmentalized all those feelings of dread and despair that had shadowed so much of her life. Now another kind of fear enveloped her, only this time it was for Wei. Song prayed to Kuan Yin that he would find his way safely to Luoyang. Why hadn't she called out his name when she'd seen him leaving the other morning? She might have been able to stop him, or at least talk some sense into him. There was no use lamenting now. *He's a smart man*, she thought, *he'll find his way*, but even she wasn't completely convinced. Song looked up at the overcast sky and couldn't help but think she'd let Liang down.

Wei

THE TRAIN LUMBERED ON THROUGH THE NIGHT. Sometime during the long pause, both he and Tian leaned back on the hard seats and slept for a few hours. Wei closed his eyes and had dreamed of Liang. In the dream, she was angry at him but he didn't know why. He woke feeling uncomfortable, knowing that they were on the verge of an argument. Their arguments never lasted long—angry words, disappointed sighs, followed by a silence that usually ended a few hours later. Thinking back, most of their disagreements originated with something he had refused to do. Only once in their long marriage did her anger remain palpable for days.

It was just before the Communist Party came into power, and he had purposely lied to Liang when she asked him to go to a political rally with her. He had told her that a new shipment of antiquities had come to the university and he needed to receive and catalogue them. In truth, he didn't want her to go; she of all people knew he had no interest in political matters. As long as his research continued, he was a happy man. He also feared the Party had eyes everywhere and he and Liang would later be considered agitators. He'd hoped Liang wouldn't go without him and she hadn't. She'd been quiet the next morning at breakfast. When he asked her if everything was all right, she had replied in a controlled voice, "I just wanted you to give me one evening of your precious time for something I believed in. I've given you a lifetime."

Tian's story had brought it all back. Why hadn't he told her that he was afraid for them? As with everything else in his life, it was too late.

Outside the window the sky had begun to lighten to a deep gray and he heard the soft murmurs of the two women in front. Wei stood up and stretched his stiff back. He was hungry. Most of all, he had to relieve himself, but he was uncertain where the toilet was in the still dark car. Wei walked slowly, unsteadily to the back of the car looking for the toilet. Unable to find one, he stepped outside to the narrow walkway between the attached cars, then braced himself against the iron bars, relieving himself quickly onto the tracks below. Afterward, Wei stood watching the shadows of the sleeping countryside emerge, breathing in the frigid air until he was fully awake and numb from the cold.

Back inside the car, the air felt warm and stale. Wei had lost track of time. He'd been riding the train for almost a full day, but it felt as if he'd left Guangzhou a week ago. He checked his satchel to make sure the rest of his money was still there. He wondered if Kai Ying and Tao were still so angry at him. Could time and distance offer some forgiveness? Now that he was farther away from them and closer to Sheng, there were other matters to begin thinking about. Wei stretched again before he sat down. Then he turned toward the window and waited for the day to come.

When the train pulled into Linxiang, Tian was sitting up and staring ahead. What must he be thinking? Wei thought. What kind of peace did this long trip back to Luoyang give him after eight years?

But when he turned toward Wei, Tian clearly had something else on his mind. "What shall we eat? I'm starving."

Even so early in the morning, the vendors were set up and waiting for the train to arrive. They bought *jook,* fried donuts, and green onion pancakes, and washed it all down with cups of hot tea until it was announced their train was about to leave. Only then did they reluctantly board again.

Tao

TAO SAT IN HIS CLASSROOM STARING AT THE BLACK-board while his grandfather was on a train going to a place called Luoyang. He'd been gone for two days now. Tao worried that his *ye ye* was not paying enough attention, that he was closing his eyes and drifting off into his own world. What if something happened to him during one of those times? He once told Tao that when he closed his eyes, his grandmother came to him. "Does she talk to you?" he asked. "All the time," his grandfather said. *Don't close your eyes, don't close your eyes,* Tao repeated silently to himself. His *ye ye* was an old man who was a long way from home, and he needed to keep his eyes open at all times.

Tao had a hard time returning to the everyday rhythm of school. It was what his mother wanted more than anything, so he didn't tell her that everything had changed. He was easily distracted now and hardly listened to Teacher Eng's droning voice. It was as if there were a barrier between him and the rest of his classmates. Tao no longer cared what Lai Hing said about him, which made Lai Hing eventually look for someone else to bully. He also tried to ignore his persistent limp, and his classmates' taunts of "Old Man Lee, Old Man Lee," whenever he trailed behind them during physical education, or when his leg cramped up from sitting too long at his desk. He learned to block their voices out, move at his own speed. Still, Tao exercised every day hoping to keep up, to be rid of his limp by the time his father and grandfather came home. As he walked to school and back, he could feel his leg growing stronger, and it was only at the end of the day when he was tired that he felt the dull ache in his bone return, his leg dragging just a bit behind.

Without much effort, Tao had caught up with his classwork and moved quickly back up to the third seat, sitting right behind Little Shan and inadvertently gaining the upper hand. Little Shan was so uncomfortable, he was constantly turning around to see what Tao was doing and getting into trouble with Teacher Eng. Watching Little Shan squirm was the one thing he did enjoy at school now, tugging at the back of his shirt or sticking notes on his back that said *Excuse my farting* or *I'm behind in everything*. It was the perfect seat for him to stay in for as long as possible. Tao was good at tormenting Little Shan, a talent he hadn't realized he had. These were all things he couldn't divulge to his mother, who would only tell him to behave himself, so he stored up all his stories about Little Shan for when his *ba ba* and *ye ye* returned.

Suyin

S UYIN PUT THE BABY DOWN IN THE BASSINET FOR her afternoon nap. She watched her squirm, turning from one side to the other before settling down to sleep. Each day with her daughter made it more difficult to give her up. It frightened Suyin to think what might have happened to them if it weren't for Kai Ying. Her recovery was all due to her strong teas and soups after the baby's birth, while she had so foolishly returned her kindness by stealing from them. Their life in the Dongshan villa with Kai Ying and her family had grown even more tenuous now, and there was no one to blame but herself.

Suyin's small stash of food hidden under the bed felt like a thorn in her side. Since the night Kai Ying had caught her stealing, they'd been uncomfortable with each other, speaking, but not speaking. She would have expected it with the old professor, but not with Kai Ying, never with Kai Ying.

Out of nervous habit, Suyin touched her cheek, feeling the scattered rough patches and scabs of her pimples that were finally disappearing. A few weeks before, Kai Ying had given her a small jar of cream to use every night before she went to bed. "You don't need a lot," she said. "Like this." Kai Ying spread a thin layer of the cream across her pimples, her fingertips gently patting Suyin's cheek like quick kisses. She had suddenly felt like crying.

"Did you make it?" Suyin asked.

Kai Ying nodded.

"What is it?"

"I'll show you another time," Kai Ying said, and smiled.

More than anything, Kai Ying's skills as an herbalist fascinated Suyin. The simple act of brewing teas and soups with the right combination of herbs gave Kai Ying the power to restore health and prevent illnesses. Suyin now realized how the natural world, which she'd taken for granted, could be used to heal. Kai Ying had already taught her there were possibilities in everything around her, and Suyin loved watching her create magic from her assortment of dried herbs and leaves and roots in jars lining the shelves, wondering if she could one day learn to be as good an herbalist.

By the end of her first week using the cream, the angry red pimples had magically begun to dry up. Suyin sat down in front of the tarnished mirror. For the first time in months, she dared to look at her reflection, seeing hints of the healthy young girl she once was. She touched her cheek again, marveling at another small miracle.

Suyin needed to find a way to make things right again.

Wei

A S THE TRAIN CONTINUED ONWARD, WEI GAZED out the window until they left the outskirts of yet another small town before he again leaned across the aisle.

"Did you ever find Ai-li?" he asked.

Tian turned to him and began talking, as if there hadn't been any pause since he'd last spoken of her. "I caught the first train out of Guangzhou on that Saturday," he said, his voice quiet and serious, "and arrived back to Luoyang on Monday, but Ai-li was no longer at her boardinghouse, and no one from her office had seen her after she packed up her belongings and left there on Friday. I walked all over the city looking for her, finally deciding to report her missing at the public security bureau. Then I rented her old room and waited for two days, foolishly hoping she might return there, although it had been completely emptied of her existence. Her landlady told me that she'd given everything away. I thought I would go insane."

"There was no one who knew where she was?" Wei asked.

Tian yawned and shook his head. "I finally remembered the address of where she attended Party meetings, but her comrades were well prepared and wouldn't tell me anything. My gut feeling was they not only knew where she was, but had most likely aided in her disappearance. On my way out, one skinny, hawk-nosed comrade remarked, 'I guess you just weren't man enough for our Comrade Ai-li!' I went crazy and hit the bastard until I was dragged away, battered and bruised and thrown out on the street."

"You never saw her again?"

Tian shook his head. "By the end of the week, even her landlady begged me to leave because I was frightening her tenants. I stayed in Luoyang for two weeks, and couldn't find a trace of her or where she'd gone. The police found no evidence of any wrongdoing, concluding that she must have simply moved away of her own volition, telling me it was best if I returned to Guangzhou and moved on with my life too. I was nothing but a spurned lover to them."

"You returned to Guangzhou?"

"There was nothing left for me to do. I didn't know if I still had a job to go back to in Guangzhou, but it was the only thing left that felt real. Everything else I believed in had been destroyed. Sometimes, I wish we had married and that we fought bitterly and grew to hate each other. At least then, I would be free of her ghost."

Tian's words hung in the air and shivered between them. He put a cigarette to his lips and lit it, inhaling, smoke emerging from his nose and mouth and rising upward.

"I was angry for many years," Tian said. "I finally decided to return to Luoyang again this year, although I can't tell you why. Perhaps because she still remains an integral part of the city for me and I need to say good-bye properly," he said, turning toward Wei. "You must think of me as an extremely foolish man."

"No," Wei said, "not at all." How could he ever explain his own demons? "Have you ever married?" Wei asked.

Tian shook his head. "I've been with several women, good

women, but I never met anyone who could make me forget Ai-li."

"It's not too late."

Tian looked at him and smiled. He appeared tired and spent. "Perhaps one day," he said.

"I married late in life," he said, as if giving testament that life did provide surprises.

"And now your son is in Luoyang?" Tian asked.

"Yes," Wei said.

He watched Tian and realized he might be one of the few people who would understand how he, too, had been led to this faraway city in search of a ghost.

"Would you mind," Wei asked, clearing his throat, "listening to a story of mine now?"

Tao

WITH HIS GRANDFATHER GONE, THE HOUSE FELT emptiest at bedtime. Tao scrambled into bed and pulled up his covers, listening for his mother. She was the one who would tuck him in now, the one who would calm his fears and read him stories at night.

His *ma ma* usually read to him from books, while his grandfather often told him stories from memory, or made them up right there in front of him. *History is a series of stories pieced together,* he once told Tao. *And art is a living record of it.* His grandfather's voice rose in a happy rhythm as he spoke on and on, and it was the first time Tao realized how much his *ye ye* must have missed being at Lingnan teaching, and how lucky he was to be his only student now.

For as long as Tao could remember, all his favorite stories, *The Monkey King* or *The Romance of the Three Kingdoms,* were read to him by his father or his grandfather before bed. His *ye ye* would also read to him other world classics like *The Arabian Nights* and *The Three Musketeers,* which he said Chairman Mao wouldn't approve of, so they kept the books their secret. One by one, the books lovingly appeared in his grandfather's hands each night, only to disappear again once he had finished reading them to Tao. A nagging thought suddenly worried him; what if he never found out where his grandfather had hidden all his books?

Tao wanted his *ba ba* back, but not if it meant his *ye ye* had to leave. He just wanted everything to return to the way it was. Before his grandfather left, Tao wanted to apologize to him for what he'd said. He never realized how the word *hate* could fill an entire room, swallow up all the air. But every time he had tried to approach his grandfather, his tongue twisted and his lips sealed and the words wouldn't emerge. A rush of conflicting emotions moved through Tao that he wasn't able to control, and even if he did want to say something, it felt like his *ye ye* was too close and too far away from him at the same time. And now he was afraid it was too late.

* * *

Tao was still adjusting to all the changes. His mother didn't read to him with the deep professor voice of his grandfather or the funny voices his father used to make him laugh, but he liked her calm, cool mother voice. It was soothing. Tao imagined it was the same voice his mother's patients heard to put them at ease and to quiet their worries.

He turned in his bed to face his mother as she chose a book and opened it. Tao didn't really know what to believe anymore. For as long as he could remember, his *ma ma* had always been the one to teach him about what was right and wrong, how to behave and be well-mannered, or how to fold his clothes and make his bed neatly. She also told him the names of herbs and flowers and leaves that would stop his cough or settle his upset stomach. Even when he was a very little boy, she reminded him it was important that he always be able to take care of himself. Tao had wondered why, when she and *ba ba* and *ye ye* were there to take care of him. "Because there will be a time when we aren't,' she said, putting her warm palm on his cool cheek. "Not now," she added, "but a very, very long time from now."

Before his mother began reading to him, Tao wanted to tell her that he wasn't ready to take care of himself yet. Instead, he pressed his lips together and held the words in. He didn't want to upset her, but he wished he could say them aloud—*I'm still a little boy and it hasn't been a very long time like you promised, so why are both* ba ba *and* ye ye *gone?*

Kai Ying

WEI HAD BEEN GONE FOR THREE DAYS AND THEY still hadn't had any word from him. Kai Ying could feel Auntie Song's anxiety by the number of times she visited each day, checking to see if she'd had any word from him. "Tomorrow, I'm sure," Auntie Song said when she left that evening, an edge of disappointment in her voice.

Kai Ying pulled out a pair of Tao's pajamas from his bureau. She had allowed Tao to stay up later than usual with Auntie Song and Suyin, and now she was exhausted and hoped he would get to sleep quickly.

"Tell me a story?" Tao asked.

"Which book would you like me to read to you?" She went over to his bookshelf.

"Not any of those," he said. "Tell me a story about your life?"

Kai Ying paused a moment in thought. Reading to Tao was one thing, but she was tired and storytelling had always been left to Wei and Sheng. She was much more comfortable curing a headache or upset stomach. Kai Ying thought back to her childhood and asked, "Did you know that Zhaoqing, the city where I grew up, means the beginning of auspiciousness and happiness? It's called the City of Happiness."

Tao shook his head. "Were you happy there?" he asked.

She pulled off his T-shirt and slipped his pajama top over his head. "Yes, I was. It was a wonderful place to grow up. Remember I told you the city of Zhaoqing surrounds Star Lake, which is actually divided into five smaller lakes with seven mountain peaks surrounding them. It's beautiful there. Auntie Lan and I grew up riding boats and going swimming in the lakes."

Tao had met his mother's younger sister only a few times, when he was too young to remember much about her.

"And then you came to Guangzhou and married *ba ba*."

She nodded. "And now I'm happy here with you."

"And *ba ba*."

"And *ba ba*," she repeated.

"And *ye ye*?"

She hesitated for moment. "Yes, of course, *ye ye*, too," she answered.

"Because he'll be back soon," Tao added, his voice rising. He turned to her and asked, "Was it my fault *ye ye* went away?"

"Of course not," she said. "Why would you think that?"

"I said something mean to him."

Kai Ying helped him into his pajama bottoms. His eyes watched her intently, an anxious look on his face.

"Your *ye ye* loves you more than anything else in this world. You could say a thousand mean things to him and it wouldn't change the way he feels about you."

Tao hugged her and his body slowly relaxed. "You know, we always planned to take you back to Zhaoqing for another visit," she said, changing the subject.

"Tell me a story about Zhaoqing?"

Kai Ying settled him into bed and pulled up his covers.

"Let me see," she said. "When I was about your age and Auntie Lan was not more than five, my father always told us one story in particular, called 'The Bright Pearl,' before we went to sleep. It was our favorite fable because our *ba ba*, your other grandfather, told us it was exactly how all the lakes and mountains of Zhaoqing had come to exist a long time ago."

"Tell me that one," Tao said.

Kai Ying hesitated and then sat down on the bed beside him. "All right," she said. "But only because it's a very short story.

"There was once a magical white pearl that fell from the heavens to the ground and turned into a beautiful lake. It wasn't just any magical white pearl; she was coveted by the white jade dragon and the golden phoenix, both of whom couldn't bear to leave the pearl when she turned herself into a lake. So instead, they turned themselves into the mountains that surrounded the lake so they could always stay by her side. And that's what your Auntie Lan and I thought every time we looked at Star Lake, that it was the magical white pearl and the surrounding mountains were once the white jade dragon and the golden phoenix."

Kai Ying stopped abruptly and realized she hadn't told it very well. "It was too short, wasn't it? I'm afraid I'm not the storyteller your *ba ba* and *ye ye* are," she said, her eyes watering and her throat closing. She looked away so Tao wouldn't notice her tears.

"I like the story," he quickly said, reaching out for her hand.

Of course he would notice, she thought. And then Tao repeated to her what she had just told him in his own words, embellishing it in places that instantly added life to the same story. And for the first time, Kai Ying realized that he already had the same gift of storytelling handed down from Wei to Sheng, and now to Tao. She couldn't help but think how proud they both would be of him.

"Are the mountains in Zhaoqing as big as Cloud Mountain?" he asked.

Kai Ying shook her head. "They're much smaller, but they're still very beautiful. They rise above the lake as if they're floating just above the water. I can't wait until you see them."

She could feel her spirits rising as she talked about Zhaoqing. It must be the city of happiness, if it could make her feel better during such a difficult time.

"Can we go there when *ba ba* returns?" Tao asked, leaning closer to her.

She smiled and hugged him again. "Yes, when *ba ba* comes home," she said.

"And *ye ye,* too?" he repeated.

"Yes, and *ye ye*," she said. "And Auntie Song and Suyin and the baby, too, if they'd like to join us," she added.

She saw the smile grow on Tao's face, something she'd hadn't seen in a very long time. Hopefully she'd also improve at storytelling, just until Wei and Sheng returned.

Waiting

November 1958

Tao

EVERY MORNING IT STILL SURPRISED TAO TO SEE that their lives had continued on as usual. The void left by his father's and his grandfather's absences seemed to fill up each day with his mother's patients, the kitchen overflowing with their voices and the steamy medicinal smells. School still dragged on, and Auntie Song continued to work in her garden while Suyin and her baby had slipped into their household. Now that the girl was well, she helped his mother clean and run errands, and his *ma ma* seemed happier having a baby in the house. Tao still wasn't quite sure how he felt about Suyin, not that it mattered what he thought.

Tao's world had suddenly shifted to a house full of women and a different kind of family, one that he was still getting used to. Only when he saw the kapok tree looming tall and silent in the courtyard could he feel his *ba ba* and *ye ye* still close by.

Kai Ying

K AI YING HADN'T EXPECTED TO SEE SUYIN SITTING at the kitchen table waiting for her so early in the morning. Ever since she had caught her rooting around the kitchen a few nights ago, she'd taken a step back, disappointed in being taken advantage of, realizing that *Lo Yeh* had been right. They didn't know a thing about the girl.

"Is everything all right?" Kai Ying asked. She heard the slight edge of strain in her voice that she couldn't seem to hide.

Suyin nodded. "I just need to talk to you," she said.

"What is it?" Kai Ying didn't sit down at the table, instead busying herself by putting on water to boil for tea, taking down the herbs she would need.

Suyin paused a moment before she sat up straight. "I know it was wrong to have taken the food. It's just that I didn't know when you might want me to leave. I was afraid of being so hungry again, especially with the baby. I just needed a little to get by until I figured out what to do. I'm sorry," she said.

Suyin lifted a cloth bag onto the table. From it she pulled out biscuits, some peanuts, dried plums and apricots, putting each in a separate pile on the table just like Kai Ying did with her herbs. "That's all of it," she said. "I promise it won't happen again."

Kai Ying nodded.

It was a step in the right direction, she thought. She hadn't realized Suyin's constant fear of being on her own again, and could only imagine how harrowing her life had been on the streets. Kai Ying walked over and took the empty cloth bag from the girl. Then she went through the cabinets, putting in the rest of the biscuits and other dried foods until she'd nearly filled the bag.

"Keep this," she said, softening her tone, "so there's no need to worry." She handed the bag back to Suyin, who appeared surprised.

Then Kai Ying opened the door to the courtyard and stepped out into the morning, the fresh air a relief as she went to unlock the front gate and let in her first patient.

Wei

THE TRAIN HAD ARRIVED IN LUOYANG JUST AFTER dawn. The two older women sitting toward the front of the car, whom he had first noticed boarding back in Guangzhou, had gone the entire distance with them and were now disembarking. Wei felt strangely bereft, as if some intimate journey they had all taken together was coming to an end.

Wei carried his satchel and stepped down from the train. His legs were weak and he felt suddenly adrift for the very first time since he'd left Guangzhou over two days ago. The sun was shining and the sky was clear, although it felt terribly cold. It was a dry, mountainous terrain that was so different from Guangzhou. A sharp, icy wind blew, and for a moment Wei thought of putting on the woolen sweater he'd brought along for Sheng, but he pulled his padded jacket closer and decided to keep the sweater fresh for his son.

Tian followed closely behind him. Wei waited on the platform and watched the younger man pause at the bottom of the train steps, his eyes looking first left and then right, scanning the platform. Wei saw a look of unguarded vulnerability that flashed across Tian's face. Was this the moment of hope and resolution he had come all the way to Luoyang for? Did he really believe Ai-li might be there waiting for him? Wei's heart suddenly raced with the possibility. After so many years, what a joyful reunion it would be for him. Nothing was impossible. But as the train platform emptied, the moment faded with Ai-li nowhere in sight.

"Come this way," Tian said, quickly recovering. He stepped away from the train and took hold of Wei's arm, leading him through the station building and out onto the street. "Let's get something to eat, and then we can decide what you should do next."

Luoyang wasn't what Wei had expected. He'd anticipated darkness and desolation, but instead found a bustling city just like any other, filled with people and bicyclists moving through their lives as a new day was beginning. There was something so familiar in seeing a mother walking her child down the street to school. He thought again of Tao as he watched them round the corner, disappearing out of sight. Wei felt homesick and wondered how Kai Ying and Tao were faring. All these years they had provided a lifeline for him, and now, he hoped to give them something back. He drew courage in knowing he'd be seeing Sheng soon and bringing news of him home to them.

Not far from the train station, they sat in a small noodle and dumplings shop. Wei was relieved to be sitting down in a warm room without the constant rattle of a moving train car rumbling through his body. The room buzzed with the distinctive Luoyang dialect, which sounded similar to a more complicated singsong version of Mandarin. Tian didn't seem to have any trouble communicating with the tall, broad-faced waitress. After they ordered, Wei closed his eyes for a moment. He was exhausted and felt his head spinning with all the change.

"Are you feeling all right?" Tian asked.

Wei opened his eyes. "Yes, yes, I'm fine."

"It's a different world here."

"Yes, I'm just finding my footing," he said. "You're very good with the dialect."

Tian laughed. "I just try to imagine myself as an actor in a Peking Opera," he said. "It's the same, more archaic form of Mandarin used in operas."

Wei listened to the voices and recognized the similarities. "I hear it," he said.

Their waitress returned with a tray carrying their soup and noodles.

"I was determined to learn the dialect when I was living

here," Tian continued. "Ai-li spoke Cantonese, but I still felt it was important to learn."

"I imagine it would be even more difficult living in a place without the language," Wei said.

Tian nodded and continued eating his noodles and dumplings. "I've been thinking," he said, looking up. "It might make the most sense to visit the public security bureau here first, to see if they can locate your son, and if you can arrange a visit through them."

Wei didn't know what he would do without Tian's help. Even with all his education and know-how, he felt like a child dropped in a strange place and asked to blindly find his way.

"Yes," Wei said gratefully. "That sounds like a very good plan. Thank you, Tian."

Tian had made no judgments on the train when Wei finished telling him his story about Sheng. "You must think very little of me," Wei said when he finished. The lights had dimmed and he could barely see Tian's face, though he saw the glow of his cigarette and the outline of his shadow as he leaned across the aisle. "I imagine if I were your son," Tian said, "I would have done the same thing."

"Would it be possible to send a telegram home?" he asked Tian. "My daughter-in-law will be worried."

"Of course," Tian said. "We'll stop by the telegraph office before the public security bureau."

As expected, it was a long wait at the public security bureau. When Wei finally sat down in front of a uniformed clerk, he was told to fill out a form and return the next day. The clerk, Hu, spoke a bit of Cantonese and said he would need time to look up the inmate's file before he could give Wei any more information.

"Do you know if I'll be able to see my son soon?" Wei asked.

The thin, middle-aged man barely looked at him as he continued to shuffle through files. "I have no idea where your son is," he answered. "It might be a few days, a few weeks, or even months."

"Months!" Wei said, his anger rising. "I don't have months!"

"Then I suggest you go home and let me do my job," the man said.

"Who do you think you are?" Wei asked. He stood and looked down at the man.

Clerk Hu finally stopped what he was doing and glanced up at him. "I'm the man who's telling you to go home and come back tomorrow. There's nothing else I can tell you right now."

Tian stepped up and took hold of his arm. "Thank you, comrade, we'll be back tomorrow. We appreciate all you can do to find Mr. Lee's son."

It was cold and dark by the time they arrived back at the same boardinghouse Tian had stayed in years before, the room damp and musty smelling. Wei could barely see, he was so exhausted, his body just needing to rest. In the morning, everything would be clear again. It was just tiredness, he told himself. Not despair, not failure. Wei tried not to think beyond the step right in front of him or else he would surely stumble. He hadn't been in Luoyang for one full day, although it felt as if he'd been there for a week. Tian took hold of Wei's arm and led him to a small, narrow cot where he fell into a deep and dreamless sleep.

Tao

TAO WAS TIRED OF WAITING. AFTER THREE DAYS, they still hadn't heard from his grandfather. When he finished his schoolwork that afternoon Tao went outside to the courtyard and sat on the stone bench where his *ye ye* always sat, but even then he felt restless. The kapok tree stood silently watching. Without saying a word, Tao stood up and limped quickly out of the courtyard and down the street, as he imagined his grandfather had done on one of his long morning walks. The more he walked, the less apparent his limp felt. Tao was like any other boy walking to the store, only he'd already broken two rules: earlier, he'd snuck into his mother's room and taken two coins lying atop her bureau. There were other coins, so she wouldn't even miss them, he'd thought. And now, he'd left the house alone and without permission. There was no turning back.

Tao decided against going to Mr. Lam's store; he'd already brought him home once, just after his *ba ba* was taken away. It wasn't going to happen again. Instead, Tao decided to go to the store on the other side of the park. It was farther but no one would know him there, and if he hurried, his mother might not even realize he was gone.

His *ba ba* once told him about the little boy who went into the park alone and never came back out again. "What happened to him?" Tao had asked. His father had meant it as a lesson for him never to wander away. "He was never found," his father said, "so you mustn't go anywhere without telling us." Tao was young then and never thought to go anywhere alone. Things were different now, he thought, he was older, and the only man left in the house. Besides, they were the ones who had left him alone.

Tao came to the park entrance and paused. What if the boy was still in there, circling and circling, never able to find his way out again? *Stay on the path*, Tao told himself. *Just stay on the path and you'll come out on the other side of the park*, he repeated. He picked up his pace and entered.

The sky had cleared by late afternoon, a burst of sun emerged that brought out crowds of people strolling in the park; soldiers in their green uniforms and old people sitting on benches, young women and men and children, stray dogs sniffing through garbage. There was a whole world of people right there in front of him; Tao had nothing to be afraid of. Already his mind was spinning as to what he would buy at the store, rice paper candy or dragon's beard candy, made of sugar and peanuts. He kept walking until the open space soon gave way to a more wooded area, where there were fewer people and the tall trees cast shadows so that the air suddenly felt much cooler. *Just stay on the path,* he reminded himself. Tao realized he'd left the house so quickly, he hadn't taken a jacket. He began to walk faster, hoping for warmth, but his leg was beginning to feel tired, and when he came to a fork in the path veering off to the left and to the right, Tao thought of the little boy who went into the park alone and was never seen again. When he turned around, there was a young soldier standing a few feet away from him.

"What are you doing here all by yourself?" the soldier asked. He wore a long heavy military coat that appeared too big for him.

"I'm going to the store," Tao quickly answered. "For my mother," he added.

"And what are you buying at the store?"

Tao put his hand into his pocket and gripped the two coins, wondering if the soldier wanted to rob him. He looked around to see that they were alone on the path, and his heart began to pound in his chest. Maybe this was the man who had taken the boy who never came out of the park. Tao looked closer to see that the man wasn't a soldier at all, his hair was too long and greasy and he wore sandals, not boots. He took a step back.

The man watched Tao and smiled, slipping his hand inside his coat.

"I have to go," Tao said.

"Don't you want to see what I have here?" the man asked.

He flipped open his coat just as Tao turned to run, his leg dragging just a bit behind. *Follow the path, follow the path,* he repeated to himself. From the corner of his eye, he saw the man holding what he'd once heard Auntie Song call his *turkey neck* in the palm of his hand.

Song

WHEN SHE HEARD A KNOCK ON THE DOOR, SONG looked up surprised to see Suyin standing in her opened doorway. The girl had ventured back to her garden and rooms only once or twice, either to bring her a message from Kai Ying or to gather some needed vegetables for their dinner. Now her shadow wavered unexpectedly in the threshold.

"Come in, come in," Song said.

Suyin stepped into the room and out of the bright afternoon sunlight. She appeared like a different girl from the one Song had first spoken to in Great-Auntie Shu's room. She no longer reminded Song of an underfed dog, shivering in the streets. But it wasn't just a physical change Song could see; there was an energy and vigor emanating from her again. Song could see it in her eyes.

"Auntie Song, have you seen Tao?" Suyin asked.

"What is it? Is everything all right?" she asked, pushing her bowl of pea sprouts to the side.

After all the turbulence of the past year, Song's first thoughts had naturally bordered on dread. *Not again*, she thought. *Not again*.

"Kai Ying can't find him. She thought he might be back in the garden with you."

"No, no, he was with me yesterday," Song said, "not this afternoon. Did you look upstairs?"

Suyin nodded.

"He can't have gone far," she said.

Voices came to them from the courtyard, and Song smiled. "That must be him now," she said.

They looked at each other and without saying another word, hurried in the direction of the voices.

The courtyard gate had just closed and Kai Ying stood alone in the courtyard holding a piece of paper in her hands.

"What is it?" Song asked.

Kai Ying looked over at her. "It's finally a telegram from Wei," she said, relieved.

"At last!" Song exclaimed.

She suddenly felt her blood flowing again, the warmth spreading through her body. *He made it,* she thought to herself. The old fool had actually made it all the way to Luoyang.

Kai Ying held a thin, yellow piece of paper out to her that read:

ARRIVED SAFELY IN LUOYANG. WEI

They all looked again when the courtyard gate opened and Tao hurried in, sweating and dragging his leg. He looked on the verge of tears.

"What happened? Where have you been?" Kai Ying asked.

Tao kept silent.

"Are you all right?" Song asked.

He nodded and limped over to his mother. He pulled two coins from his pocket and put them in her hand before going into the house.

Tao

WHILE IT WAS AUNTIE SONG WHO WALKED TAO TO school every morning, it was Suyin who stood by the front gate waiting for him every afternoon. Ever since Tao had gone to the park alone, he'd had to go directly home after school to do his homework. Tao hadn't told anyone what had happened, and he didn't care if he never stepped foot into that park again. He was secretly happy Suyin was waiting for him after school. She wasn't so sickly-looking anymore and her skin had cleared. Walking next to her, he realized she was almost as tall as his mother and thin all over. Tao couldn't imagine how a baby could have come from her. She usually wore a dark cotton tunic and pants and he recognized one of his mother's sweaters that she was wearing.

Tao liked walking home with Suyin; it made him feel older. He liked the way she nodded at him without saying a word, without making a fuss the way Auntie Song did trying to help him with his books or forcing him to put on his jacket as the days grew cooler. Suyin kept things simple and to the point. If he didn't feel like talking to her, she never pushed.

"Ready to go?" she said.

Tao nodded that he was.

"I need to make a quick stop for your mother," she said. "It'll only take a few minutes."

"Sure," he said, following her as she turned down the street and away from home.

As the days went by, he also liked the way Suyin reached across and helped him with his book bag without saying a word, and how she purposely walked slower so he could keep up with her, but never in a way that seemed deliberate. Once in a while, she asked him a question about school and what he had learned that day, but she never asked about his father or his grandfather and he never asked about her family.

As they weaved in and out of the pushing crowds, she leaned over and took hold of his sleeve so he wouldn't be pulled away from her. She'd never know how grateful Tao was as he hurried to keep up.

"How's your leg feeling?" she asked.

"Better."

Suyin leaned closer and asked, "Where did you go the other day when we were looking for you?"

The question was so unexpected he paused for a moment before he said, "I went for a walk."

"It looked more like you were running away from someone, or something," she said.

Tao stayed silent. His mother had been angry at him for taking the coins and leaving the house without telling her, but she assumed he was on his way to the store before he simply changed his mind and returned home. Tao wasn't sure if he should tell Suyin about the man in the park, but when he finally decided he would, he realized she had let go of his sleeve and was no longer walking beside him. He turned around to see that she had paused at the corner and was staring at something down the street.

"Is everything all right?" Tao asked.

Suyin didn't answer.

"What is it?" he asked. "What are you looking at?"

Tao followed her gaze and didn't see anything particularly special. It was a street teeming with people going about their business, just like every other street in downtown Guangzhou. He watched all the people moving back and forth, a grandmother walking with her grandchild, two boys a bit older than he was standing in front of a storefront, a woman and man in a heated conversation, nothing out of the ordinary.

When Suyin finally did respond, she looked serious and sounded very far away. "You see those two boys?" she said. "They're my brothers."

Later that afternoon, Tao paused at the opened door of Suyin's room. He never thought she'd have family of her own so close by. Why hadn't she said anything about them? As much as he wanted to ask her, he knew not to, not yet. She was standing by the window with the baby in her arms and he suddenly felt sorry for her having to be all alone.

Suyin turned unexpectedly and caught him watching them. "Do you want to come in?" she asked.

Tao's face flushed warm. He was all ready to say no, but his left foot led and he stepped in.

"How's your baby?" he asked, trying to sound more grown-up.

She laughed. "Growing. She's getting bigger every day, and her rash seems to be disappearing. See?" She held the baby out toward him.

Tao took another step into the room. With the drapes drawn, a harsh sunlight illuminated everything. It was the first time he'd seen the room in the clear light of day, the water stains like dark puddles across the ceiling, the peeling paint that curled along the edges of the wall, the faded armchair that sat in the corner of Great-Auntie Shu's old room.

Standing in the middle of it all was Suyin and her daughter. The baby was so small, he thought, with a full head of black hair sticking up. She opened her eyes wide and raised her tiny fist up, reaching out toward him.

"I think she likes you," Suyin said.

Tao touched her hand with his finger and smiled. "What are you going to name her?" he asked.

"I don't know. I'm not sure . . ."

"*Ma ma* says you're supposed to wait a month," he said, remembering what he'd heard.

"I'm afraid I've missed that deadline already," she said. "She's almost seven weeks."

"You'd better start thinking," Tao said.

Suyin looked down at the baby and then back at him. "Maybe you can help me find the right name for her."

Tao thought for a moment. There once was a stray cat that wandered into their courtyard that he'd named Mao, not for the Premier, but because it had the same sound as the word *cat* in Chinese. Mao came every day for months until he began to think of the cat as his. And then one day, Mao stopped coming and he never saw him again. Tao had cried when the cat hadn't appeared by the third day, but his grandfather sat him on his lap and told him Mao was a very busy cat and had other children to visit. Some cats strayed from one place to another, never forming attachments, he said, so the fact that Mao stayed for so long visiting him was already something very special.

Now Tao wondered if Suyin and her baby would suddenly just disappear too.

"I'll think about it," he answered, slowly backing out of the room.

Wei

WEI AWOKE JUST AFTER DAWN. FOR A MOMENT HE couldn't remember where he was until he heard Tian snoring softly in the cot across from his. He was in Luoyang waiting to see Sheng. His back ached and when he stretched out lengthwise, his feet hung off the end of the small cot, which must have been someone's childhood bed, a child Tao's age. Just the thought of his grandson made his eyes tear up in the dismal room.

When Wei was a boy, it was a different world, one that was now condemned by Mao and the Party as extravagant and wasteful. But he also remembered the beauty and intellectual curiosity of a country that could have easily caught up with the rest of the world, if she weren't always being dragged backward. And now he didn't know if Tao would ever experience any of China's glories, other than in the stories from the books he read to him. In the China his grandson was growing up in, just surviving each day left very little time for much else.

Wei pulled the thin blanket closer against the cold, thankful he was still fully dressed, or else he might have frozen to death during the night. Wei looked around the cell-sized room, the two small cots, a wooden chair and table, a small coal stove in the corner. From one side of the ceiling, a long zigzagging crack ran across it and all the way down one wall. He had hoped things might appear better in the daylight. Instead, it looked sadder and dingier as light filled the room and everything came into focus. Wei's heart sank at the thought of returning to the police bureau for another long day of waiting for any information about Sheng.

When Tian coughed, Wei knew he was awake.

Wei watched Tian drop a few pieces of coal into the little corner stove to heat some water for tea. When it was ready, he made the tea and pulled one of the cots closer to the wooden table where Wei sat in the only wooden chair, rubbing his back.

"Did you sleep well?" Tian asked.

Wei nodded. "For the most part," he said, his hands cupped around the hot tea. It was the most warmth he'd felt in days. On the table was their breakfast: the package of dried plums and tin of biscuits he had bought back in Guangzhou. "It's much colder here in Luoyang," he added.

"I'll ask Mrs. Lai for a couple of extra blankets tonight," Tian said. "I forget how this dry cold settles into your bones here."

"I don't know how to thank you," Wei said. "I don't know what I thought. It's obvious I came without planning everything thoroughly. I wouldn't have known what to do if it wasn't for you."

Tian smiled. "I knew there was a reason to return to Luoyang now. It's good to know that something will come out of this trip."

Wei had spent his life holding on to the past, trying to preserve the old and failing to live in the present. And now he would give whatever was left of his life just to know that Sheng was all right.

"It's time we both moved forward," Wei said.

Tian smiled and sipped his tea.

Wei felt better after he'd eaten. He prepared himself for the long day ahead while Tian stood up and cleared the table. Wei watched him move easily through the tiny room and didn't dare ask when he would be returning to Guangzhou. At the moment, he was just grateful that Tian had enough enthusiasm to carry them both through the day.

Tao

T AO HEARD SOMEONE ON THE STAIRS AND LOOKED up to see Suyin standing in his doorway carrying her baby. "What do you think about the name Meizhen?" she asked. "Your *ma ma* calls her that when she doesn't think I can hear," she said, and laughed. "Now I find myself calling her Meizhen, or Mei Mei, too."

"It's all right," he said. He felt good having her confide in him. "I like it."

"Me, too," Suyin said. "Good night then." She nodded again and was gone.

Suyin

S UYIN WALKED QUICKLY DOWN THE STREET. ONCE OR twice a week she ran errands in the morning for Kai Ying while Auntie Song watched Mei Mei. Dongshan appeared different now that she was actually living there, the villas behind the tall walls no longer a mystery. They were filled with families and problems just like in Old Guangzhou. But instead of the multitude of voices all screaming at once from the crowded apartments, there was a quiet seething just below the surface in Dongshan. Upon closer scrutiny, she saw the cracks in the stone walls, the big houses crumbling slowly behind them in need of repair or paint or new tiles. All Suyin's illusions of grandeur had suddenly disappeared. She would never be the same wide-eyed schoolgirl walking down the street for the very first time, and the thought brought both a sigh of relief and a moment of sorrow.

It was a mild morning. Most of the trees that lined the boulevard were now stripped bare of leaves. The last time Suyin had stumbled down the street in the rain was almost two months ago, the baby pushing her way out into the world. The pain had been unbearable. Suyin didn't know what she would have done if she hadn't made it to Kai Ying's house.

The vendors were just setting up when Suyin arrived at the marketplace. Kai Ying had asked her to buy a lean piece of pork before they sold out. Pork was the main ingredient for most of her soups, providing taste with little fat. If there wasn't any pork, she was to bring back a chicken.

Suyin wondered if any of the vendors recognized her as the pregnant beggar girl scrounging for their throwaway fruits and vegetables. Only with close scrutiny would they find any resemblance to the girl she once was, and Suyin knew they'd never paid her that kind of attention. It shouldn't matter to her now what they thought, but it did.

Suyin bought a piece of pork from a woman who had once

given her a bag of soup bones, not thinking she didn't have any means to make soup with them. She had gnawed on the bits of dried, raw meat, sucked out the bone marrow, and had given what was left to a hungry dog afterward. The same woman now pushed the wrapped package of pork at her and took her coins without a second glance.

From the marketplace, Suyin began walking in the direction of Old Guangzhou. It was still early. Ever since she'd seen her brothers, she longed to see her mother again. If Suyin hurried, she might catch a glimpse of her *ma ma* leaving the apartment for work.

It had been more than eight months since Suyin set foot in Old Guangzhou, the only home she'd ever known. The familiar streets she knew so well lay before her: the Qilou buildings with their shaded corridors, lined with the cramped and cluttered shops of her childhood, the pulsating mix of voices and smells and people who all lived together in the small, teeming area.

Suyin paused across the street from her family's two-story apartment building and stood behind a pillar, hidden away in the shadows of the overhang in front of a vegetable market her mother sometimes shopped at. The foot traffic had picked up, early-morning shoppers and people on their way to work. Suyin inhaled and exhaled slowly, trying to stay calm, knowing that at any minute her *ma ma* would come out the door and she would be no more than fifteen feet away from her. All Suyin had to do was walk across the street, throw her arms around her, and tell her she was a grandmother. The thought filled her with hope when the door to their building opened and her mother appeared, looking thinner and older. She was smiling and talking to someone following her down the stairs. Suyin wondered if it was one of her younger brothers.

Suyin stepped out from behind the pillar and the words *ma ma* rose to the tip of her tongue, just as her mother turned back toward the doorway. In that instant, Suyin saw him. Her step-father came bounding out to the sidewalk after her mother, and just seeing him again brought back the ugly memories: the look on his face, his sweaty palm over her mouth. Suyin felt sick to her stomach as she watched them walking down the street together. She leaned against the pillar and couldn't move. A cool breeze had picked up and she felt the cold hand of winter coming. Suyin knew now that she'd never be able to return home. She pulled Kai Ying's sweater tighter as she walked away from Old Guangzhou.

Kai Ying

K AI YING FOUND THE NIGHTS WERE ALWAYS THE most difficult, lying in bed in despair with the darkness wrapping around her. In the daylight, everything appeared as it always did. Kai Ying worked hard to make it stay that way for Tao, though there was hardly a moment she hadn't felt anxious since they'd received Wei's telegram last week saying he'd arrived in Luoyang.

Kai Ying didn't dare allow herself to hope for news of Sheng. What if it was news she didn't want to hear? What would she do then?

Sometimes, she could almost feel Sheng's body pressed against hers, his breath on the back of her neck, the coolness of his skin. She missed his touch, his hand on the curve of her hip. It frightened her to think that she and Sheng might never know that same intimacy again. There were no herbs to make time stand still, to retrieve the time lost. They'd each been through so much in the past year, created their own individual histories that veered away from the life they once shared together. Would they still know each other? Kai Ying knew she was just feeling sad, but the distance and the silence had also brought along dark thoughts. If only she could heal her fear and restlessness as easily as she did indigestion or constipation.

Kai Ying sat up when she heard a faint cry and then nothing. Sometimes Mei Mei slept through the night, or else Suyin, who was becoming a very good mother, was there to pick her up. Kai Ying loved having a baby in the house, another new life to make them think of the future. She couldn't help but wonder if things might have been different now if her other baby had lived. The child would have been three years old now. Kai Ying had miscarried so early, she never knew if it was a girl or another boy. Would two children have changed their fates? Kept them all too busy to attend political meetings or write letters to the Premier? It wasn't like her to feel sorry for herself, and still she did. Kai

Ying knew how fortunate she was. All she had to do was look at Tao to be reassured that Sheng was always with her.

Tell me he's alive, she thought. She lay back down and closed her eyes, willing Wei to hear her. *Tell me he's coming home soon*.

Wei

FOR TWO DAYS WEI SAT AND WAITED ON A HARD wooden bench in the drafty hallway of the public security bureau. He felt perpetually cold in Luoyang, his *mein po* buttoned all the way up to his neck. He found if he sat very straight, his back hurt less. The cot he slept on at the boarding house was too soft and after his first, exhausted night of sleep, he hadn't slept well since.

Most of the time, Tian kept him company, although he frequently went out for walks, often returning with something for Wei to eat. Who could blame him? All Wei had done since he arrived in Luoyang was sit at the bureau and wait. Wei closed his eyes, hoping Liang would come and comfort him, but she didn't. He opened his eyes and looked around the dreary building, too distracted by the despairing thoughts and the constant noise in the busy hallway to concentrate. Why was everything taking so long? If Sheng was right there in Luoyang, wouldn't they have found him by now?

Clerk Hu had told him that he would first have to locate Sheng, and then have someone authorize Wei to visit his son. He also reminded Wei that there were others already waiting ahead of him for authorization. But rather than remain antagonistic, Wei decided to change his tactics and thanked the clerk politely. "Yes, of course, I understand," he said, almost cordial.

"I see you're learning," Tian had said, leaning in close and teasing him.

It surprised Wei how easy it was to talk to Tian, who had been a stranger to him less than a week ago.

Wei cleared his throat and said, "Have you heard the saying, *'The wise adapt themselves to circumstances, as water molds itself to the pitcher'*? It seems I've been the pitcher most of my life. I've forgotten how to be fluid. It feels as if I'm finally learning now," he said.

Tian smiled. "You remind me of my own father," he said, "although I'm afraid he never did learn."

By the morning of the fourth day, when Tian had gone out to get them something to eat, Clerk Hu stood up from his cluttered desk in his small cubicle and approached Wei sitting in the hallway.

"Permission has been granted for you to see your son," he said, thrusting a thin yellow piece of paper toward him.

It took Wei a moment to realize what Clerk Hu was saying.

"You found him?" Wei asked.

"Of course," Clerk Hu said. "I told you it would take a bit of time."

He could see his son. It meant Sheng was alive in Luoyang. Alive. "Alive," he whispered, looking up at Clerk Hu.

Until that moment, Wei hadn't let himself think otherwise. But as the days wore on, he'd begun to lose hope. He even imagined that Sheng had died because of his cowardice. Then what would he tell Kai Ying and Tao? Now that he knew his son was really alive, Wei felt warmth spread through his body, and for the first time in almost a week he didn't feel cold.

Wei stood up and grasped the piece of paper, struggling to find his voice. "Thank you," he finally said, although Clerk Hu was already halfway back to his cubicle.

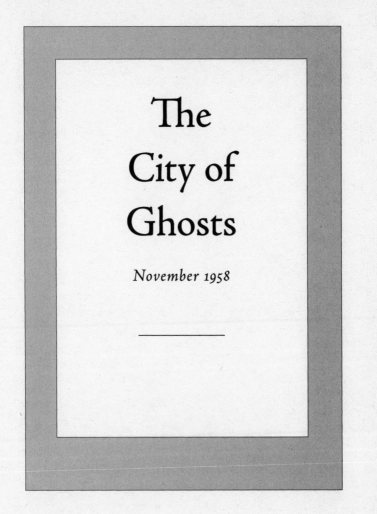

The
City of
Ghosts

November 1958

———————

Wei

WEI WAS SCHEDULED TO SEE SHENG THE FOLLOWing afternoon at the Ruyang district correctional facility, an hour's distance from Luoyang by public transportation. Clerk Hu said it was a town near the stone quarry where Sheng worked and on the city bus line. It was the most helpful he'd been all week.

When he and Tian left the public security bureau and walked down the crowded street, Wei felt as if he were a completely different man from the one who had entered the building a few hours earlier. Sheng was *alive*. The thread of hope they'd all clung to for almost a year was now a reality.

"What would you like to do now?" Tian asked.

Wei wanted to tell Kai Ying and Tao the good news, but decided to wait until he'd actually seen Sheng.

"Can we check on the bus schedules for Ruyang?" Wei asked. "I would hate to come this far, only to miss the bus that takes me the final distance."

Tian smiled. "I don't believe anything would make you miss that bus tomorrow."

"Don't say another word," Wei said, "we don't want to tempt the gods."

"I believe the gods have already spoken."

Wei laughed. "Then we don't want them to change their minds."

The bus to Ruyang left every other hour according to the schedule. From there Wei could walk to the correctional facility. Wei told all of this to Tian, half expecting him to say he would accompany him, but he simply nodded in response and otherwise kept silent. That afternoon as they walked through the Wangcheng Park, visiting the famous peony garden, Wei learned that Tian would be returning to Guangzhou early the next morning. By the time he'd be boarding the bus to Ruyang, Tian would already be on a train heading back to Guangzhou.

"I'm sorry," Wei said. "I've taken up so much of your time here in Luoyang."

"Not at all."

"It can't have been much of a trip for you, babysitting an old man most of the time."

"I welcomed the company," Tian said. "Sometimes the best lessons are in the journey, regardless of the outcome."

Wei watched him light a cigarette. Tian was everything he wasn't.

"Did you find what you were looking for?" Wei asked.

"I found there's nothing left here in Luoyang," Tian said, inhaling on his cigarette. He blew out smoke and smiled. "So, yes, I found what I was looking for. Returning helped me to finally realize that the Ai-li I knew and loved no longer exists." Tian cleared his throat. "We used to come here all the time to see the peonies, but even they seemed brighter in my memories."

"I've been a master at living in the past," Wei said. "It's a very lonely place. Take my advice, if you will: go home and live your life."

Tian smiled and nodded. "Yes," he said.

They came to a fork in the path and Tian guided him to the left.

"You've been such a big help to me," Wei said. "I don't know what I . . ."

"You would have done exactly the same thing on your own," Tian said.

"Why is it that I can speak so easily with you, while I have no idea what I'm going to say to my own son when I see him?" Wei asked.

"The fact that you've traveled all the way to Luoyang to see him already says a great deal," Tian said. "The rest will come naturally. So come now, let's celebrate by having a nice meal."

The sky had lightened as they emerged from the park, although Wei's spirits remained somber at the thought of Tian's departure tomorrow. It felt as if he were letting go of one son for another.

Suyin

A LMOST EVERY AFTERNOON WHILE MEI MEI SLEPT, Suyin stole back downstairs to the fragrant, steamy kitchen. During the short lull right after lunch, Kai Ying continued to teach her about herbs. Suyin took every opportunity she could to learn. The more she understood, the more fascinated she became by the meticulous process, thankful that Kai Ying put up with her, always beginning the lesson with the same mantra, "Always remember, if you keep the immune system healthy, you can avoid illnesses before they begin. It's the foundation of all herbal medicine."

Suyin heard the words in her sleep.

She'd begun to help Kai Ying package the basic herbal ingredients that patients came to buy for their everyday use. Suyin learned that along with the basic ingredients of ginseng, wolfberries, Chinese yam, and astragalus, other herbs, such as licorice root, ginger, and ephedrine were added to soups, depending on what area of the body was lacking in *qi,* the energy that kept all the vital organs working smoothly. The ingredients were all simmered together with a piece of lean pork or white fish for added flavor, if you were lucky enough to have the money, or could find them at the market.

Suyin carefully took down several jars and extracted the herbs, measuring them out onto the white sheets of paper, wrapping them up into two perfect square packets.

"Good," Kai Ying said. "Mrs. Wong will be coming by to pick these up at any time now."

Suyin beamed. She hadn't realized how much she missed being in school and learning. Kai Ying was the first person since then who took the time to teach her, and she wanted more than anything to prove that she was a worthy student.

"Thank you," she said.

"I should be the one thanking you," Kai Ying said, "for distracting Tao the night after *Lo Yeh* left when he was asking so many questions. Sometimes I just don't have all the answers."

Suyin watched her take down a glass jar from the top shelf and take out a more complicated-looking dried fungus that she thought resembled a shriveled ear.

"I have two younger brothers," Suyin suddenly blurted out. It was the first piece of family information she'd volunteered since she arrived. "They ask a lot of questions, too."

Kai Ying stopped what she was doing and looked at her. "No wonder you're so good with Tao," she said.

Suyin felt herself blush, the warmth coloring her face. Her two younger brothers were close in age, and she never thought of herself as anything but an older sister who broke up their fights and threatened them when they were bad. They were always the most difficult during the long afternoons after school when she was in charge of watching them. Suyin wondered if her mother ever thought she was good with her brothers. If so, she'd never once told her. Still, everything had been fine until her mother remarried.

"My *ma ma* raised the three of us for several years on her own," Suyin continued. The words she'd kept to herself for so long suddenly fought to push their way out. "My *ba ba* left for work one day when I was eight years old and he never returned. My mother remarried when I was twelve."

"Is your family in Guangzhou?"

Suyin hesitated. Perhaps Kai Ying would want her to return home if she knew they lived in Old Guangzhou. And yet, it seemed pointless to lie now; Tao had already seen her brothers. "Yes," she finally answered.

"Does your mother know about the baby?"

Suyin shook her head. "I left when I began to show." She tasted a tart bitterness on her tongue and tried not to think about her stepfather.

Kai Ying put the jar of fungus ears back up on the shelf and turned to her. "So she has no idea where you are, or how you are?"

Suyin shook her head again.

"Or that she has a granddaughter?" Kai Ying asked, her voice rising slightly with the question.

Suyin remained silent. Her hand unconsciously rose to her cheek, the rough patch of skin barely detectable now. Suyin felt a dull ache in the middle of her stomach, knowing that her time in Dongshan was coming to an end. What was she supposed to do now; she was fifteen years old with a little baby. She couldn't return home and live in the same apartment as that monster.

It was Kai Ying who spoke again. "We'll work something out," she said, before she reached over and gently pulled Suyin's hand away from her cheek, holding on to it.

Suyin didn't move. It had been such a long time since anyone had held her hand. Kai Ying's hand was warm and soft and Suyin held tightly on to it as if she were falling, as if the wall she had built up so meticulously during the past year was suddenly plummeting all around her.

"He came home drunk one afternoon," Suyin began. Her heart raced. "I didn't know what to do. Before I knew what was happening, he had grabbed me and pushed me to the ground and was on top of me," she said in one breath.

"Who?" Kai Ying asked. "Who hurt you?"

In the weeks following the rape, Suyin daydreamed that she had fought back, that she had reached out and gripped one of her father's old hammers and swung with all her strength, hitting her stepfather again and again until he no longer moved, pushing his bloody deadweight off her as the room spun around and the daydream ended with a moment of pure relief before the feeling disappeared again.

"My stepfather," she said, spitting out the words.

Suyin didn't dare look up when she felt Kai Ying's hand suddenly pull away. She stared down at the table, her tears falling on the stained, scratched wood, realizing her hunger wasn't just about food. All these months she'd been starving for warmth and shelter and family. Suyin couldn't stop crying until she felt Kai Ying come over and wrap her arms around her, pulling her in from the cold.

"It's all right," Kai Ying whispered into her ear. "You can stay here for as long as you like. You'll always have a home here."

Suyin tried to say something but all that emerged was a choking sound. *A home*, she thought, which made her cry even harder.

Wei

THE DAY BEGAN BITTERSWEET. WEI SUGGESTED they stop for breakfast on their way to the train station. It would be a nice walk before Tian's long trip home. Wei memorized the streets so he wouldn't get lost when he was alone again. They had already arranged to meet back in Guangzhou when Wei returned. He'd forgotten that life could still surprise an old man, how he had to travel all the way to Luoyang to find a new friend from Guangzhou.

At the train station, Wei didn't think it would be so difficult to part with someone he'd barely known for a week. "Thank you, Tian, for all you've done for me," Wei said. "Your guidance has been invaluable."

"I did nothing," Tian said. "I'm only sorry I won't be here to hear about the reunion with your son."

"I'll tell you all about it when I return to Guangzhou."

"I'll look forward to it."

Wei shook Tian's hand and the younger man boarded the train, turning back to wave before he disappeared into the car. Through the windows, Wei could see scattered passengers sitting throughout. He watched Tian move past them, choosing a window seat toward the back of the car, seeking quiet away from the others now that his story had found an ending.

Wei turned when a woman selling greasy fried donuts tugged at his arm, but he shook his head and pulled gently away from her. Discouraged, she tapped on the train windows, hoping a passenger might buy something from her. Wei stepped back and waited. When the train began to move slowly out of the station, he looked for Tian but no longer saw his friend sitting by the window. Still, he raised his hand to wave anyway.

Tao

IT WAS LITTLE SHAN WHO APPROACHED HIM FIRST IN the school yard one morning. Although it wasn't very cold, Shan was bundled up in a sweater, padded jacket, and a woolen scarf wound around his neck. Tao knew it was what his grandmother always made him wear every year after the Mid-Autumn Festival, whether it was cold or not. He was reminded of the heavier Little Shan he once knew.

"What is it?" Tao asked bluntly.

"I think we should call a truce," Little Shan said. He kept his hands in his pockets, shifting from one leg to the other as if he really were cold.

Truce. It was what they always said when they were still friends and had a disagreement, neither of them wanting to give in and say they were sorry.

Tao thought about it. Little Shan had betrayed him to be one of Lai Hing's stray dogs, and now he wanted to be friends again. Mao would have sent him away for less, just like he did his *ba ba*. He looked up and studied Little Shan's face, trying to understand what had happened during the past few months, how his entire life had been turned upside down ever since he'd fallen from the kapok tree. Yet, here he was, standing upright. Little Shan hadn't totally abandoned him, having saved him from being pummeled by Lai Hing and his gang. *Best friends are hard to come by,* his grandfather had said. His *ye ye* was hard to come by. There would never be anyone else like his grandfather, and Tao wanted him back, but until then, Little Shan stood bundled up and waiting in front of him.

"Truce," Tao said.

Kai Ying

KAI YING KEPT TO A REGULAR SCHEDULE, TRYING not to think beyond what she needed to do from day to day. She waited anxiously for another telegram to come from Wei telling her Sheng was alive and well, but there had only been another week of suffocating silence.

She found her most fulfilling moments came every afternoon when she taught Suyin about the herbs, watching her listen intently to everything she said, quizzing her on simple remedies and basic treatments. They had fallen into a comfortable rhythm and Kai Ying enjoyed teaching. She now under-stood the satisfaction that Wei and Sheng must have received from their students, as each day her lessons with Suyin grew a little longer.

"What herb would you prescribe for a sore throat and fever?" she asked Suyin.

The girl's face grew serious in thought. Kai Ying saw a moment's hesitation, which quickly turned to certainty.

"The root of the Chinese foxglove," Suyin answered.

"Yes," Kai Ying said, and smiled.

Suyin's face lit up with joy.

"Why would you prescribe the root of the foxglove?" Kai Ying asked.

She didn't hesitate this time. "It helps to remove the heat from the body and cool the blood."

Suyin was a natural.

At the end of their lesson, Kai Ying went upstairs and searched through her bureau drawer, finally finding the cotton pouch. In it were the pearls she had taken from Herbalist Chu when she studied with him. Kai Ying always meant to put them back, but she knew now she'd kept them for this very reason, to pass on to the next student.

Downstairs, she poured the tiny translucent pearls into the palm of her hand.

"What are those?" Suyin asked.

"Each pearl represents the time it'll take for you to learn the basics of herbal work."

Suyin looked confused.

"Do you remember the skin cream I gave you?" Kai Ying said.

Suyin nodded, her fingers brushing across her cheek, the once dark patches now almost undetectable.

"The pearls are the secret ingredient I told you about," Kai Ying said, placing a small pearl in Suyin's hand. "By the time you have collected all these pearls in the palm of your hand, twenty-four months will have passed, and you'll have learned more about herbs than you ever wanted," Kai Ying explained. "That's if you want to," she added.

"Yes," Suyin said, closing her hand around the pearl. "I want to."

Wei

WEI LEFT FOR RUYANG ON THE NOON BUS. HE checked and rechecked his pocket for Clerk Hu's permission slip from the camp managers to visit Lee Weisheng at the Ruyang correctional facility that afternoon. Seeing his son's name printed on the slip had instantly brought Sheng back to life, making it all a reality. On Wei's lap was a bag that contained the woolen sweater he had carried all the way from Guangzhou. He had no idea if his son was allowed to accept anything from him, but he was determined to give him the sweater one way or the other.

The bus was crowded and noisy with day laborers going

to work. He sat by a window near the front and closed his eyes for a moment against the bright sun. Since his first night on the train, Liang hadn't returned to him. His greatest sorrow was that he loved her better in death than in life.

Wei opened his eyes and gazed out at the flat, dry plains surrounded by tall mountains in the distance. He wondered if the famous Longmen Grottoes and the Fengxian Temple, with its many carved stone Buddhas, were over there. It was the first time since arriving in Luoyang that Wei thought about it once being the cradle of Chinese civilization, where many of the finest Chinese poets and writers also gathered and had produced great works of literature. At one time, Wei's heart would have raced with joy to know that he was so close to so many ancient art treasures, but now it was only an afterthought, a distant place where Sheng had been taken to be reeducated.

The correctional facility was a three-story, whitewashed building surrounded by a high wall trimmed with barbed wire. Wei held the letter of permission nervously in his hand, then watched as it was passed from one uniformed officer to the next, until he was finally ushered down a darkened passageway and told to wait in the room at the end of the hall. "Your son will be brought down shortly," the woman told him in a flat, tired voice. And then she was gone.

The room was stark and cold and windowless. Several dim lights hung from the ceiling. There were three rows of five wooden tables with chairs facing each another. Wei sat down at a table closest to the door, while another older woman sat at a table on the other side of the room. She looked over at him and then away again. Wei was told that he'd been given special visiting rights, since visitors were usually allowed only at the beginning or the end of the month. He wondered if the woman had come from far away, too. Wei was tempted to make conversation, to raise his voice and ask her who she was there to see, but they had chosen tables far apart from each other for privacy, and he thought it better to keep it that way.

When the door finally opened, Wei's heart leaped. He took a deep breath and held it in, only to let it seep slowly out again when he saw a thin young woman with a shaved head walk in with a female guard. She was hunched over and moved slowly, as if in great pain, but raised her head just long enough for Wei to see her black eye and swollen lip and just how young she was. She wasn't much older than Suyin. When she walked past him, a foul stench emanating from her accosted him, and Wei quickly turned away.

The older woman immediately rose from the table, but the guard held up her hand to stop her. The woman, who he assumed was the girl's mother, hesitated, then sat back down again. Wei could see how anxious the woman was to get up and go to the girl, but she gripped the edge of the table instead and waited. The guard pushed the young woman down in the chair across from her and stepped to the side.

"Fifteen minutes," the guard said.

Respectfully, Wei looked down at the table. There was nowhere else to escape. He knew well that privacy could be found only in small gestures, by closing his eyes, or turning his body away, or dropping his gaze to the tabletop. It provided emotional distance if nothing else. He looked down at the sticky and worn tabletop. Someone had further added to the despair by making a deep gouge in the table that ran in a curving line from one end to the other. But the longer Wei studied it, the more it appeared to follow the same route as the Yellow River flowing through Central China. He had spent more hours than he could count scrutinizing maps and tracing the artifacts in this area where so much of China's civilization began. The river wound through nine provinces from Qinghai to the Bohai Sea, where the table ended. Wei might have been imagining it, but he was delighted with the discovery. The Yellow River represented the spirit of the Chinese people, and it was not only fitting, but inspired that someone would have scored it into the tabletop as a symbol for all those visiting their loved ones. Even if he were the only one ever to make the connection, it lifted his spirits.

He studied the tabletop closely, wondering how the gouge had been made and by whom, the visitor or the inmate. With a pen? A sharp object? Out of rebellion or despair? It must have required thoughtful planning and cunning not to have been seen and stopped by the guards. He imagined the room crowded with visitors, voices raised to be heard, the guards gathered together smoking, ignoring the reunions. Wei's finger traced the line and he smiled at the secret of it. He had been thoroughly searched before he was allowed into the facility, and had the presence of mind to wear Sheng's sweater rather than carry it in. He wondered how many others had prepared intricate plans of defiance on their visiting days.

When Wei looked up again, the girl across the room had laid her head down on the table as if she could no longer hold it up. Her mother reached out and began to stroke the girl's head as her voice hummed quietly. Wei listened to the dialect and thought he recognized her saying something about time and patience. In the moment afterward, a frightening moan erupted from the girl. *"Quiet now, quiet now,"* the older woman soothed, raising her voice to let the guard know she had things under control. Just then the door whined open again and he turned to see if it was Sheng who had stepped through the doorway.

The guard who approached Wei was a large man, with close-cropped hair and sleepy-looking eyes. He leaned against the table, just enough to pin Wei between it and the chair he sat in, the guard's shadow falling over him.

"Lee Wei?" he asked. His voice was surprisingly high for such a big man.

Wei nodded. "Yes, I'm Lee Wei."

The guard stood straight to his full height. "I'm afraid there was a mix-up. Your son left for the stone factory this morning before he received word of your visit. He isn't here."

Wei was confused. "Are you saying I won't be able to see my son today?"

"Not today," he said.

"But this letter of permission," he said, pulling it from his pocket. "It's dated today. Today, see? Can I see him over at the stone quarry? If not, will I be able to use it tomorrow?"

The guard shrugged. "Visitors are received only here. You'll have to either reapply with the unit manager or through the police security bureau."

Wei sat in disbelief. He'd come this far, he was so close to seeing Sheng he could almost hear his voice, see his boyish smile. Instead, he would have to start all over again. "It can't be," Wei muttered to himself, but the guard had already closed the door behind him.

* * *

Across the room, the female guard moved closer to the girl, signaling her time was up. Wei heard a sharp scream come from the girl when the guard grabbed her arm and lifted her from the chair. "Go quietly, go quietly, I'll return soon," her mother said, pleading. The girl grabbed on to the woman's hand for as long as she could before she was dragged away.

Song

SONG SURVEYED HER GROWING GARDEN, KNOWING that the cleared area where Tao had just planted new seeds would soon be brimming. By early spring the garden would be thriving, providing them with a new crop of vegetables for the months ahead. She saw it day after day already in the form of cabbage and chives and pea shoots sprouting. She prayed to Kuan Yin that Wei would have returned safely by the time she cut the chives, and that Sheng might be home by the next harvest.

The past few years had been bountiful and she was grateful. But Song wouldn't forget that anything could happen, that nature had a way of taking as well as giving.

* * *

The only year Song's garden didn't bloom was during her second year at the villa. It had rained incessantly for weeks and the land she worked so hard to clear had flooded, becoming a small pond, the earth swelling and bloating from all the water, the new seeds she'd planted rising to the surface like tiny corpses. Any signs of growth afterward would be a miracle.

When the rains finally stopped, Song had rolled up her cotton trousers and waded barefoot into the muddy mess, wanting to see how deep it was and if anything could be salvaged, her feet sinking into the muddy sludge below her ankles. Every time she tried to lift a foot, she sank a little deeper into the mud, a sucking sound raising air bubbles to the surface. She needed something to grab on to for leverage. Song wanted to laugh at her own stupidity, and couldn't help but wonder if this was what it felt like to be sucked under in quicksand. What if she couldn't get herself out, would she die standing upright encased in dry mud? What a silly way to go, she thought.

"Can I help?" Sheng had asked.

He appeared out of nowhere, a tall, gangly teenager then. She hadn't heard him at all, didn't realize he was standing there and watching her, amused.

"Of course you can," she said, reaching out for his hand, grateful beyond words that he was there.

He leaned over and grabbed her hand, first one, and then the other, and pulled her slowly out. As her feet made their final kick free of the sucking mud, it splattered all over Sheng's clothes. He began to laugh and it was the first time Song realized Sheng was growing up and becoming his own person, full of life and mischief. His temperament was so much like Liang's, even more so as he grew older. Unlike Wei, they were both able to laugh at themselves. Sheng never told anyone about her being stuck in the mud, and they kept it as their private joke throughout the years. Afterward, he never failed to check on her after every big storm.

Song hadn't thought about that day in a very long time and it brought sudden tears to her eyes. Weeks later, she remembered being surprised to see a few green shoots sprouting from the once sodden earth—the remaining seeds finding their way toward the sunlight. She marveled at nature's resiliency, its sheer stubbornness to survive.

She thought no less of Sheng.

Wei

BY THE TIME WEI RETURNED TO LUOYANG, IT WAS too late to go back to the public security bureau. It would take at least two or three days to process another letter of permission, and that was if the fates were with him. Wei wasn't sure if he had the energy to go through it all again. He was tired and hungry and he wondered how many times he'd have to go through the endless bureaucracy before finally getting to see Sheng.

The room felt emptier and colder with Tian gone, the presence of defeat in every corner. Still, as Wei sat on the sagging cot, he heard Tian's voice encouraging him to continue: *Come now, you're tired, tomorrow you'll go back and Clerk Hu will issue you another letter of permission. You know what to do now, and you'll see your son the next time.* Wei tried to smile, though he could have just as easily wept, his heart so heavy with loss.

The next morning, Clerk Hu reacted with little or no sympathy. He filed another form and instructed Wei to wait as he had before. But he must have felt some pity toward him. Two days later Wei was on the same bus heading to Ruyang. He was beginning to feel like a nomad, moving from one place to another without a home like the *Hakka*, the Chinese Han known as the "guest people," who migrated southward through the dynasties due to the social unrest. The new letter of permission was in his pocket and he didn't allow himself to think of what he would do if he wasn't able to see Sheng again. Wei's money was running out and he had enough for one, maybe two more nights at the boardinghouse and a train ticket back home. What then? He couldn't return to Guangzhou and to Kai Ying and Tao without having seen Sheng. What would they think of him? Wei cleared his head to dispel any other bad thoughts.

As the bus traveled on, Wei closed his eyes. At first there was only darkness and then everything began to lighten. *Do you remember,* he heard Liang's voice ask him, *when Sheng was a little boy and he was determined to fly his dragon kite even when there was no wind?* He nodded at the memory, at the calm, cool watery sound of Liang's voice, and how she had finally returned to him after so many weeks. *Yes,* he said. Wei could see her smile. *Remember how he ran up and down the street trying to get enough wind until he finally gave up,* she reminded him. *And how you were the one who told him the wind would return again in no time, but he had to be patient. The wind will return again,* Liang said. *You've come this far, just listen to your own words.*

Wei wanted to reach out for Liang, but was afraid she would disappear if he did, and remained content to feel her there beside him again. Not long after, the bus made a sudden sharp turn before it jerked to a complete stop and Wei was forced to open his eyes. He blinked against the bright daylight to see that they had arrived at Ruyang's city center, a short walk from the correctional facility.

Kai Ying

K AI YING HAD JUST FINISHED WITH A PATIENT, HIS wife leading him out through the courtyard, his eyesight almost completely gone. There was little she could do for the old man, who had refused to see a medical doctor, but offer him a sweet tea made from Chinese wolfberries and chrysanthemum flowers known to help vision-related diseases.

While Kai Ying waited for her next patient to arrive, she took stock of what herbs were running low. The house was quiet during the pause in her busy morning, and it gave her a moment to gather her thoughts. Tao was at school, Auntie Song was with Meizhen in the garden, and she'd sent Suyin out using the last of their monthly coupons to buy rice and cooking oil.

Kai Ying glanced up at the ceiling when she heard what sounded like footsteps from the room above. It was followed by a creaking sound on the stairs, although no one else was at home. *It's just the old villa playing tricks, shifting and sighing with age,* she thought. Or maybe it was the ghosts of Wei's servants, Sun and Moon, lurking about. She smiled to herself. In the ten years Kai Ying had lived at the villa, she'd never seen either of them. Perhaps they were finally paying her a visit.

Kai Ying walked from room to room. There was no one upstairs. "What's becoming of me?" she whispered to herself. The only room she hadn't checked was her father-in-law's, which she had avoided ever since he'd left for Luoyang almost two weeks ago. Now, even though there was no one in the house but her, Kai Ying knocked on his door and waited a moment for Wei to answer, knowing a reply would not come. She opened the door slowly and stepped in.

The room was dark and had a moldy, closed-in smell of old books and traces of the ginger and sesame oil liniment she had mixed for Wei. The bottle sat on his desk and she fretted now that he didn't have it with him when his back acted up. The drapes were parted just enough for a sliver of light to fall across his dark wood desk.

Kai Ying opened the drapes and a dusty morning light flooded the room, making it appear drab and tired. She was usually in and out of his room quickly to clean, or to bring *Lo Yeh* his tea. Now she stood in the telling light and took a good, long look around. The bookshelves that lined the walls with overflowing volumes gave the room a heavy, insulated feel. On his desk were papers, a book of poetry by the poet Tu Fu, a photo of Liang and Sheng when he was a little boy. It was the photo he'd kept in his Lingnan office for over thirty years. She imagined him glancing at it every day and wondering where all the time had gone.

Like much of the old villa, the room was in a sorry state. Kai Ying looked up and noted the water stains across the ceiling, the peeling paint, the intricate molding along the walls now hidden under years of neglect. The grand villa was only a tired shell of what it once was.

Kai Ying closed her eyes and imagined what it must have been like for Wei growing up in the villa at the height of its beauty and his family's prosperity, when the idea of Mao and his Party were inconceivable. Later, Liang and the university had been Wei's life, and Kai Ying had never stopped to realize how lonely he must feel with them both gone, clinging on to what little of the past he had left. She wouldn't have been able to forget either.

Kai Ying opened her eyes and leaned over Wei's desk to straighten his papers and pens. He must have written the letter right here, she thought, feeling only sadness. She carefully closed the book of poetry that lay open, a long-ago gift from Sheng. Her hand rested gently on the cover for a moment before she turned and opened a window, letting in the fresh air.

Dear Kai Ying,

There's little time for me to explain everything to you. It's not quite 5 A.M. and I was just about to leave for the stone quarry, when Hou, my unit manager, informed me that my father's petition to visit had been granted and I would be seeing him for a short time this afternoon. I couldn't believe what I was hearing. My father. It seems I've been gazing at a dark sky for so long, I'd forgotten there are always glimmers of light. I only have a few stolen moments to spend with you in this letter, and it feels as if I'm stumbling over all the words I want to say. My work unit will be leaving in a matter of minutes and then there won't be any time to write you again. For the first time in so many months, I'm a happy man, knowing my father will be bringing this letter back to you.

It was the leader of my work team who stopped sending my letters to you, and it was the same bastard who withheld all the letters and packages you must have sent to me. I was frantic the first few months when I didn't receive any of your letters, thinking something must have happened to one of you. Instead, another inmate told me my letters were being destroyed by one of the managers here. From the beginning, he and I were like two alley cats who had taken an instant dislike of each other, even when I tried to remain invisible and keep out of trouble. But there are times when you can't avoid the storm, which led to some small altercations. Had I known that the result of my convictions would be the loss of your letters, of your voice, I would have been wiser. But please understand too, that without our own moral standards, where would we all be?

Forgive me, Kai Ying.

Every day since, I've worried about you, thinking the worst—that I had turned into a shadow you could no longer see or hear. I'm here. I'm as well as I can be. All I can promise you is that I'll survive this place because of you and Tao; the long arduous work days which begin in darkness and end in darkness, the crowded, squalid conditions, the endless steam buns and cabbage, the desires and the needs. Time is simply made up of the days passing until I can return to you.

Do you remember when we first married and we went to Zhaoqing to visit your family? We took a boat across Star Lake to explore the mountain crags and we were separated from each other onto different boats. I remember seeing you from across the water and asking myself, what did I do to deserve such great fortune? Think of the joy we felt when we were reunited that afternoon. Think of it again when I return home.

Until then, I'm here. I'm here.

Wei

WEI WAITED FOR SHENG IN THE SAME STARK, windowless room of the correctional facility. He was alone this time, no other visitors to capture his attention. He sat down at the same table by the door, his finger automatically tracing the route of the Yellow River scored across the table. It somehow brought him calm, a quick means of escape.

Wei heard footsteps coming down the hallway and looked toward the door, but the steps passed and faded. Not long after, more voices rang down the hallway as the room grew warm and stuffy. He took off Sheng's sweater and draped it across the back of his chair. His clever plan was to hand the sweater to Sheng when they parted as if it had been his all along.

Another half hour had gone by, when finally, the door swung open and he saw a thin, gaunt Sheng with a shaved head standing in the doorway. He glimpsed the young boy who stood quietly at the doorway of his library again, too shy to speak to him. Wei's heart pounded at the sight of Sheng. He wanted to say his name out loud to make sure he was really there and not a figment of his imagination, but Sheng's face appeared hard and closed, and Wei instead whispered his name to himself. Only then did it occur to Wei that his son might not want to see him.

The guard pushed Sheng forward and he walked toward Wei and sat down in the chair across from him. Only when

Sheng was seated and facing him did he relax and appear more himself again.

"*Ba ba*," Sheng said, his voice low and hoarse, his eyes softening. "You're really here."

"I had to come," he said.

Wei reached across the scarred table and touched the sleeve of his son's thin cotton tunic. He needed to touch Sheng, to have proof that he was really there sitting across from him. Wei could see how Luoyang had taken its toll on him. Sheng had aged; he was too thin, his skin pallid, his eyes sunken, his hands scraped and calloused, dried blood on his knuckles, the stubble on his chin and the shadow of growth on his shaved head making him appear even sicklier. And for the first time, he saw traces of his own father in his son's dark eyes.

Wei cleared his throat. "We haven't heard from you in so long, we didn't know what to think. I had to come," he repeated. "I had to make sure—"

"I know." Sheng quickly finished his sentence. "I'm thankful. There was nothing I could do. My work team manager stopped sending my letters. I never received any of yours after the first few."

"But why?" Wei asked.

"It was his way of punishing me."

Wei refrained from asking too many questions. There was too little time now for long explanations. It was a world that made no sense to Wei, and he needed to remember only what was important to bring back to Kai Ying and Tao.

"How are they?" Sheng asked. "Kai Ying and Tao? Auntie Song?"

It was as if he had read his mind. Wei heard an edge of desperation in his son's voice.

"They're well," Wei answered. "They miss you." He quickly told Sheng all the important details, including the arrival of Suyin and her baby, while downplaying Tao's fall from the kapok tree and breaking his leg.

"But he's all right? *Sai Lo?*" Sheng asked, sounding worried.

"He has a limp, but it'll get better with time and exercise. He's been a very brave boy."

Sheng ran his hand across his head. "What was he thinking?" he said under his breath. "Why would he suddenly climb the tree?"

"He's a boy," Wei said. "I recall you were quite a climber in your day."

"Yes," Sheng said, and finally smiled.

When the guard stepped back to light a cigarette, Sheng leaned closer to Wei. "I have a letter I need you to bring back to Kai Ying."

"Yes, of course."

Wei hadn't thought about what Kai Ying would have wanted him to bring to Sheng: a letter or message, herbs, anything that might help to keep him going. Once again he'd failed her.

"Kai Ying had no idea I was coming to see you," Wei said. "I was afraid she would try to stop me. I left a note." He paused for a moment and then said, "I should be the one in here, not you."

Sheng shook his head.

"Kai Ying knows I wrote the letter," Wei continued. "They all do. I've created a world of grief for all of us." He swallowed.

"*Ba ba,* you don't need to explain—"

Wei waved his hand to interrupt. "You're here. I've seen you, touched you. At least I can bring that back to Kai Ying. But can you ever forgive me for writing the letter?" he asked. His fingers felt for the gouge in the table, following it to the edge.

Sheng leaned even closer to him. "Forgive you? You don't need to ask for forgiveness for writing the truth. I would have done the same, given time. I'm here for the both of us. We're more alike than either of us knew."

Wei saw the color return to Sheng's face again as he spoke. *We're more alike than either of us knew.* His words hung in the stale air of the ugly room.

Sheng continued to talk. "The most difficult thing has been not having contact with you and Kai Ying. Everything else I'll survive." He turned around to see the guard smoking and quickly took the letter from inside his tunic and passed it to Wei, who slipped it into the pocket of his *mein po*. "You'll tell them I'm well."

"Yes, yes, of course I will. I'll see that Kai Ying gets this," he said, patting his pocket. "Is there anything else I can do?" Wei asked.

"You can give Tao a hug for me. He must have grown so much I'll barely recognize him when I see him."

"It's been difficult. He misses you," Wei said. "He hates me for what I've done to you."

"When Tao's older, he'll understand what this was all about," Sheng said. "And he'll be proud of his grandfather for walking into the storm."

Wei smiled, remembering his own words.

"It's time," the guard said, suddenly back and hovering over them.

"Please, a moment more," Wei pleaded.

"It's time," the guard repeated.

They both rose from the table and Wei reached over and placed his hand on Sheng's cheek. "I'm sorry," he said, "I let so many years slip by." He felt the tears pushing against the backs of his eyes.

Sheng squeezed his hand before letting go. "Tell Kai Ying and Tao that I miss them. I'll see them soon, I promise."

Wei nodded. He patted the letter in his pocket.

Sheng smiled before he was led out of the room, the door clicking closed behind them.

Wei sat back down and stared at the door, hoping Sheng might return even when he knew it wasn't possible. *We're more alike than either of us knew.* Even if Sheng had forgiven him, how could he ever forgive himself?

It wasn't until Wei finally stood up that he realized he'd forgotten to give Sheng the woolen sweater that still hung on the back of the chair.

Wei

WEI OPENED HIS EYES. THE HOLLOW, ROCKING motion of the train had lulled him to sleep. It was dark outside. He shifted on the hard seat, his sore back a constant reminder that it was still a day's journey until he arrived back in Guangzhou. Wei looked across the aisle at the empty seat, wishing Tian was sitting there again, sipping from his bottle of rice liquor, ready with another story of love and loss. Before Wei left Luoyang, he wanted to send Kai Ying another telegram, but he barely had enough money for the train ticket back home.

Wei pushed himself up and rubbed the tiredness from his eyes. It was almost Tao's bedtime and he suddenly wondered who'd been reading stories to him since he'd been away. Wei couldn't remember the last time Kai Ying had read to Tao. It had always been Wei's favorite time of each day, and he hoped it might be the one moment Tao would think kindly of him again.

Wei reached into the pocket of his *mein po* and touched the edge of Sheng's letter for Kai Ying, the most important accomplishment in his long career, a letter that would bring his daughter-in-law some much-deserved happiness. It was a thought that eased the ache of having left Sheng behind. Even with his son's forgiveness, there would always be the guilt, the precious time he'd stolen away from Sheng and his family. It was his burden to carry and he would try to make it up to them in any way he could. Wei sat back and looked out the window, his own weary reflection staring back as the train traveled onward through the darkness.

Kai Ying

KAI YING WALKED OUT TO THE COURTYARD. FOR the very first time since Tao had fallen from the kapok tree, she paused in front of it. It seemed as if an entire lifetime had passed in the five months since. She had collected all the green leaves that had dropped and the flower petals before them, and now the tree stood skeletal, the branches remaining bare until the nut-sized pods miraculously appeared again by the New Year, followed by blooming red flowers in the spring. It was always Sheng's favorite time of the year, the sweet perfumes and the hum of bees filling the air. Although Kai Ying knew it was foolish, she still dared to hope that they would all be together again by then.

Kai Ying stepped closer to the tree. At least let her hear from Wei soon, she thought. The gash that her father-in-law had left in the trunk was a scar now, slightly deeper in color and hardly noticeable if you weren't looking for it. Kai Ying's fingers traced the smooth wound. She thought of it as just another example of nature's genius; the kapok tree had healed itself.

From the kitchen, she heard Tao's and Suyin's voices and smiled. She turned at the sound of the gate whining open, although she wasn't expecting another patient so late in the afternoon. Instead, Kai Ying's heart skipped a beat when she saw that it was Wei.

Wei

WEI WONDERED IF HE LOOKED AS TIRED AND DE-feated as he felt. When he stepped off the train, his legs were still shaky from the long trip. He could hardly believe he was back in Guangzhou, but as he pressed his way through the swelling crowds, the sheer tremor of bodies and voices, the smell of exhaust and the pungent aroma of roasting chestnuts made him step to the side and stop for a moment to take a breath. His satchel, still bulging with his clothes and the woolen sweater he'd carried back, suddenly felt too heavy. It was only on the walk back to Dongshan that he'd begun to feel himself again. By the time Wei pushed open the gate to the courtyard, it was with both relief and trepidation. He hadn't expected to see Kai Ying standing by the kapok tree.

"Lo Yeh," she said. He heard the surprise in her voice as she moved toward him.

"Kai Ying," he said. He couldn't imagine how disheveled he must appear. He put his satchel down where he stood.

"I was so worried . . ."

Before she could continue, he quickly reassured her. "I'm fine . . . and so is Sheng."

"You saw him?"

Wei nodded.

"He's alive," she whispered.

"He's alive and well," he said. "I wanted to send a telegram, but the train ticket back took everything I had left."

"But why, why haven't we heard from him in all this time?" she asked.

"They've been withholding his letters," Wei said. From the pocket of his *mein po,* he extracted the folded piece of paper. "He asked me to give you this letter."

A small cry emerged from Kai Ying and she turned away. When she turned back to take the letter from him, he saw the tears in her eyes. Without saying another word he embraced her, her body stiff at first, before slowly relaxing against his. A moment after, she leaned in closer and whispered into his ear, "Thank you."

Later that evening the house was quiet when Wei returned from walking Song back to her apartment. He made his way upstairs to his room, exhausted. He had brought back Sheng to them, every little detail saved for this evening, as if he'd been holding his breath all the way back from Luoyang and finally able to exhale. He stopped on the landing when he saw a sliver of light coming from Tao's room. His grandson had been almost shy upon seeing him, saying very little all evening. Wei knocked once lightly and opened the door.

"Shouldn't you be asleep?" Wei asked, and then smiled.

Tao lay in bed and shrugged. "Will *ba ba* be coming home soon?" he asked.

"As soon as he can," Wei answered.

"Did he say anything about me?"

"He misses you terribly."

Wei watched his grandson. His hair had grown back in the weeks since he'd been gone and he appeared older. He couldn't imagine what Sheng would see when he returned, a boy where there once was a small child. It suddenly stung him to realize that he wouldn't be there to know Tao as a man, although he could already see Sheng in him, a bit of the storm, who might one day have his own son and understand how important these past months were to Wei. He swallowed and stepped into the room.

"How's your leg feeling?" he asked.

"I still limp," Tao answered.

"Well, it takes time," Wei said.

"Maybe by the time *ba ba* returns," he said.

Wei nodded and smiled.

"You're not going anywhere again, are you?" Tao suddenly asked.

"Not for a while."

"You promise to tell me the next time you do?"

"I promise."

"*Ye ye?*"

"Yes."

"Will you tell me a story?"

Wei hesitated. "It's late," he said, but then sat down on the chair by his grandson's bed and stroked his whiskers.

"What do you want to hear?"

"Houyi and Chang'e," Tao answered.

Wei glanced out the window, the shadows of the kapok tree looming. It would still be standing long after he was gone, and the thought brought solace.

"There's no moon," he said.

"There's still the story," Tao said, ready to listen.